"IS THIS HOW YOU TREAT ME, WOMAN? LEAVING ME AT THE ALTAR JUST BEFORE OUR WEDDING?"

Fanny glared at the duke in shocked outrage. "Put me down this instant!" To her dismay, her eyes filled with exhausted tears.

"Be still, lass," Malen said breathlessly, as the girl in his arms twisted furiously. "I promise I'll put you down if you promise not to run away again. We could both use a good night's sleep."

Fanny's wild thrashing came to an abrupt halt. "In a real bed?" she whispered hopefully. Could she trust the duke to keep his distance? Probably not. "Do you promise all we'll do is sleep, your Grace?" Pinning him with her gaze, she searched his face.

Malen hesitated. This was one vow he didn't know if he could keep.

Lucky in Love

REBECCA ROBBINS

AVON BOOKS ◆ NEW YORK

LUCKY IN LOVE is an original publication of Avon Books. This work has never before appeared in book form. This work is a novel. Any similarity to actual persons or events is purely coincidental.

AVON BOOKS
A division of
The Hearst Corporation
1350 Avenue of the Americas
New York, New York 10019

First Avon Books Printing: April 1994

AVON TRADEMARK REG. U.S. PAT. OFF. AND IN OTHER COUNTRIES, MARCA REGISTRADA, HECHO EN U.S.A.

Printed in the U.S.A.

RA 10 9 8 7 6 5 4 3 2 1

Author's Note

This is a work of fiction. Any resemblances contained herein to places and people existing or living at this time or in the past are purely coincidental. Although the Glencoe massacre did take place in 1692, this story is purely imaginary, and the author makes no claim to know the true character or sentiments of those individuals involved in the actual historic event or that of any of their descendants.

Prologue

Raising her nose slightly, sixteen-year-old Lady Fanny MacDonald sniffed the humid breeze that skimmed down the steep Scottish peaks. Thick with the scent of rain, it heralded a storm approaching over the mountains. An occasional grumble of distant thunder competed with the sparrows chattering in the apple tree overhead. The apple's delicate branches danced and waved, the birds perched therein bobbing up and down among the new leaves like unusual fruit. It wouldn't be long, Fanny suspected, before the sparrows were blown from their playground and forced to seek sturdier shelter.

Although she and her grandfather, Lord Ian Mac-Donald, often sat in this corner of the estate, Fanny had an ulterior motive for wanting to come here today. In fact, she had made certain to spend some of every afternoon in this same place for the last six days.

Fanny MacDonald had fallen in love.

Absently toying with the emerald satin riband twined through her poppy-red hair, Fanny wondered who the object of her affections—the young man hiding behind the low stone wall some fifteen paces from the bench—could be and why he had spied on her for the past week. He looked to be several years older than herself, and, from what she was able to see, he was extremely handsome.

Trying to appear nonchalant, Fanny reached down and stroked the ears of the huge gray dog sitting adoringly near her pale-green-slippered feet. It was an Irish wolfhound bitch, whose swollen belly attested to her advanced pregnancy as she rolled onto her back to have

1

her stomach scratched. The dog was due to whelp in about two weeks, and Fanny had been looking forward to the puppies with an excitement topped only by her curiosity about the young stranger.

Next to learning family history from her beloved grandfather, the most important pursuit in Fanny's life was raising her dogs. Her first wolfhound had been a gift from Lord MacDonald on her ninth birthday, the finest pup in all that year's litters. That dog, a male, had died almost two years ago but had sired the female at Fanny's feet.

Irish wolfhounds were rare in Scotland, and the finest in the country came from the kennels at MacDonald Manor. Thus the envy of his friends, Lord MacDonald occasionally loaned out the huge canines for wild boar, wolf, stag, or elk hunts. Since the large dogs had short life spans, and since some were lost on hunts, the pack never grew beyond manageable size.

The matter of hunting was the single bone of contention between Fanny and her grandfather. Lord MacDonald enjoyed the sport, while Fanny believed chasing deer or other wild creatures until they were too exhausted to run any farther was unforgivably cruel, not to mention unfair, since the long-legged dogs had been specifically bred to run farther and faster than any prey they might pursue.

In all the years she had had dogs, Fanny had steadfastly refused to allow them to be used for such entertainment. Rather, she considered wolfhounds ideal companion and protection dogs, often citing as her argument the ancient description of the breed: gentle when stroked, fierce when provoked.

Now, scratching the dog's stomach, Fanny wondered why the bitch hadn't complained at the stranger's presence. Rather, the animal's tail wagged each time the lad appeared. Perhaps that was a good omen. Dogs could instinctively read people's intentions.

But why would the young man hide? Why not introduce himself? There must be some reason. Might he belong to a lower class—happy to admire but too wise to approach the granddaughter of the rich and powerful

Lord MacDonald, laird of the entire MacDonald clan? The thought was bleakly disappointing. Still, it was all Fanny could do to keep her eyes from straying, time and again, to the top of the wall.

Fanny patted the dog's belly and, lifting her hands to her lap, smoothed her green-and-white skirt with lady-like precision. She tossed her head. Let him watch. She wouldn't give him the satisfaction of acknowledging his presence. *She* was too old for such games. But even as she carefully schooled her features in what she hoped was an expression of casual hauteur, she could not help but notice that the young man's gaze was definitely ad-miring, and, despite her tender years, Fanny was al-ready woman enough to glory in the attention.

Just then a lone cardinal, brilliantly scarlet among its dowdy companions still frantically bobbing amid the undulating apple limbs, caught Fanny's attention. As several sweet-smelling blossoms slid down the moist currents of air and settled like dainty pink-and-white butterflies on the carved stone bench where Fanny and her grandfather sat, she tipped her head back to get a better look at the bird. Startled by her movement, the cardinal, along with the sparrows, departed with scold-ing cries and another shower of petals.

Gathering the velvety flowers in her hand, Fanny buried her nose in them and breathed in their heady perfume. Then, spreading her fingers, she allowed the rapidly cooling wind to sweep the petals away.

One of the liberated blossoms came to rest atop the low stone wall. Fanny gasped with surprise as the young man's hand shot out and seized the flower. She gasped again as he clutched the flower to his chest like a price-less treasure and blew her a kiss to rival those thrown by Romeo to Juliet during the play a wandering troupe had recently enacted at the manor.

Demurely folding her hands, Fanny jerked her gaze to her fingers and tried to cool the slow burn rising in her cheeks before her grandfather noticed her inner dis-array. The young man really was most attractive. His hair gleamed blue-black like a raven's wing, and his eyes, easily discernible even from this distance, flashed a peculiar mix of sage-green and teal-blue.

Who could he be? A new groom? A tenant's son? Or, she thought with a rush of hope, a new neighbor from one of the nearby estates and thus a member of her own class, merely too shy to approach until he'd been properly introduced?

With a quick, giddy breath, Fanny lifted her eyes from her hands and glanced at Lord MacDonald to see if he had noticed their skulking observer. Apparently he had not, for he was looking into the northern sky with an expression of concern. Fanny's gaze followed his as thunder rumbled ominously.

Rolling back onto her stomach and lifting her big head, the wolfhound growled in tepid response, then simply laid her head between her enormous front paws and dozed.

With a sudden burst of speed the first fluffy clouds scurried across the sun, transforming the sky from a far-flung canopy of robin's-egg-blue to a bowl of white spun sugar. The breeze, so refreshingly cool only moments before, now turned chilly.

Shivering, Fanny pulled her brightly colored India shawl more closely about her shoulders, remembering what she had wanted to discuss with Lord MacDonald before she'd been distracted by the young man.

"Grandfather," she said hesitantly, "Papa told me this morning that I shouldn't hate all the Campbells because of the Glencoe massacre. He says enough time has gone by that we should forgive and forget. He says you are wrong when you say 'The only good Campbell is a dead one.' "

She watched as Ian MacDonald, magnificently dressed in full Scottish regalia, reared up against the bench. His kilt, made of wool in the clan's tartan, sported wide red-and-black bands complemented by narrow yellow stripes. His shirt was of breeze-soft linen in a pale saffron. His thick white beard bristled, and his burnt-umber eyes flashed with rage.

"What! Forgive those bloody bastards? Forgive them for murderin' our fellow MacDonalds after we offered refuge from the winter storms? Forgive them for deliberately trickin' our clansmen, for killin' my grandfather in his oon bed and bitin' the rings from my grandmother's fingers? For rippin' the MacDonald luckenbooth from her nightdress afore puttin' her out o' her misery by thrustin' a sword through her heart? Forgive them? May God may forgive their heathen souls," he snarled, "for I will not!"

Fanny's eyes widened at her grandfather's fury, which never failed to fill her with amazement and awe. Usually he was a mild, gentle man, but whenever the subject of the Campbells was raised, he became a completely different person.

The massacre of which he spoke had taken place over a hundred years ago, in 1692, and Fanny agreed with Lord MacDonald's opinion that just because King William of Orange had instructed the Campbells to wipe the unruly MacDonald clan from the face of the earth, the Campbells should have had more loyalty to their fellow Scots than to William. William, a German, had obtained the English throne by marrying James II's daughter, Mary II, who had replaced her father as monarch when the Scottish-born king was deposed.

In contrast to her grandfather's thickly accented pronouncements, Fanny spoke in words that sounded delicately English, for her mother had come from the south of England and had taught Fanny to enunciate carefully so that people would know she was Quality. "What do you think became of the MacDonald luckenbooth after it was stolen?"

Narrowing his eyes, Lord MacDonald gazed off into the distance. "That fine silver brooch was passed doon from MacDonald laird to MacDonald heir for generations afore the Campbell blackguards stole it awa'. Ye remember the tale, how each time the eldest son o' the MacDonald laird married, he pinned the luckenbooth tae his bride's bodice—sort of a love token in lieu of a ring."

Fanny nodded. "Yes, I remember. But what do you think the Campbells did with it? It was silver, not gold, you say, and couldn't have been worth all that much to anyone but another MacDonald."

Lord MacDonald sighed. "God only knows where the brooch is now. But I can tell ye one thing for certain. The way our people feel about its theft, there will be nae peace between our clans till the brooch is returned. And if it be in the hands o' some drunken Campbell sot, 'twill probably never happen."

Fanny frowned. "There must be some way to get it back."

Lord MacDonald smiled in reminiscence. "When I was young, I tried for years tae find it. I wanted tae pin it tae my own bride's bodice, but 'twas not tae be. My grandmother was that fond o' her brooch and loved tae tell the story o' how my grandfather pinned it tae her bodice on their weddin' day. She wore it at all times, e'en on her nightrail. She always said wearin' it tae bed made her feel closer tae her husband, especially when he was awa' from home."

He paused, raising an eyebrow in Fanny's direction. "Ye'll be rememberin', o' course, that the brooch was already quite old and rich wi' family history when she received it."

"Yes."

"Well, the day before their weddin', my grandfather had both their names engraved across the back: Duncan and Francesca MacDonald. And the date: 1689. My grandmother thought it was a verra romantic gesture, inscribin' their names like that."

He grunted suddenly as he pulled himself back to the present. "But enough sentimentality. Yer father is a blasted fool, Fanny. I know ye're but a lass, and perhaps I shouldna speak so frankly, but ye're a wise bairn and I'll no mince words wi' ye. I've said it afore and I'll say it again: The only good Campbell is a dead Campbell, and ye musna forget it."

He gazed at her fiercely. "Ye are our hope for the future, lass. Nay, more than that. You *are* the future o' the MacDonald clan, the only grandchild I have. Sure, if somethin' happened tae ye, a cousin or some such would be more'n happy tae take yer place as the

MacDonald heir, but it wouldna be the same as the true heir takin' vengeance on the Campbells. For that is what I want ye to do someday—make those bloody bastards pay!"

Thinking about her romantic ancestors, Fanny stared wistfully into the distance. "Oh, I do wish I could find the luckenbooth. I would love to have my future husband pin it to my wedding gown." She grinned suddenly. "I realize the honor was usually performed by the eldest MacDonald son, but since I'm the only MacDonald heir, I think we could make an exception to the rule, don't you?"

Lord MacDonald chuckled. "I'd like tae see anyone talk you out of anythin' once ye've put yer mind tae it. 'Twould be more than I've ever been able tae do. I canna remember a time when I wanted ye tae do somethin' you were against that I didna have tae explain my reasons in detail. And if ye didna agree, ye still wouldna have anythin' tae do wi' it."

He shook his head fondly. "The most logical lass I've ever met, ye are, and the most intelligent. I canna count the times I've had words wi' yer papa on the matter. He's always seemed tae think ye'd comply wi' his wishes if he simply forced ye. Oh, he loves ye, but he canna seem tae get past the fact that ye're a lass. One o' these days I fear ye will show him just how wrong he is tae believe that ye're biddable just because ye're female and not because ye respect him as yer papa." He chuckled. "And I dinna ken I want tae be around when ye do teach him that lesson."

Fanny laughed. "He doesn't seem to understand my temperament, does he? But I cannot imagine him forcing me to do anything I was dead-set against. At least, he never has."

Smiling tenderly, Ian MacDonald chucked her under the chin. "I'm not so certain that isna because ye've always seen fit tae obey him, me darlin'. But ye mark my words: The day will come when ye balk, even tae him."

Fanny couldn't help hoping the young man hadn't seen her grandfather's affectionate gesture. She loved Ian MacDonald deeply, and he accorded her more intellectual respect than did her father, but he still treated her like a child.

Suddenly the thought occurred to her that if she could see the young man's clothing, she might be able to discern his station. Frowning, she shot a glance toward the wall. No, she could see nothing but his face. To her mortification, when he noticed her glance, the young man winked. Hot-cheeked, Fanny redirected her attention to her grandfather, who was speaking again.

"Yer mother tells me yer tae have a Season next year."

Making a moue of distaste, Fanny nodded. "Yes. I suppose I must."

"Ye dinna sound too pleased wi' the notion."

"Oh, I am excited to see London. But I don't understand why anyone would want to leave Scotland. It is so beautiful here," she said softly, looking toward the mountains. "And the air smells so clean and fresh. If I could, I'd spend the rest of my life in Scotland and never go to England." She sighed. "Neither Mama nor Papa seem to understand that all I *really* want to do is raise wolfhounds."

Lord MacDonald barked with approving laughter but then grew serious. "Remember, lass," he said solemnly, "when yer mother tries tae marry ye off tae a suitable Englishman—and she will—ye must resist. The man ye choose must be a Scot, tae preserve our heritage. Preferably a fellow MacDonald. An Englishman isna the same as a Scot. If ye canna find a full-blooded Scot, a half-blood will do. But nae less."

Fanny laughed. "But *I* am only half Scottish, Grandfather."

"Aye, but ye are full Scot in yer heart, lass. And ye must bear many children tae preserve our future. Ye must make certain the treacherous Campbells never have the power tae smite the MacDonalds again. Promise me, lass, that ye'll nae forget my words today."

Fanny kept her glance from skittering to the wall, embarrassed that the young man might have heard the comment about child-bearing. She replied quickly, "I promise, Grandfather. I'll never forget how deceitful or dangerous the Campbells are. Never. And someday I'll make them pay for what they did to our clan."

"I'm glad tae hear it, lass," Lord MacDonald said with satisfaction. He climbed to his feet. "We'd best get inside. 'Tis goin' tae rain."

Thunder rumbled balefully.

Looking up at the sky, where the cottony clouds had turned to coal, Fanny nodded and stood up. Out of the corner of her eye, she glanced toward the wall. The stranger was still there, his strangely colored eyes watching her with an odd intensity. As her gaze met his, the young man grinned roguishly and tipped his head in greeting.

Tilting her nose toward the sky, Fanny tried to ignore him. Laying a hand on her grandfather's arm, she began walking sedately toward the house, the pregnant wolfhound ambling lazily alongside. She hoped the stranger got caught in the rain, insolent bumpkin that he undoubtedly was, nodding at her like that without benefit of introduction. Then a rueful smile curved her lips as she silently admitted that perhaps his seeming lack of desire for an introduction, rather than his familiarity, had set up her hackles.

Suddenly the clouds split open and the deluge began. A bolt of blue-white lightning rent the sky, and thunder ripped through the air. One of the apple tree's branches, wrenched from its socket by the gusting wind, fell with a splintering crash beside the bench as the old man and the girl burst into a run.

Detesting rain, the wolfhound soon outdistanced the humans, making for the stables and shelter. So close to whelping, the bitch preferred a comfortable nest of hay in the stables to her usual place beside Fanny's bed.

Sheets of rain tore from the black sky as Fanny attempted to hurry Lord MacDonald along. Unable to keep up, however, he pulled his hand from hers and pushed her forward. "Run, lass!" he gasped. "I'm right behind ye!"

And Fanny ran. Water streamed down her hair and pelted her eyes. Her gown, saturated and slick, clung to her slender body like a second skin. When she was but ten paces from MacDonald Manor's front door, another flash of lightning, so bright she was momentarily blinded, cleaved the sky. The ensuing crash pushed her legs out from under her and nearly shattered her eardrums.

An instant before she hit the sodden ground, an arm caught her about the waist and swung her into the air. The rain, like a million relentless needles, stabbed her cheeks, and she pressed her face into her savior's neck as he raced toward the house.

Just as she realized it was the young man who had come to her rescue, a shaft of flame slammed into the ground directly where she had fallen, making the wet earth spit and hiss. Then they were inside, and the lad set her down.

Craning her neck, Fanny tried to see past the stranger. Where was her grandfather? Her eyes sought his tall, invincible form amid the driving rain. Then she saw the motionless figure lying on the saturated earth, oblivious to the howling storm, and she began to scream.

She tried to dash back out into the gale, but the young man's fingers closed tightly on her wrist. "Nay, lass! 'Tis too late! Ye can't help him! Ye'll only get yerself killed! Ye can't go out there. Remember, the future was everythin' tae him, and if ye get yerself killed, 'twill all be over!"

The young man's eyes blazed into hers, and Fanny gazed up at him in confusion. "But he's not dead! He's not! I was just speaking to him! He can't be dead! It's not possible!"

"Ye must be brave, lass," the young man said softly.

"But . . ." Her voice trembled.

Firmly gripping her shoulders, the young man shook his head. "No buts. Lord MacDonald is gone. He would expect ye tae be brave. Ye canna fail him. Be strong, Lady Fanny, for his sake."

Suddenly he looked past her as, from within the house, footsteps approached. Making an irritated sound, he hurried on. "Listen tae me, lass. I'm in love with ye. I know this is a terrible time tae tell ye this, but

I'm leavin' the area tonight and wilna have another chance."

The footsteps came nearer.

"Wait for me," he whispered urgently. "I'll come back for ye when ye're old enough tae wed, if ye will have me. I know ye are at least a little interested in me, since ye've come tae the garden every day for the past week, as if watchin' for me." He smiled. "I would hae spoken tae yer father if 'tweren't for . . . certain circumstances and the fact that ye're so young. Ye must trust me. Say ye will marry me when I return."

Overloaded with pain and surprise, Fanny gaped at him, unable to speak. Was he mad? Or was she, for feeling a sudden delirious thrill at his words, with her beloved grandfather's body not even cold? Despite her pounding heart, she nodded stiffly. She could not deny her interest in this commanding young man. Her breath caught as his lips, cool and firm, swept down to claim hers in a brief caress. Then he was gone, vanishing into the hammering rain.

With his departure, agony over her grandfather's death swept over her like a tidal wave. Shoulders trembling with each wracking cry, she flung an arm over her face and slid weeping to the vestibule floor as her father entered the hall.

"Fanny? Dear Lord, what is it? And where is your grandfather?" As the new Lord MacDonald looked out into the sheeting rain, his cheeks paled to match the white marble pillars abreast the door. "Holy Mary," he whispered. "Mother of God."

1

"**I** tell you I'll not have him! I'll not wed some murdering Campbell, duke or no! I don't understand how you could even invite one of them here, much less suggest sacrificing your only daughter to the leader of those bloodthirsty heathens! Grandfather must be rolling in his grave!" Lady Fanny MacDonald's eyes flashed and her lips compressed as one ginger kidskin–slippered foot stamped the parquet floor for the third time in as many minutes. Shaking her thick red curls, she turned to stare mutinously at the towering bookshelves lining the walls of the library.

Near the fireplace, reclining on a vividly colored Chinese rug, a gigantic wolfhound raised its head and growled menacingly, warning that no one had better anger her mistress further if he valued his life. Fiercely loyal, Dagmar was Fanny's only dog at this time, although Fanny had been diligently searching for a suitable mate for the almost-two-year-old bitch since its birth.

The MacDonald family had come to England nine years ago, two weeks after the untimely death of Ian MacDonald. Fanny's father, finding himself the new Lord MacDonald and the owner of numerous Scottish titles as well as the earldom of the English town of Carlisle, had wasted no time in leaving Scotland to take up his seat in the House of Lords.

The estate where they now lived, Carlisle Cottage, lay on the edge of the town bearing its name and opened on the north to a large wood that stretched to the Scottish border. Far from resembling a cottage, the house, built as a fortress named Eagle's Rest in the sixteenth century, looked more like a castle, with its stone battlements and long, narrow windows, but it had long since been renamed.

Fanny had been just sixteen when she, her mother and father, an enormous retinue of servants, and one pregnant wolfhound bitch had left MacDonald Manor in Dumfries, Scotland, and made the move to Carlisle Cottage. Although transplanted to England at such a tender age, Fanny had never lost her Scotch loyalty.

Perhaps even more important, she thought now, she had kept her vow to her grandfather, elicited only moments before his death, never to forgive the Campbells for massacring her clan that snowy night in 1692 in the village of Glencoe, Scotland. That her father had invited the laird of the Campbell clan here to woo her without informing her of his intention galled bitterly.

When several minutes passed and no response was forthcoming, Fanny cast a veiled glance toward her father. Lord MacDonald sat behind a large oak escritoire littered with books, papers, and half-melted beeswax candles, which bespoke his scholarly bent. Just now his ordinarily indulgent countenance was as stiff as carved granite, and his normally kind eyes had constricted to determined slits.

Seeing her glance, Lord MacDonald erased the doggedness from his face and smiled appealingly. When he spoke, his words were cajoling. "Come, Fanny," he pleaded, "can you not give Argyll a chance? He does you a great honor by wanting to make you his duchess. Certainly you cannot still hold him responsible for what his forefathers did. I know you always agreed with your grandfather on the matter, but I'm sure that was only a childish whim. You have grown up and, I trust, gained wisdom with your years."

Fanny shot him a furious glare, but Lord MacDonald continued in a reasoning tone. "Besides, I should think you would want the match if it might save the lives of our clansmen."

Saying nothing, Fanny raised one eyebrow.

Speaking confidentially, the earl went on. "You must know that since the old duke's death the Campbells have developed a notion that, because our clan has grown powerful, we intend to destroy them all, and that they must destroy us first."

Fanny's other eyebrow joined its raised companion. "Now, there's an idea. Let's massacre them as they did our forefathers."

"I'm going to pretend you didn't say that," Lord MacDonald huffed. "Truly, Fanny," he continued sincerely, "there is no other way but this union to stop the violence. I am sorry the match is so distasteful to you, but there is no other choice. Argyll and I have met numerous times with men of our respective clans, but each time we came to a stalemate. Until His Grace hit upon this solution, we were at our wits' end. I beg you to reconsider."

Lowering her eyebrows forbiddingly, Fanny retorted, "Even if he is not a murderer, the Duke of Argyll is a scoundrel! A rake! A roué! He is an acknowledged womanizer, and I am horrified to think you believe him an appropriate mate for me. Besides, you had no right to discuss my marriage without informing me first. I am no longer a child. I repeat, I will not have him."

Clearing his throat uncomfortably, the earl shifted in his chair. "I know I shouldn't have taken these steps without informing you, Fanny, but you weren't here to ask. You were still in London when I met with His Grace. As you must remember, the Season had three weeks to go, and you and your mother didn't return to Carlisle until yesterday. There was no opportunity to solicit your opinion. Besides, I was certain you would see that this marriage is our only solution."

Turning, Fanny impaled him with her truculent gaze. "Haven't you heard of that wonderful thing called the post? Being a member of Parliament, you could even have written to me without any cost."

"Fanny, I—"

She interrupted mulishly. "No, you simply did not want to tell me anything until you had things squared away with your precious duke! And you just as obviously thought I would go along with your *fait accompli* like a docile lapdog. Simply because I wear a gown instead of breeches! Well, I may have been a tractable daughter until now, but I'm afraid this time you've overstepped the bounds of my obedience. I've always tried to do what you wanted, Father, but I will not agree to this."

She drew a heaving breath. "Also, the stories of the Duke of Argyll's scandalous escapades during the last several years are horrifying. The women! The gambling! The drunken orgies! You must know that the mothers of eligible daughters breathe a sigh of relief with each passing year the duke remains in Scotland rather than return to London. I have always thanked God that His Grace left Town before I made my come-out, so that I would be spared having to be in the same room with him."

When Lord MacDonald merely blinked, Fanny made an impatient gesture. "Surely you must remember the tale of how he thoughtlessly ruined two young debutantes in quick succession and then refused to marry either of them? No, instead of doing the honorable thing, he ran back to Scotland with his tail between his legs rather than face the censure of the *ton*. And the matter has never been forgotten!"

Lord MacDonald gave an exasperated grunt. "You speak of matters you know nothing about. A *tale* is precisely what it was, no matter what the drawing-room biddies say. Both of those girls recognized the duke as an ideal catch and endeavored to trap him into marriage. One young *lady*," he said disparagingly, "crept into his bed during a house party her parents gave in Devonshire and had to be forcibly removed by her own father! And the other passed around a rumor that His Grace had seduced and then discarded her. It so happens that he'd never even met the chit."

"Of course he hadn't. I'm quite certain such a paragon of virtue could never have misbehaved," Fanny muttered caustically.

Lord MacDonald ignored the comment. "Neither story was true, although both young women managed to have themselves ostracized from polite society. As for your insistence that Argyll ran away from the *ton*, you couldn't be more mistaken. His Grace returned to his family estate in Scotland to tend his ailing grandfather—the old duke, who died shortly thereafter. Believe me, daughter, the Duke of Argyll is not the sort of man to run from a fight. If he hasn't returned to Town, he must simply prefer his native lands to the rush and roar of London. Much, if I may add, like you."

Throwing herself into a chair, Fanny scowled. Since her father was correct in saying that she also preferred Scotland to England, she could hardly fault Argyll's choice in the matter.

A movement near the fireplace drew her attention, and she watched as the wolfhound bitch rose from the rug and moved lazily to rest her massive head on her mistress's knee and gaze up at her with soulful black eyes. Raising a hand, Fanny patted her absently.

The sole reason she'd remained at Carlisle Cottage for so long was because of her attachment to her parents. Especially her father. Although she loved her mother dearly, Edward MacDonald was the one who had filled the void left by her grandfather's death. Even though they'd had their differences during her younger years, Fanny had thought he'd finally begun to understand she preferred being reasoned with as an intelligent human being to being pushed about like a chess pawn.

But now he was trying to relegate her to the position of imbecilic female again, just as if all their understanding had never existed! You'd think she was sixteen rather than going on twenty-six! She shook her head. "Even so, the girls did remain unmarried, and they were ruined."

Lord MacDonald threw up his hands. "It was their own fault! I specifically interrogated His Grace on the matter. How could I do less and give him my only child?" He shook his head. "No, Fanny, the gentleman I met in Inveraray, Scotland is not the type to trifle with young ladies of quality and then jettison them without a second thought."

Fanny snorted. "He should not have allowed either girl to suffer. If he *were* a gentleman, he would have married one of them. That he did not simply proves he is an uncaring, unprincipled knave—like all Campbells!" She tossed him a smug smile.

Lord MacDonald shook his head again. "His Grace returned the girls to their parents and went his own way. And you may be interested in knowing that, after talking to him on the matter, I did even further research on the incident. I spoke to one of the girls' fathers."

Fanny shot him a surprised glance.

"It turns out that Argyll had to be talked *out* of marrying her, so determined was he to save her reputation, despite her foolishness. Now then. I am satisfied with his explanation, and so should you be. I know of no one but you who still believes the tales to be anything but ridiculous. The facts, according to those who would know best, state that the girls were ostracized not because of *his* behavior but for their own."

With a disbelieving sniff, Fanny redirected her attention toward the floor.

"As you said, the incidents took place years ago, just before your come-out, and so should be forgotten. Besides, I am certain the only reason you cling to the stories is because you want to think the worst about a man you have never met—just because of his surname. And that, my dear Fanny," the earl finished with a pointed glance, "is far more reprehensible than the imagined wrongs you believe His Grace to have committed. *You* have no cause to question Argyll's ways—not when you haven't even troubled yourself to discover the truth before vilifying him."

Unable to think of a suitably acerbic rejoinder, Fanny hurriedly picked up her thread of negative counts. "Even if the stories about the two girls are untrue, Argyll is still not husband material. Why, he has been known to have three mistresses at once—in the same house! Can you even conjecture what he did with three women at the same time? I have tried, and I must say the thought is beyond even my vivid imagination."

The earl's eyes glittered, and Fanny realized she had made a tactical error.

Hunching over his desk, Lord MacDonald stabbed a menacing finger at his daughter. "Mind your tongue, my girl. As a man, His Grace is allowed more license than a woman, and as for his keeping mistresses, most gentlemen of my acquaintance do. But no *lady* would ever allow such a vulgar thought as that to cross her mind, much less her lips! I will allow your indelicate comment to slide by this once, but you will not speak so crudely again!"

Biting her lip, Fanny turned away, fingers plucking distractedly at the rust silk of her gown.

Smiling suddenly, Lord MacDonald tried to inject some humor into their conversation. "Oh, by the way, Sir Blanden Fitch called here this morning, but the wastrel must have run mad. Said *you* had asked *him* to marry you."

Fanny's eyebrows flew to her hairline. "Really? How is it I did not see him?"

"He came while you were out riding. Naturally I had Beddoes toss him out on his ear. The dandy looked like a blasted peacock in that hideous ensemble he was sporting—green and blue and yellow with lace all over. Can't fathom where he got such a ridiculous idea as to think *you* would want *him*."

"No, neither can I." Then a stunned look crossed her face. Fanny threw her father an agonized glance. "Oh, dear."

Drawing a hand across his brow, Lord MacDonald groaned. "Lord preserve us. Every time you say 'Oh, dear' in that tone of voice, I know something terrible is about to descend. Please, Fanny, tell me the man's claim had no grounds."

"Well, it didn't, really. It's just that I ran into him last month at Lady Brannigan's house party. One of the gentlemen there jokingly asked me to marry him. Of course he wasn't serious, and no one took him so. I laughed and told him that the only one in the group I could possibly marry was Bland, since Bland was the only full-blooded Scot among them. You remember, the Fitches lived not far from us in Dumfries."

Her face fell as she remembered the real reason she had refused every suitor who had ever begged for her hand. For nine years she had waited for her hazel-eyed young man to return. He'd seemed so sincere. And from his voice, she had been certain he was a son of Scotland.

But, she thought now as her heart gave the familiar painful thump it always did when she realized he was never coming back for her, he had obviously been trifling with her emotions. And for him to have done so on the heels of her grandfather's death was despicable. If she ever saw him again, she would spit in his eye. Before ripping out his blackguard's heart.

Her father's voice jolted her out of her reverie. "And?"

"And then the subject changed, and I forgot all about it. But just as I was leaving, Bland came up to me and asked if I would give him the black velvet riband I wore around my neck—you remember, that bit I used to hang Mama's cameo from?"

The earl nodded.

"Well, Bland was standing with a group of other young bucks, and, not wanting to embarrass him, I removed the cameo and gave him the riband, saying it was the least I could do for the only eligible man in the room. He bowed and then left, saying the usual things about seeing me later and all that. Apparently he assumed more from my gesture than I had intended."

Lord MacDonald burst into annoyed speech. "The devil and all the hounds of hell! You really must learn to think before you act, my girl. It's no wonder Fitch got the wrong idea. And here I thought the man's wits had gone a-begging! I certainly could not countenance his implausible claim that my daughter—who until this moment I believed to have impeccable standards—had agreed to marry him. At least he was mistaken, thank God."

Ignoring her father's repulsed grimace, Fanny scratched the wolfhound's ears and replied calmly. "No, I wasn't serious. At the time. But now that I think on it, it doesn't seem such a bad idea at all. He is of our class. He is a Scot, and a full one, which was one of Grandfather's stipulations. I might add, as I did at the party, that he is the *only* full-blooded Scot I've met in London in the nine years I've gone to Town for the Season. And I have no doubt that if I married him, he would leave me alone to live my own life without feeling he had to keep track of my every move."

Her face showed her growing excitement. "After all, why would he? Other than my money, he has no more interest in me than I have in him. He is fashionable enough to agree that husbands and wives needn't live in each others' pockets." She looked thoughtful. "You know, the more I think on it, the more I like the idea."

The earl glowered. "Fanny, don't even consider it."

Looking up in mock surprise, Fanny replied smoothly, "I'm sure I don't know what you mean. I am of an age to choose my own spouse, am I not?"

"Good God, Fanny," Lord MacDonald groused, "you are the most vexing child! My daughter could not be such a feather-brain as to want to marry that buffoon. The man is a coxcomb of the first order. A—a macaroni. Surely you couldn't be so cruel to your mother and me as to bring that—that *dandy* into the family! Why, he'd go through your inheritance in a month, the way he spends money on fripperies. Besides, the man has no idea how to dress without making himself a laughing-stock."

Glancing pointedly at her father's subdued clothing, Fanny tipped her nose toward the ceiling and glared down its bridge. "I fail to see where *you* are fashionable enough to mock a recognized tulip of the *ton.*"

"Those lacy handkerchiefs he carries around, for example," the earl grumbled with a disparaging wave of his hand. "He's forever pressing their scent-laden folds to his nose as if everything and everyone around him smelled of the stables." Holding an imaginary kerchief to his nose, Lord MacDonald screwed up his face as if something in his study had gone rancid. Then he dropped his hand to his side. "And speaking of lace, I do not think a single item in the man's wardrobe isn't dripping with the stuff. Lace! Makes one wonder if he isn't a man of a certain type," he said in a nauseated tone.

Fanny glared, but her lips twitched slightly. "Bland is

a sensitive gentleman. He carries scented handkerchiefs because he has a more acute nose than most. And many gentlemen wear lace. On their cravats, for example."

"If he has such a sensitive nose, why doesn't he bathe more often? Then he wouldn't have to drown himself in perfume. As for lace, most men do *not* go about looking like a full card of the stuff!"

Fanny coughed to hide her smile.

The earl rolled his eyes, then turned to pierce his daughter with a serious gaze. "No matter. Make no mistake. I will not countenance a match with him. I could not allow my grandsons to grow up in that lacy fop's footsteps! Granddaughters, perhaps, for lace looks nice on little girls. But lace on my grandsons?" He shuddered. "Good God, the very thought! No! Absolutely not!"

Relieved the discussion had taken a lighthearted turn, Fanny bit the inside of her lip to keep from chuckling.

"Anyway, it is common knowledge his estates are foundering and he must needs marry an heiress. You must have taken leave of your senses to give him grounds to think you might truly entertain his suit. You, who have refused offers from some of the most highly thought of men in England! Perhaps if you were telling me you had chosen a man other than that—that exquisite, I would feel differently. But what woman in her right mind would want to marry a man who thinks himself more beautiful than she?"

Biting her lip harder, Fanny managed to look affronted. "Bland has told me often that he admires my beauty."

"I'll wager," Lord MacDonald acquiesced. "For you are a diamond. But tell me true, Fanny, did he or did he not, immediately after acclaiming *your* beauty, pull out that gold-plated hand mirror he always carries tucked in his breast pocket and admire his own reflection, an act designed to force you to admire *him* in return?"

A tiny gurgle of laughter escaped Fanny's lips. "Actually," she said grudgingly, "he did."

"I thought as much. And he lisps! And wears shoes two or three sizes too small, which, from the way he glowers at everything and everyone, I imagine pinch excessively."

"Oh, Father, really! You are being most unkind."

"I am being honest! For God's sake, Fanny, as if everything I've said were not damning enough, he minces! No! You will not marry that prancing swisher! The matter is closed. Although I will agree that it is high time you married—Argyll."

Fanny returned with a vengeance. "I can see that the only way to get you to realize I am old enough to make my own decisions, even about which husband I will choose, is to prove it to you. Grandfather always said this day would come, and, while I doubted him, this time you leave me with no alternative."

The earl sniffed. "Your being *old* enough to choose your own husband is not the issue. The issue is whether you are *mature* enough to choose a suitable one! And you are obviously not."

Somehow Fanny kept her tone even. "I realize you still think of me as a child, Father, but I am an adult. And as an adult, I remember the vow I made to Grandfather and take it very seriously, even though you think it was a childish whim. Honestly! You know me well enough to realize I would never, ever consider marrying a Campbell, so I don't know why you have even suggested it."

She went on matter-of-factly. "As for Blanden's lack of funds, I have money enough for both of us with the legacy Grandfather left me. Nearly ten thousand a year."

"No amount of money would last long with that spendthrift," Lord MacDonald rumbled.

Brushing his comment aside, Fanny was struck with an exciting idea. "And you know, since I'm sure Bland wouldn't expect to manage my every move, I could return to Scotland! I have always wanted to live where I could raise dogs—you know how difficult it is keeping an Irish wolfhound in our London town house during the Season. I'm certain Blanden would want to stay in London, so, other than siring the heirs Grandfather

wanted," she said with a fiery blush, "I'd never have to
see him at all. I could remove to MacDonald Manor!

"After all, as you said yourself," she declared, gazing
out the library window, "I far prefer solitude to Town
life. I have only gone to London every spring because
you and Mother expected it. But now that I'm an adult
and you apparently don't care if I stay here with you or
marry some disgusting reprobate who would carry me
off to northern Scotland so that I'd probably see you
once a year at most, perhaps it is time I reconsidered
my priorities. At least if I lived in Dumfries, you and
Mother could visit often. After all, MacDonald Manor
isn't all that far from here."

Pulling himself erect, the earl lowered his eyebrows
and leaned over the desk. "Never! You will not marry
that fashionable fribble!" he said dangerously. "A marriage with Sir Blanden Fitch will come about only over
my dead body! I will not have it! Rest assured, I will do
everything in my power to keep you from marrying
that sorry excuse for a man—and to see that you marry
the Duke of Argyll!"

Slowly, Fanny turned to look into her father's eyes.
"Father, I am twenty-five years of age—too old to brow-
beat or to be forced into marriage. I thought you'd
learned long ago that force doesn't work with me. Perhaps if you'd tried reasoning with me before taking
matters into your own hands, I might feel differently. I
doubt it, but it is possible."

The earl set his jaw. "Fitch is not the man for you," he
said unequivocally. "And don't threaten me. You may
not be terribly intelligent about choosing a husband, but
you're far too bright to cut off your own nose to spite
your face. You wouldn't marry that fool just out of anger at me."

Fanny gritted her teeth so hard her jaw ached.

Seeing her rebellious expression, the earl burst out,
"Good God, Fanny, you cannot seriously want Fitch.
Why, as a child, you hated him! So don't try to tell me
you really do want him, for I shan't believe you. Admit
it—you are merely being stubborn and trying to teach
me a lesson so I shan't interfere with your affairs."

Although he was right, Fanny didn't acknowledge it. Fists clenched at her sides, she spoke stiffly. "I'll thank you to allow me to choose my own husband, and I choose Bland."

"No, you don't." The earl spoke with such fierce conviction that Fanny bit down savagely on her tongue, somehow quelling the almost overwhelming urge to thump him over the head with one of the legion books on his desk.

Oblivious to the looming danger, Lord MacDonald gave her a self-satisfied smile. "Besides. It is too late for you to choose another besides Argyll." He sighed blissfully.

Fanny froze. "Too late? What do you mean, 'too late'? I've not married your precious duke yet!"

"Ah, but you will. Now let us have no more nonsense. You may be twenty-five, but you're still my daughter and as such will do my bidding. You owe me that much respect."

"And you owe me none?" Overwhelmed by the impression that she was careening toward the edge of the world without hope of rescue, Fanny grasped at her last argument. "Father, the duke is a Campbell! That fact alone should have made you refuse to hear his suit! No man should revolt your senses more than a *Campbell!*"

Lord MacDonald eyed his daughter forbiddingly. "Don't be a booby. I've already told you it is precisely because he *is* a Campbell that I have accepted him for you. Matters between our clans have grown too grave to allow yourself to be caught up in ancient history. Only those with no hope for the future dwell on the past. And you, daughter, hold the future of the MacDonald and Campbell clans in the palm of your hand. Whether or not you are wise enough to know what to do with that future remains to be seen."

The earl's words about the future brought back with blinding clarity the memory of sitting with her grandfather in the garden only moments before his death, and Fanny's eyes burned with unshed tears. Her head drooped. A moment later she snapped to attention as her father continued.

"But as much as I want you to marry the duke to do our people good, I do not want you to think I have entertained His Grace's offer solely for the clan's sake."

Fanny's voice was harsh as she spat out the reason most other fathers married off their daughters to men of their choosing. "Let me guess. You want me to wed that miscreant to increase the acres your grandchildren will inherit. Well, if that is your main reason for wanting this marriage, you should feel more disposed toward Blanden, whose lands not only adjoin ours but are said to be in far better condition than Argyll's properties. Everyone knows the cad ran through his fortune when he became the duke and is now a pauper. Or am I mistaken and he has suddenly come into a fortune?"

Papers, inkstand, candelabrum, and quills rattled violently as Lord MacDonald slammed one hand down on the top of his desk. "You exasperating, headstrong chit! If I wanted you married off to increase my lands, I'd have wed you to some unfortunate fellow long ago when you were too young to refuse!" He sighed suddenly. "I do not want you to marry to increase the family holdings. I want your happiness, and I want peace for our clan."

Fanny slapped her forehead with the open palm of one hand. "Oh, now I understand. Oh, dear Father, forgive me. I thought you were being unreasonable, but now I see you were really only interested in my wellbeing! Well, now that you know I would not be happy with the duke, I suggest we consider the matter closed." She smiled brittlely. "Anyway, you couldn't have forced me to wed him, you know."

Lord MacDonald's eyes flashed with something Fanny thought looked suspiciously like guilt. Her own eyes narrowed. What wasn't he telling her?

Carefully avoiding her scrutiny, the earl turned his gaze back toward his desk. "While you were in London for the last three weeks, I visited the duke's home, Inveraray Castle, which, as you've already stated, is in northern Scotland. The estate is the most beautiful place I have ever seen and is definitely not in disrepair, which shows that, unlike Fitch, His Grace has used his funds to build a household rather than a wardrobe."

Fanny sniffed dubiously.

"He may not be flush in the pocket right now, but that is only because when his grandfather died and His Grace inherited the dukedom, he poured every spare penny into rebuilding the estates his grandfather had let fall into disrepair. The old man gambled on anything from how fast a raindrop would slide down the windowpane to whether a certain man's mistress would throw a girl child or a boy. *He* was the reprobate, not his grandson."

"Perhaps that unfortunate trait runs in the family," Fanny retorted mordantly. "Would you truly want your grandchildren to possess it?"

Lord MacDonald waved a hand in dismissal. "At any rate, by the end of my visit I had discovered what I hoped I would when I went to Scotland: that His Grace is a man of honor and integrity and, most important, that he is the man for *you*."

Fanny spoke with conviction. "The Campbells are filth, and I shall never willingly wed one of them, even if Argyll's heart is snowy white as you would have me think. And I do not believe my fellow MacDonalds would be pleased by my marrying a Campbell. But apparently that doesn't concern you. Possibly because you, Father, have shown yourself to be a traitor to our clan by even suggesting such a revolting solution."

Lord MacDonald sank back in his chair, suddenly looking old and very tired. Running a hand over his eyes, he murmured softly, "A traitor, am I, Fanny? For wanting the best for both my clan and my beloved daughter?" His hand trembled, and he hid it in his lap.

Her father's unexpected vulnerability frightened Fanny, but she managed to hide her fear behind righteous indignation. "What are you going to spring on me next? That His Grace is one hundred years old and has two heads? Or worse, that he is an imbecile like King George?"

Lord MacDonald drew a shaky breath. "You have the tongue of an adder. I almost pity the duke."

Seeing how deeply she had wounded her father by calling him a traitor, Fanny felt her staunch refusal to marry the Duke of Argyll waver. She fought down the urge to throw herself into her father's arms and agree to anything. She opened her mouth, but nothing came out. She cleared her throat. "You are correct. I do not truly want to marry Sir Blanden Fitch. But rest assured, I will marry Bland before I agree to marry Argyll, so don't push me."

Looking at her, the earl shook his head grimly. "I will not allow you to waste yourself on a worthless shred of a man like Fitch. Apparently you have yet to learn the most important fact of life. It is this: No man or woman can survive all alone. If you marry Fitch, you will be alone forever, for the man has no more intelligence or caring than a squid."

He paused significantly before continuing. "On the other hand, if you marry the duke, who I am certain is the perfect mate for you, you will have a happy life, a life like your mother's and mine, filled with all the joys of a loving relationship. You will bear children you are proud to bear, since you will respect and love your husband."

Fanny's lips twisted.

The earl sighed. "You have asked me if I would condemn my grandchildren to carrying Campbell blood. Can you honestly say you would be willing to mingle your blood with that of Fitch before marrying a fine man like Argyll? Don't you remember what a cruel child Fitch was? How he loved to torture small animals?"

He saw by her expression that he had touched a nerve, and he pressed his advantage. "Could you, who love your animals so dearly, survive in such a marriage? What would you do if he took the notion to mistreat your dogs? Or your bitches' puppies? You would be unable to stop him. As your husband, he would have every right, since your property would become his. No, I am sorry you feel so strongly against marrying Argyll, but you *will* marry him, and you will *not* marry Sir

Blanden Fitch. No matter what I have to do to see these things come to pass."

Distraught at her father's implacable determination and her need to defy him to honor her childhood vow, Fanny felt a single tear slide down her cheek to drip onto her rust silk bodice just over her breaking heart. Her voice quavered, but she swore, "I will not wed a Campbell."

Lord MacDonald's voice turned gravelly with emotion, and he blinked rapidly. "I love you, Fanny. And I love the clan MacDonald. Please believe that if I didn't know in my heart you would be happy with His Grace, I would never, ever have considered this match. But you *will* marry him, or may the devil take you!"

Fanny rose and moved sorrowfully toward the library door. Like an enormous gray ghost, the wolfhound followed. As she reached the threshold, Fanny turned to gaze back at Lord MacDonald through her tears. "So be it. I'll see you in hell."

2

Ｈis Grace, Malen Patrick Ross Campbell, Viscount Lorn, Knapdale, Islay, Jura, and Cowall, fifth Earl of Bute, fourth Earl of Gigha, Colonsay, and other minor islands, sixth Duke of Argyll, paused as he neared the Scotch-English border.

Squinting in the bright afternoon sunlight just breaking through the rain clouds that seemed to have plagued him and his manservant ever since they'd left Inveraray Castle, he gazed down on the English town of Carlisle. At his side, his manservant pulled a set of bagpipes from its protective leather sheath and set about skirling a familiar tune.

After studying the small town far below for a moment, the duke reached into his sporran, the large, fur-covered leather bag hanging from the waist of his brightly colored tartan kilt, and removed a small object that gleamed in the brilliant June sunlight. His eyes narrowed as he stared at the ancient piece of jewelry.

Turning the luckenbooth brooch over, he examined it thoughtfully. Two finely wrought silver leaves curved upward, protectively surrounding a large amethyst carved to resemble a thistle. The outermost edge of the brooch was a delicate heart, which was, in turn, topped with a dainty silver crown.

He frowned suddenly, remembering how he'd meant to pin the brooch to Lady Fanny's bodice and claim her for his bride so many years earlier—the year she had made her bow to Society, her first Season. She'd been seventeen. He'd been twenty and almost uncontrollably eager to wed—and thus bed—the fire-haired beauty with the glowing pansy-brown eyes.

Only a few weeks before that fateful Season began, the old duke, Owen Campbell, had fallen seriously ill. As the ducal heir, since his own father was recently deceased, young Malen Campbell was forced to forget his romantic plans and return to Scotland without a bride. The old duke had died shortly after his heir's arrival at Inveraray Castle, and Malen had suddenly found himself responsible for an entire clan's happiness, safety, and good fortune. He had stepped into the position as if born for it, which he was.

At first he had hoped to return within six months to claim Lady Fanny's hand. In the end, however, it was years before the Argyll properties, which the old duke had nearly bankrupted through his unfortunate gambling habits, began showing a meager profit, and by then Malen was penniless, having poured every pence of his personal finances into estate restorations.

Finding himself a pauper, and having already left Lady Fanny on the shelf for years—he knew she hadn't married—he had tried to put all thoughts of matrimony out of his mind. Despite an infatuation of half a decade's duration, by sheer force of will he had managed to banish many of his memories of Lady Fanny.

After a bit longer, he had succeeded in convincing himself he didn't really want to marry at all. After all, the Campbell clan was extensive enough that he needn't worry about producing an heir. Indeed, had not necessity dictated his action at the present date, he might have settled down quite happily to a life of comfortable bachelorhood.

Still, although necessity *had* dictated his present course, Malen had no intention of allowing a wife— even the beauteous Lady Fanny—to curtail his bachelor entertainments. He liked staying at his northern estate, Inveraray Castle. If his duchess wanted to go to London for the Seasons, let her go alone; he would not bestir himself for her benefit. Nor was he about to give up his numerous flirtations. No, he had no intention of curbing his masculine habits. But if Lady Fanny behaved like all the other women in his past, he wouldn't have to.

Although he didn't consider himself vain, Malen

knew he was a fine specimen of manhood. Too many women had shared his bed without remuneration—indeed, he'd had no money whatsoever to lavish on them in years—for him to doubt his attraction for them. Thus he felt quite certain that even Lady Fanny would readily forget any unhappiness he had caused her in the past for the honor of sharing his bed and his title.

And marriage to Fanny MacDonald would have benefits for him as well. Although it had been years since he'd seen her, her sweet violet scent still clung to his memory. If he closed his eyes and breathed deeply, he could almost smell her perfume now. And if her childhood promise of beauty had blossomed, it would be a pleasure to teach his bride-to-be the ways of love.

He no longer felt guilty about returning to Lady Fanny at such a late date, for surely she had realized that he'd been but a green boy stupidly infatuated with an unknown girl at the time of his proposal. Of course, it hadn't felt like mere calf-love at the time. Ye gods, it had been terrible. The dreaming of her, the longing to be at her side, the overwhelming desire to marry her. Thank God he had outgrown those distressingly urgent feelings.

Besides, it was not as if he demanded a great deal of his future duchess, so why should she expect anything of him? His only mandatory requirement—one shared by every gentleman of his acquaintance, and not an unreasonable one—was that she be a virgin, so that any heir would be unquestionably his. Other than that, let her do as she pleased, so long as she didn't embarrass him.

At the thought of bedding Lady Fanny his loins throbbed expectantly, and he shifted in the saddle. It had been far too long since he'd had a woman in his bed. His three mistresses—and no, he was not ashamed of having three women in his household at once, for they had all been well served and had enjoyed their stay—had left the morning after he'd informed them of his intention to wed. Thus he was determined that Lady Fanny would submit to his desires immediately after the ceremony.

Images of the ways his bride would make amends for the dispatching of his concubines rose in Malen's imagination, causing a surge of fire in his loins that was echoed by the jewel's sparkle as he polished the luckenbooth against his wool jacket.

It wasn't as if he had a choice about marrying her at this late date, after all. His clan was in danger of being wiped out. The MacDonalds seemed to have decided that, now that they were rich and powerful, the time had come to seek revenge for the Glencoe massacre. That was how he came to be on his way to claim Lady Fanny as his bride today, in the hopes that an alliance between their two houses would bring peace. As laird of the Campbell clan, it was his duty to ensure the safety of his people.

But whether peace did or did not come, he reiterated silently, he would not allow Lady Fanny to dictate his life-style or curb his enjoyments one iota. In return, as long as she gave him an heir or two, he would allow her all the freedom she wanted.

As he made to put away the luckenbooth, Malen noticed a small tear in his kilt and frowned at the reminder of how hard he had had to struggle to reclaim some of the wealth Owen Campbell had gambled away. Well, no matter. Although he wouldn't be flush enough in the pocket to enjoy an extremely elaborate ducal lifestyle for two or three years yet, his finances were improved enough that he wouldn't need money from his bride-to-be, heiress or not. He was aware that many men of even higher station than he married to secure fortunes, but he had no intention of being one of them.

He laughed self-disparagingly as he remembered how foolishly romantic he'd been when he'd first proposed to Lady Fanny. He'd had this ridiculous idea that it was necessary to have sufficient finances to give her the world—without having to hand her the bill.

At that moment his massive chestnut stallion whinnied and stamped impatiently, eager to move on. Malen's legs tightened automatically around the rearing horse, and he thrust the luckenbooth into his sporran and nudged the stallion forward. As if on cue, the servant put his pipes away, and the small party began their descent down the muddy mountain road.

So violent was Fanny's headlong flight that she nearly ran into her mother, who was just then entering the library.

"Oh!" the countess gasped, putting a slender hand to her breast. "You startled me, Fanny."

Seeing her mother usually brought a smile to Fanny's lips. Lady MacDonald was a slim, fluffy, feminine creature with deep-red curls much like Fanny's own. Her eyes, however, were a vivid, sparkling periwinkle rather than velvety brown. Just now the countess wore her favorite lilac laces and ruffles, and her silky hair was dressed high upon her head. She smelled faintly of lavender water.

Today, though, no smile rose to Fanny's lips. Lowering her eyes, she tried to move around the countess. "I'm sorry. Excuse me."

Lady MacDonald caught Fanny's elbow just as her daughter stepped past. "Where are you going, my dear? An illustrious guest has just arrived and awaits your pleasure in the Egyptian room." The countess beamed. "Your father did tell you the good news, I hope."

Fanny gaped. "Good news? So you are against me, too? How could you, Mother? Do you care so little for me? How can you, who have had such love with my father, toss me so callously into marriage with that rake?"

Lady MacDonald's large eyes widened in surprise. "I beg your pardon?"

The earl surged out from behind the desk. "Don't you dare speak to your mother like that, my girl!" he said sharply. "Even if you are angry with me, there is no cause to strike out at her."

Lady MacDonald glanced covertly toward the adjoining chamber. "Fanny, Edward, do you think you might lower your voices? The duke is sure to overhear if you are not a bit more reserved."

As though she knew her mistress was going nowhere, the wolfhound headed back to the fireplace. She circled twice, then lowered herself to the Chinese rug with a heavy sigh.

The countess smiled soothingly as Fanny glared at the offending wall. "As for His Grace's being a rake, daughter, you may take it from me that what they say is true: Reformed rakes do make the best husbands." Lady MacDonald paused, gazing at her daughter's face. "Please think carefully about all this, my dear. The Duke of Argyll is a fine figure of a man. Why, if I had met him before I was married . . ." She laughed softly. "But no, I never would have married anyone but your father."

Edward MacDonald beamed.

"At any rate, my dear," the countess went on, "you would do well to avail yourself of your father's wisdom in this matter. At least do not reject His Grace sight unseen."

Sudden suspicion nibbled again at Fanny's thoughts. Why couldn't she shake the feeling that her father's handling of this situation was even more devious than she had first imagined? Turning toward Lord MacDonald, who was gazing in rapt adoration at his gracefully aging wife, Fanny raked him with a wary gaze. "There is more to this than you are telling me, is there not?"

Tearing his attention from his wife's face, Lord MacDonald moved to stand beside one of the long library windows. Twitching aside the burgundy velvet curtain, he peered out as if intent on the scenery.

"Father?"

Lord MacDonald avoided Fanny's eyes. "The banns proclaiming your betrothal to the Duke of Argyll were read in the parish church here in Carlisle and also in Inveraray at His Grace's chapel for the first time three weeks ago, while you were still in London. They have been read and duly recorded each Sunday for the past three weeks."

Fanny gasped, unable to find words to express her outrage.

The earl cleared his throat. "You are legally bound to the duke. Unless he agrees to cancel the betrothal, which isn't likely, since it was his idea to begin with, you will marry him tomorrow morning."

"You had no right!" Fanny finally cried furiously.

Lord MacDonald gazed at her expressionlessly. "You're correct. I had not. But if you value our family name, as well as your station in Society, you will go through with the ceremony. Otherwise you will be ruined, as will we. Your mother and I won't be able to raise our heads among our friends if you refuse. I hope you will consider your mother's reputation, even if you don't yours or mine. Everyone we know has congratulated us on your splendid match. Why, the Regent himself sent a note declaring his pleasure. Word of our clans' troubles has apparently reached even his illustrious ears."

Feeling trapped and desperate, Fanny clutched the back of a wing chair and stared at the earl, her face the color of Dover's chalk cliffs. "I don't believe you. You're just saying all this so I will agree to your plans."

"Who knows," Lord MacDonald continued in a firm voice, "you might even like His Grace if you give him a chance."

For a moment Fanny couldn't speak. After what felt like an eternity she managed to murmur brokenly, "Oh, Father, how could you? I have always trusted you, with my very life! I . . . I thought you loved me!"

"I do love you. And I want only the best for you. I think in your heart of hearts, you know that."

Fanny's voice was ragged with pain and sarcasm. "Oh, Father dearest, thank you so very much for relieving me of the burden of making my own choices in life and love. Now I see how truly you love me!"

Although his lips tightened painfully and his eyes shone with unshed tears, the earl did not rise to the bait.

Whirling, Fanny struck out at her mother a second time. "And you! You knew about this but did not tell me? What kind of mother are you?" Her voice broke on a sob. "But how can I expect you to understand how I feel about marriage to that—that devil? You're not really a MacDonald!"

Lord MacDonald was suddenly standing in front of her, his face inches from her own. "That will do!" he said in a voice as brittle as flint. "You will not speak to your mother that way. Like myself, she has your best interests at heart. Never say she has been less than an ideal parent. You will apologize at once!"

Cheeks flaming with mortification at having lashed out so vilely at her gentle mother, Fanny apologized.

Lady MacDonald gave her daughter an understanding smile. "That's all right, darling. I know you must feel betrayed by everyone just now. But it is not such a calamity as you imagine, I promise you."

Placing a hand on his daughter's shoulder, the earl patted it with uncharacteristic awkwardness. "It will all work out for the best, you'll see."

Fanny shoved his hand away as though it were a spider. Lord MacDonald stiffened and looked back out the window. He took a deep breath, and Fanny braced herself for his verdict.

When the earl finally spoke, resolution emanated from his voice. He gestured toward the chamber door. "As you already know, His Grace awaits your pleasure in the Egyptian room. You will meet with him immediately after finishing your business here. And Fanny," he said with an edge to his voice as his daughter turned sharply away, "as I have already said, you will accept him. As laird of the clan MacDonald, I *order* you to accept him."

Fanny forced her next words through frozen lips. "And if I do not?"

Her father was silent for a moment. Then he replied softly, pain resounding in each rigid word, "You know the Scots law when a clan member refuses a direct order from his chieftain. You will be cast out of our clan."

Fanny was nearly overcome with shock. Cast out? Cast out of the clan? For several moments she said nothing. At last, even though her heart contracted painfully, she turned to face the earl. "Well, then, I suppose I should adjourn to the Egyptian room. If you will excuse me?"

Neither parent moved, but Fanny could feel their vigilant gazes boring into her back as she turned away. Tipping her chin up, she raised her long skirts slightly and walked toward the door. The wolfhound kept her place, merely lifting her massive head to watch her mistress's departure. For Fanny, this last betrayal was nearly more than she could bear.

She closed the library door behind her and felt the full force of her aloneness. Swallowing a sob, she raised a trembling hand and brushed back her unruly curls, then smoothed her silk skirts. Drawing a quavering breath, she stepped toward the Egyptian room.

3

For several long, delirious moments, Fanny thought the room unoccupied. Had the duke heard her acrimonious ravings and beat a hasty retreat? Her gaze slid over the room's nooks and crannies, resting on sarcophagi and statuary, a multitude of gold and lapis lazuli figurines, ancient carnelian and agate jewelry nestled securely in a long crystal box, and several divans with headrests shaped in the guise of various animals.

Her slippered feet sank deep into the thick cobalt-and-crimson rug stretching the entire length of the chamber as she walked to the far end of the Egyptian room. There she pivoted slowly. At last a cool, self-satisfied grin turned up her lips. He wasn't here! He had run away, just as he'd run from the *ton* after ruining those two girls. What a coward! Just wait till she told her father how lionhearted his precious duke had turned out to be. Giving a happy skip, she moved back toward the door through which she had come.

From where he stood, half-hidden behind an Egyptian sarcophagus, Malen Campbell watched his future bride with surprised delight. She was even more beautiful than he'd remembered. A deep dimple decorated her right cheek, while a small black mole to the left of her lush mouth emphasized the sensuous quality of her generous lips. Her eyebrows were dark and finely arched. Her lashes, sooty and thick, formed a veritable forest around shining pools the color of a mourning-cloak butterfly's wing. Her teeth were startlingly white behind lips the shade of a damask rose, and her hair, a lush copper torrent filled with fiery highlights, cascaded in wild curls over slim shoulders to her tiny waist. How delicious it would be to wrap the rich locks around his fingers and pull her close for a long, deep kiss.

In short, the bud of youthful loveliness he remembered from nearly a decade ago had blossomed into a gloriously beautiful woman. Suddenly his nostrils flared, and he breathed deeply. Violets. She still wore his favorite scent.

And not only was she lovely but, judging by the way she had argued with her father, she was a spitfire as well. While at first heartily dismayed to hear her violent disclaiming of his person, he had quickly shrugged off his concern and reminded himself that she would come around once she met him. Or at least, he thought with an anticipatory smile, once he bedded her.

She would probably have been horrified to know that her outspokenness had merely stirred the desire more fervently in his loins, until he could think of little but her extraordinary body writhing in ecstasy beneath his. He was certain she would be passionate; given her temper and that flaming hair, she could be little else. His eyes glowed at the prospect of teaching her the exotic delights he had learned during the last few years.

And what sons she would give him! Fiery leaders such as the world had never known. And daughters beautiful enough to rival the maharanis of India. She was delectable—and soon to be all his. Had any man ever been so lucky? Suddenly it didn't matter that he was still nearly penniless or that he would undoubtedly be castigated vehemently once she recognized him for the boy who had jilted her years before. Nothing mattered but that she belong to him, body and soul.

His gaze continued devouring her body. His eyes widened. Lady Fanny's breasts, thrusting emphatically from beneath their rust-colored silken veil, were pleasingly generous. The loose folds of her Empire-waisted gown did nothing to conceal her lush curves. She obviously wore no stays or corset; her voluptuous body needed no artificial aids.

After considering the narrowness of her waist, his eyes flew to her hips to investigate her child-bearing capacity. It wouldn't do if they were too slim. He breathed a sigh of relief. Her hips were delicate but wide in the right places. Since, as he had discussed with her father, their offspring would help heal the deep rift between their two clans, it was necessary that she be a good breeder.

Her legs, emphasized as she strode confidently toward the door, were long and firm. No excess flesh there.

A faint curiosity at how she would respond to his kiss flitted through Malen's mind. Not one to refuse himself anything, he pushed off from the dead Egyptian. The girl, who had just placed her hand on the doorknob, whirled, dismay altering the aristocratic planes of her face.

Suddenly the duke grinned in unabashed delight. He'd been afraid she would have outgrown the faint sprinkling of freckles cavorting across her nose and cheeks. Rather than detracting from her beauty, they gave her a gamine quality he found irresistible, and he could not help but wonder if they also frolicked over her full breasts.

His lips turned up in a deceptively lazy grin, and he moved forward. "My bride, I presume?"

Fanny gaped. The duke's voice, she noticed, while not particularly deep, contained a suggestive, velvety quality that made her eyes widen and her temperature soar. Appalled that she should have been observed dancing toward the door in obvious pleasure at what she took to be his absence, Fanny felt her mouth open and close dumbly as the cad's assessing gaze drifted from the top of her curls to the toes of her soft ginger kid slippers and back again. She flushed violently as his eyes came to rest on her breasts and his nostrils flared appreciatively. Such impertinence!

Her hands flew up to cover her bosom, but she stopped them in midair. Determined not to reveal how his hawklike examination unnerved her, she lowered her arms to her sides in what she hoped was a relaxed manner. Tilting her chin haughtily, she returned his brazen inspection, allowing her eyes free rein over his figure, starting with the hollow at the base of his neck, since she could not yet find the nerve to stare him directly in the eye.

The Duke of Argyll was not extraordinarily tall, nor extremely broad-chested. He wore a blindingly white linen shirt open at the neck, with its ties hanging freely on either side in arrogant abandon, and to her surprise, Fanny's belly tightened as she noticed several alluring black curls peeping out of the V.

Over his shirt the duke sported a short, pine-green jacket of fine Scottish wool that hung easily on his shoulders. These shoulders, although not stunningly wide, whispered strength rather than shouting it, and Fanny found their quiet confidence somehow disturbing. Her gaze slid downward.

His hips were slim, the hands that rested upon them long-fingered and elegant, sensitive and somehow artistic. A small green cap with a red pom on its crest and a long pheasant feather protruding from its brim dangled languidly from his right hand.

Altogether, there was thus far nothing obviously unsettling about the man. So why was her stomach quivering? With an irritated murmur at the unfamiliar sensations coursing through her, she forced her eyes to continue their downward trail.

The duke wore a kilt in his clan tartan, mostly green with wide black bands, blue squares, and narrower yellow and white stripes. The Campbell tartan made her want to spit. Quelling the urge, she clenched her teeth.

The kilt came to just above his knees and was cinched at the waist with a wide leather belt. Hanging from the belt was a large furry sporran.

Her nostrils flared slightly as her eyes came to rest on the long, muscular legs only partially covered by the kilt. Like splendid peaks the duke's knees were bare, while his well-muscled calves were covered by superbly woven wool stockings—also in the Campbell tartan. Black curls like those on his chest graced the exposed inches of his splendid thighs.

Swallowing, she forced her eyes from naked flesh to the duke's right stocking. Just above its hem peeped the braided leather handle of what looked to be a small knife. On his feet were flat-heeled shoes with silver buckles. He stood with his legs wide, an unnervingly masculine stance.

At last there was nothing else to look at. She drew a deep breath and raised her eyes to the Duke of Argyll's face.

A few curls had escaped the leather thong that held his unfashionably long hair at the base of his neck. Obviously this man gave little weight to popular styles. The short black wisps swirling around his cheeks lent him the look of a rogue pirate, and Fanny wondered, suddenly, what the Campbell duke would look like with his dark, silky hair flowing free.

The duke's eyes gazed at her piercingly from beneath sculpted brows of raven-black. His lashes were so long as to be almost obscene on such an unmistakably masculine face. His eyes were an odd mixture of teal-blue and sage-green, and they sparkled mischievously. Strangely, they seemed almost familiar.

His nose was long and sharp, aquiline, his nostrils wide. Or were they merely flaring under her scrutiny?

A thick rug of ebony curls covered the remainder of his face. Fanny stared. Since beards had gone out of fashion many years earlier, she hadn't seen above two or three since her grandfather's death. Most self-proclaimed dandies like Beau Brummell or Sir Blanden Fitch shaved several times daily so as to avoid even the faintest shadow of beard.

The duke's high-planed cheekbones were visible, but just barely. His lips, appearing soft and smooth, peeked intriguingly from the forest of curls. Her fingertips itched with an unbidden desire to touch those slightly mocking lips. She quickly dispelled the wayward urge.

A mellow, self-satisfied chuckle reminded Fanny she had been examining the duke for several minutes. Dragging her rapt gaze away from his mouth, she cleared her throat and searched for the right words with which to put this arrogant devil in his place. At last she tipped her chin higher and stared frostily straight into the Duke of Argyll's unusual eyes. "You presume incorrectly, sir."

Somehow Fanny managed to hide the flood of pleasure she felt upon seeing surprise wipe the confidence from those sanguine features. With frank interest she watched the smile curving his bold lips falter. Like all attractive men, she thought smugly, he must have expected her to take one look at his magnificence and fall into a swoon. She ignored the thought that she had come uncomfortably close to doing just that.

Continuing in the same matter-of-fact voice, Fanny added, "If you think you can simply come waltzing in here"—she waved a hand around the room—"and inform me of my luck in becoming your wife, you have cobwebs in your skull."

Lady Fanny smiled sweetly, and, through his surprise, Malen felt a renewed prickle of desire as the tip of her salmon-pink tongue darted out to moisten her full lips.

Fanny smirked. "I fear if that's what you expected, Your Grace, you are doomed to disappointment."

Crossing his arms and baring his teeth in a cool smile, Malen replied lightly, "I fear luck has little to do with it, my lady. Resolve yourself. You *will* be my bride." His smile broadened as he watched a slow flush climb her cheeks. " 'Twould take more than a shrewish tongue to make me release a tasty morsel like you. Nay, you will not escape me that easily."

The duke's words were spoken with the same amused inflection as his first sentence. Although she realized he was deliberately trying to provoke her, Fanny could not repress the twisting serpent of fury that coiled in her chest and blew a hot red haze before her eyes. "And what makes you so certain of that, Your Grace?"

Malen chuckled. "Certain of what, ma'am? That you will be my bride or that you are a tasty morsel? As for the first, I would think that is obvious, since the banns have already been read. As for the second, one need only look to see that your lips would taste most sweet to the man fortunate enough to claim them."

Fuming, Fanny gnawed at her lower lip—on the inside, so the outrageous knave would not see how badly he could upset her. With iron resolve she forced herself to ignore his twigging and, willing her voice not to quake, replied calmly. "Mayhap the banns have been called, Your Grace, but that does not mean I will marry you."

She thought rapidly, then smiled. "Not only was my father's act of having the banns called highly unethical, but he also apparently failed to inform you of something quite important. I am betrothed to another." She watched with satisfaction as the duke's haughty face paled.

"Betrothed?" What treachery is this? Your father gave you to me!"

At his choice of words, Fanny burst into angry speech. "Why is it that everyone speaks of me as if I were a sack of goods to be traded from one man to another?" she sputtered. "First my father, and now you! It is disgusting! I am a twenty-five-year-old woman, and as such I will make my own choices. I am no longer a sixteen-year-old chi—" Her voice broke off, and she stared at the Duke of Argyll with dawning realization.

A chill seeped into Malen's bones as he watched all color drain from Lady Fanny's exquisite features. One small hand fluttered up to clutch the rust silk at her neckline, and a tiny squeak of astonishment slipped from between her lips.

Fanny felt as if she were living her worst nightmare. As if the discovery that her father had sold her out to the hated Campbell laird were not enough, now the precious dream she had secretly held to her heart these last ten years had been shattered. Was it really possible that the sweet young man who had saved her life and then stolen her heart was *this* hateful creature? Suddenly his failure to reappear to claim her hand was much easier to understand. After all, Campbells had no honor. It had all been a horrible trick. He had done it on purpose!

It was not until she gasped that she realized she'd been holding her breath. Without thinking, she reached behind her and grabbed the first object her fingers touched—a valuable Egyptian urn of pale-green alabaster. "You!"

"Now, Lady Fanny," Malen began. "If you'll just give me a moment to explain—"

"You!" she repeated. "You . . . blackguard!" The urn rose menacingly.

"Get a hold of yourself, my lady!" Malen said sharply as he eyed the vase clutched inauspiciously over the beauty's head. "There is a perfectly good explanation!"

"I'll just bet there is, you selfish bastard! And as soon as I've cracked your damned skull, I'll be happy to listen to it!" The urn flew from her fingertips, a missile aimed at the Campbell laird's pate.

Malen ducked, and the resounding crash when the vase hit the wall behind his head made his eyes widen apprehensively. "For God's sake, Lady Fanny!" he cursed as another airborne object—this time a small bronze statue of the Egyptian jackal-god, Anubis—nearly took off his right ear. "Give me a chance to explain!"

In the back of her mind Fanny realized tears were streaming unchecked down her cheeks. Filled with shame and mortification, she whirled away, hands pressed to her burning face.

After waiting a moment to make certain she wasn't trying to trick him into approaching so she could slam something into his skull, Malen approached cautiously. When he saw that her shoulders were trembling, an unexpected surge of guilt washed over him. God, had he really hurt her so badly? He hadn't meant to. He'd been so certain she wouldn't want to marry a pauper. Despite all his arguments for remaining a bachelor, he realized abruptly, he had never forgotten her; he'd only wanted to. "Lady Fanny?"

As his hand touched her shoulder Fanny turned to scorch him with a scathing glance. Shrugging off his hand, she moved a few steps away. "Don't touch me. I hate you. No, I more than hate you. I'd like to kill you for what you did to me. Do you realize I waited for years—*years*—for you to come back?"

Malen sighed heavily. Placing his hand on her arm, he squeezed gently when she tried to shake him off again. "Look at me." When she wouldn't, he forcibly turned her body toward him. Her lovely brown eyes were filled with tears and refused to meet his. "Lady Fanny, I didn't mean to hurt you. I didn't know I had. I wasn't even sure you would want me to come back. Please, listen to me." He shook her slightly. "I've never had the chance to tell you what—"

"Only because you n-never b-bothered!" Fanny cried brokenly.

"That's not true. Weak as it is, there was a reason. Will you hear me out?"

After what seemed an eternity, Fanny nodded faintly.

"Good. I was nineteen when my father brought me to the Dumfries area on a hunting trip." He laughed suddenly. "I don't know what he thought when he rose every morning to find my bed empty. How could he know I had risen with the sun to seek far more fascinating quarry?"

Fanny glanced up at him, then away, wanting to believe he'd found her fascinating but unable to get past her prejudice against his Campbell heritage and his broken promise.

"We were leaving Dumfries the day after that dreadful storm," he continued. "I meant to seek you out in London the year you had your come-out. But that same year first my father, then my grandfather died, leaving me in possession of the family estates. My grandfather was an inveterate gambler, and it took every penny from my father's estate to pay for the damage my grandfather had inflicted on our properties."

Against her will, Fanny felt a flicker of sympathy. "I'm sorry about your losses. But I fail to see how estate troubles kept you from fulfilling your promise."

Malen stared at her in astonishment. "Why, I was certain you would want nothing to do with a pauper. Besides, we were children when I asked you to marry me. I didn't think you really took me seriously. At any rate, upon further reflection, I realized that the insensitive *way* I had asked you, with your grandfather dying only a few steps away, had probably outraged your sensibilities and showed my vow for the childish selfish, impulse it was."

Fanny glared. "But you never bothered to ask *me*. You merely presumed that I was so materialistic I would send you away. And because you assumed I was as childish as you were, you dismissed me from your mind. But, as a woman of her word, Your Grace, I took you at yours. I am afraid I wasn't experienced enough to realize what I had received was only the inflamed promise of a green boy."

Bowing his head, Malen murmured, "I can only say I am sorry. I hope someday you will forgive me." He looked up. "But just now we have matters more serious than childish pains to discuss. Our clansmen are killing each other, and it is up to us to stop it."

Still too personally angry to consider clan affairs, Fanny shook her head. "I already told you. I am betrothed to another." She glared at him belligerently. "He expects me to marry him, and I intend to."

"Do you love him?"

His words took her by surprise. Her eyebrows flew skyward as her eyes widened. "Love him?"

"That's what I said. It was a simple question and deserves a simple answer. Yes or no?"

Flushing, Fanny lowered her gaze. "Let us say simply that I'd rather marry a well-dressed gentleman than a damned Campbell whose beard makes him look like a bear."

Despite her unflattering comment, Malen's heart pounded with unexpected relief. He was not such a cad as to take her away from one she truly cared for, even at the expense of their clans. But he did not think she really loved this unknown man, else she would have declared it. He sighed. "Even though I have grown quite attached to my beard, for you, my lady, I would shave it off. Then you should have no objection to our marriage."

Startled by his comment, Fanny blinked at him, then forced herself to give a derisive snort of laughter. "Shaving your beard won't help. I cannot, I *will* not, marry a Campbell. And you of all people should realize why. You were present when I gave my grandfather my vow to see that the Campbells were punished for what

they did to our family. How can I punish them if I
marry one?"

Malen's mouth tipped up at one side. "You might be
surprised."

Fanny threw him a look of disgust, then stiffened as
the duke's gaze swept over her once more. His eyes
flared like hot coals, dark desire flickering in their
depths.

"What do you want me to do, my lady? Prove that
we belong together? Make you forget this crazy idea
that you should marry another? I may have made the
mistake of releasing you once, by failing to return for
you, but I'll not repeat the error."

Fanny blushed wildly as the unmistakable hunger in
his eyes rushed through her veins like molten sunbeams. To her dismay, her breasts seemed to tingle and
her thighs to tighten with excitement. Her breath caught
in her throat when he closed the distance between them
with a single step.

Malen looked down into Lady Fanny's face. Her eyes
were wide and brilliant, her finely sculpted cheeks
flushed. Extending his index finger, he traced the deep-
pink washing up the curve of her neck.

Fanny couldn't breathe. Her face flamed more hotly
still as the duke's finger glided with torturing leisure-
liness toward her mouth. Slowly, so slowly she somehow ached for it, his finger came to rest on her lower
lip, sliding sensuously back and forth. She shuddered at
the exquisite, unfamiliar sensation, and her lips parted
with a sharp gasp. The duke then traced a path across
her jaw and down to the small, wildly pulsating hollow
at the base of her neck.

At last he breathed a sigh of apparent regret and
lifted his finger from where it lay just above her breasts.
Never taking his eyes from hers, he stepped back
slightly. "You are utterly magnificent, my lady."

Horrified by her permissive behavior, Fanny showed
him her profile. Still under the influence of some animal
passion she had not been aware she possessed, she tried
to calm the urgency that was tightening her nipples into
tiny rigid peaks.

Seeing her confusion, Malen felt a wave of longing to pull her into his arms, but he kept a firm grip on himself. In truth, he dared go no further with his seduction, or there was not a shred of doubt in his mind that he would take her there and then on the floor of her father's house. His entire body trembled with repressed ardor, and he was glad of the kilt that hid his raging desire.

Composing himself with difficulty, he spoke softly, as if soothing a nervous filly. "Lady Fanny, I'm sorry I hurt you. But don't ask me to release you from our engagement. After what we have both just experienced, you must see why I will not. You belong with me as the sea belongs to the shore. What we feel must not be denied."

Fanny shook her head slightly, attempting to clear her muddled thoughts.

"Truly," Malen said softly, entreating her logic, "you must know that even if I were not so swept away by your beauty, I would insist upon marrying you to bring peace to our clans. If our union does not bring peace, I'm certain our children will. And I intend that we have many, many children."

His gaze licked over her body once again, pausing to devour the hard points of her nipples now evident beneath her bodice. His fingers curled into fists as he squelched the desire to nuzzle the turgid peaks with his thumbs.

"Well!" Fanny huffed in an effort to mask the turmoil of her emotions. "So I am to wed you for the sole honor of bearing your offspring?"

Shaking his head, Malen smiled gently to soften his words. "Nay, lass," he said quietly, in his earnestness slipping back into the Scotch burr he had largely lost since spending time in London. "I am sure ye will find much pleasure in bein' my duchess."

Unable to deny the suggestion outright yet fuming at his presumption, Fanny snapped, ''What would a brute like you know of a lady's pleasures?"

Malen laughed, his hunger for her in all her outraged innocence rising so demandingly it was all he could do not to take her in his arms and compel her to accept his suit that way. "I may lack gentlemanly virtues, 'tis true, but your own colorful behavior in your father's house could hardly be called ladylike. 'Twould seem we are well-matched. However, if there are particular ways you would like to be pleasured, I'd be most willing to learn them," he added with an outrageous wink.

For a moment Fanny was so incensed she couldn't speak. When she regained her voice, she replied crisply. "That, Your Grace, is something you will *never* have the opportunity to discover! As soon as I can talk my father out of this insane plan of his and yours, I intend to go to Scotland, where my true betrothed and I will be wed."

The plan to go to Scotland to marry Blanden Fitch slipped from her tongue unintentionally, but as soon as she'd said it, Fanny realized it was a brilliant idea. Although she didn't know precisely how one went about it, she remembered hearing something about elopers in Scotland being married "over the anvil." Once there, she would investigate the method, which she recalled had something to do with declaring oneself a man's wife before witnesses.

As for Bland, she was certain he would comply, if only to tweak her father's nose for having him thrown out of Carlisle Cottage. With a faint smile, Fanny raised one eyebrow and stared challengingly into the duke's astonishingly blue-green eyes.

For a long moment Malen considered her words. She was lying about her desire to marry another, that much was obvious. But it was just as obvious she was dead-set against marrying *him*. And he realized with a jolt that, even had he not planned to wed Lady Fanny to save his people, the challenge to make her want to be his duchess was now irresistible.

What was it about this woman that drew him so? What was it that had captivated him years ago and now, even when he had believed himself over her, had reached out to grip him once again? Whatever it was, he had to have her; the matter had gone beyond reason. In that moment it took all his self-control to keep from proving to her, right there on the Egyptian room floor, that they were meant for each other. He grinned, suddenly thinking that this marriage would prove far more interesting than he had first believed.

Fanny's head buzzed at the duke's slow, sensuous smile and unreadable expression. Her knees turned to rubber, and she moved to lean in what she hoped was a casual pose against the fireplace mantel. Missing the marble rim with her elbow, she came close to falling flat on her face, but she recovered quickly.

Malen grinned as Lady Fanny glared at him, as if daring him to laugh at her near-accident. "I see," he said finally. "Well then, I suppose there is nothing for it but for me to escort you to Scotland."

As graciously as possible, Fanny shook her head and attempted a cool smile. She could have cursed when her upper lip stuck to her paper-dry teeth, exposing her nervousness. "I don't need accompaniment, thank you very much. I'm sure I'll be able to manage on my own."

"Aye, but your competence is not in question. While a gentleman wouldn't want to force you into a marriage that would be repulsive to you, it would be unforgivable for him to allow you to travel without protection." He raised a hand as she opened her mouth to object. "I will take you to Scotland, and that's the end of it." He paused. "Unless you prefer that I tell your father what you're plotting. I trust," he said in a conspiratorial whisper, "that you don't intend to inform him of your travel plans?"

Fanny fumed silently.

Malen smiled. "I thought not. Well, since I imagine he plans to make absolutely certain you do not flee until you are safely wed, I think you'll need my help making a successful escape."

Considering her options, Fanny studied him. Did he really think her so simpleminded? Probably. Most men thought women hadn't the brains of a peahen. Of course he planned to escort her to Scotland and then try to force her to marry him. Also, he was probably right about her father's locking her in her room, if need be, since Lord MacDonald's mild-mannered behavior had changed so drastically over this match. Hadn't the earl said he'd do anything to see this marriage come to pass?

Therefore, she assessed quickly, Argyll was correct. She would have to escape Carlisle Cottage in some way other than walking out the front door with her bags packed. She frowned. Perhaps she could use the duke's arrogance to her benefit. The question was, how hard would it be to elude him when the time came? And, more important, did she have any choice but to agree to his terms?

At last she smiled. Holding her hand out in a businesslike gesture, she said confidently, "I accept."

4

Sir Blanden Fitch, baronet, sat before a sticky trestle table in the common room of the Sauce for the Gander inn. A narrow strip of black velvet dangled from his fingers. He stared at the riband for a moment, then thrust it into his breast pocket.

He had not moved from the table since noon, having arrived just after receiving the set-down of his life from Lord MacDonald. One would have thought Fitch had suggested ruining Lady Fanny on the dining-room table while the earl looked on, the way MacDonald had lambasted him.

A double shot of whiskey, the latest in a series of such glasses the sullen, pockmarked barmaid had placed before him, rested beside his right hand. Picking it up, he took a deep pull at the glass, swishing the pungent liquid over his teeth and tongue. He swallowed with a shudder, then nervously began shredding the costly lace on one of his elaborate cuffs.

MacDonald had laughed at the coat Bland now savaged, a coat the baronet had designed especially for the interview with Lady Fanny's father. Said it was garish and vulgar. Said the colors didn't match and it had too much lace. Called him a macaroni. Said his daughter had far too much sense to shackle herself to a dressmaker's dummy. As if the old man had any sense of fashion whatsoever!

Since he considered himself a tulip of the fashion world, Bland was confident that, despite the earl's scathing remarks, emerald-and-canary brocade trimmed in aqua satin and dripping with Brussels lace looked

most striking, especially on a figure as fine as his. The
old fool was only jealous. And with just cause.

But that knowledge didn't make Bland feel much better, and he tore another strip of lace from its moorings
and threw it on the ground, trampling it beneath the toe
of one metallic gold Hessian. The action made the fili-
greed gold spur above his heel jingle merrily.

Lord MacDonald had refused his suit, and Bland
knew he'd never be able to wear this lovely jacket again
without thinking of the humiliating event. No, he
thought sulkily, his delight in the lovely coat had been
shredded, just as he was now shredding the lace.

MacDonald, the old cretin, had treated Bland as if the
baronet had taken leave of his senses. The old man had
even insisted his darling daughter would sooner look to
a slimy eel for a husband than a . . . What word had he
used? Oh, yes. *Fop.* But MacDonald was wrong. Dead
wrong, Bland thought as he gave the lace another violent tug.

He had the lady's approval. Indeed, had Lady Fanny
not thrown herself at him like a veritable harlot, he
never would have believed he'd had a chance at win-
ning her hand. The lady was rumored to have received
upward of twenty offers since her first Season, many
proffered by his personal acquaintances. But she
wanted *him.* Wise girl. She had said *he* was the only
man she'd marry!

The discovery that Lady Fanny was madly in love
with him had taken him completely by surprise, for she
had never seemed to like him overmuch. In fact, she
had appeared to despise him when they were neighbors
as children. But then, he hadn't minded her unwillingness to play with him. She had not been much fun.
She'd never wanted to play any of the games he liked,
such as catch-the-frog-and-pull-off-its-legs or rip-the-
wings-off-flies-and-toss-them-into-spiders'-webs or
smash-the-bird's-eggs.

In fact, he remembered with distaste, Lady Fanny had
been too much of a goody-two-shoes to be amusing.
Once, when he'd wanted to throw a small kitten far out
into the pond behind her house to see if it would swim

back or drown, the impudent hussy had clubbed him over the head with a fallen tree branch, giving him a huge lump that had been sore for days. Then, to top matters, that horrid monster she called a dog had chased him off the MacDonald Manor grounds.

He wasn't certain if Lady Fanny still kept the curs, but if she did, the first thing he'd do after their marriage would be to put a bullet through every one of their vicious heads—after, of course, making them suffer for what their fellow mongrel had done. He'd be damned if he'd have the nasty beasts around, but he'd have some fun with them first.

But even though he'd been amazed when she'd said she wanted him or no one, just after saying so Lady Fanny had given him a token of her esteem, a narrow black riband she often wore around her neck. Wishing to give the lady the benefit of his attentions, he had asked for the riband deliberately, and she had given it willingly, proving to him how much she cared. His companions had been astounded. Obviously, however, he had concluded as he accepted her tribute, the lady's taste in men was excellent.

And although he considered physical intimacy tolerable at best and too hideously messy to bother with at worst, he had magnanimously decided marriage to Lady Fanny would be bearable, since it was common knowledge she would receive not only a large dowry from her father, as well as his entire estate when the old boy popped off, but she had also inherited ten thousand a year from her grandfather.

Because the thought of her fortune was so delectable, he thought he'd be able to grit his teeth and give the lady what she so desperately craved—him—though as seldom as possible, of course. And if he weren't capable of pulling it off, once they were married there would be little the slut could do about it. Any suitably shaped object would deflower her, and then she couldn't argue that he'd not consummated the marriage. Why, he might just begin their marital relations that way anyway, for the sheer pleasure of her shock and humiliation.

Other than the thought of physical intimacy, the idea of marrying Lady Fanny had been most acceptable. It had pleased him so much that he had, albeit with great difficulty, forced the notion that he would be marrying an unruly romp to the back of his mind, contenting himself with thoughts of the new ensembles he would design with her riches.

Of course, he *had* had to accept that it would be quite a noisome task bringing Lady Fanny up to his standards. An unexceptional dresser, she would very likely need a completely new wardrobe merely to be seen in his presence without disgracing him. Truth be known, the image of her at his side rather put him in mind of a crow competing with a brilliantly feathered tropical bird. Then again, that image did not altogether displease him. Perhaps it would be best to allow her to continue choosing her own clothes.

And there remained the fact that Lady Fanny's offer had come at a most opportune moment. The morning before she had begged his hand in marriage, Bland's solicitor had informed him that the extensive fortune his father had left had been depleted to a measly few thousand pounds, and, unless the baronet's finances were supplemented or he learned to limit his needs for silks, satins, and laces, he would find himself in debtors' prison before much longer.

Of course he'd dismissed the solicitor for his disrespectfulness. And he had certainly not curtailed his spending. He was a baronet! A Fitch! It was his right—nay, his duty—to look splendid at all times.

It was not as if he spent thoughtlessly. He was well aware of how much blunt it took to stay on top of the fashion world. It was dashed expensive. But what could one do? One had a reputation to maintain.

As a pink of the *ton*, a blade of fashion, one of Brummell's Boys who stood in the bow window at White's with Lord Alvanley, "Ball" Hughes, and "Poodle" Byng among others, he would honestly rather die than be caught dead in anything less than perfection. The very thought that he, considered by all to be a veritable *ar-*

tiste, might soon no longer be able to indulge his creative instincts was devastating!

There was not one in his circle, he knew, whose skill came close to his ability to put together startling turnouts. Why, even though he admired that acknowledged Beau, George Bryan Brummell, greatly, Bland had always secretly wondered why everyone thought the fellow such a classic dresser. After all, the man had no flair for color and less of an eye for jewelry. Why, Brummell had even been known to say, "If someone turns around to look at you, you are not well dressed." The comment had flabbergasted Bland until he realized that, although the Beau handled somber styles quite well, he was simply not—how should one say it?—snappy.

But just now there was no time to ponder anything save how to solve his present dilemma. It was all Lady Fanny's fault that the had come to the pass he now found himself in, and she must be made to pay. Another fragment of lace joined the dingy heap on the floor.

It was her fault, not his, that he had rushed out the morning after she had begged him to marry her and purchased an entirely new wardrobe to celebrate the happy event. After all, she *was* an heiress. And he had had to have that new black-and-yellow-striped curricle, as well as the high-stepping sugar-white ponies he had gotten at the bargain price of five hundred pounds apiece at Tatt's, to set off his new clothes.

And there really had been nothing else to do but buy champagne all 'round at White's to celebrate, although he had to admit he *was* a bit annoyed when the bloods needed a fortune in drink to be convinced that the exquisite Lady Fanny, who had received and refused offers from most of them, had consented to be his wife.

Bland could not imagine why his gentlemen friends had been so amazed that the lady had chosen him. Who better than a man of his caliber to wed the acclaimed beauty of the last nine Seasons? They should have realized that, as magnificent as he was, marrying her would be a step down for him, for at twenty-five Lady Fanny wasn't getting any younger.

But now everything had been ruined. Damn Lady Fanny! What game was she playing?

Clearing his throat, he hawked on the filthy floor. Really, it was impossible to understand the actions of women. She must not have told Lord MacDonald of her desire to marry the fabulous Sir Blanden Fitch, and the earl had been taken by surprise. Without a doubt that was the only reason MacDonald had behaved as he had. But it had been so embarrassing! If he weren't in so much financial trouble, Bland thought with a sneer, he'd let the lady stew in her own juices. She'd never forgive herself for losing him forever.

When he had removed all the delicate lace from his cuffs, he sighed. After examining the damage with the aid of one of the myriad quizzing glasses adorning his chest, he sighed again and dropped the eyepiece back among its companions. Then, since there was no more lace to shred and his hands were too nervous to hold still, he jammed a fingernail between his teeth.

When his gnawed finger began to hurt so badly he could feel the pain even in his present state of inebriation, he pulled it from his mouth and clasped his hands tightly on the table before him. Hiding the ragged finger in its opposing palm, he examined his hands furtively. They were so beautiful. They had never done a moment's hard labor and were as white and soft as a dove's breast.

Damn and double damn Lady Fanny for getting him into this mess! He might actually be forced to work for a living! Him! Of course, he could always find employment as a fashion advisor, but still, work was work, for God's sake. It just wasn't fitting that a baronet become a common laborer. Why, it was downright intolerable!

He picked up the whiskey glass again, only to discover it empty. And he had no money to buy another. Actually, he had not paid for the last three, and the innkeeper's wife, standing in the kitchen doorway, had begun looking suspicious. Insolent hag. Slamming the glass down on the table, Bland stared at it balefully. Then, moving his arm in a dizzy arc, he swept the empty glass to the floor, where it shattered into a hundred pieces. That'd teach her.

" 'Ere noo!" the innkeeper's wife said sharply, moving swiftly to his side.

Sneering, he watched her come, a large, bovine creature with hips the size of a side of beef and feet like grave-diggers' spades. Her hair, stringy and gray, was pulled into a bun so tight her eyes were near to being plucked from their sockets. She was Scottish, and her voice was so thickly accented he could barely understand her. Bland turned away disdainfully. *He* had long since purged every last bit of Scottish burr from his elegant voice.

The woman stood at his side, hands settled on her massive hips. "That'll be enough, me bucko. No more fer ye. Not till ye pay yer shot. 'Tis three drinks ye've 'ad—and one broken glass ye'll pay fer."

With unlimited disgust, he noticed her hands were cracked and red. Quite revolting. In a superior voice, he retorted, "I haven't got any money with me. Put it on my tab."

For a moment the woman looked as if she were seriously considering squeezing the whiskey back out of him. Then, with a growl, she thrust out a brawny paw. Closing his eyes tightly, Bland prepared for the blow. It didn't land.

Instead, gripping him by one elbow and heaving him to his feet, the woman started toward the door. "Out ye go, ye worthless sot. I'd make ye work tae pay, but noo doubt ye'd break somethin' else."

For a moment he swayed unsteadily. Had not the woman kept a firm grip on his waistcoat he was quite certain he would have joined the lace and shattered glass on the floor. Then they stepped outside, and there was a resounding *plop* as she dropped him in the center of a mud puddle. Brushing her hands together as if completing a highly satisfying job, the woman moved back inside.

The door closed, cutting off the warm light of the inn and leaving him alone in the cold, damp evening. He remained partially submerged in the puddle until the

chilly muck began soaking through the fine jean of his
breeches, then he clambered up with a heartfelt moan.

His evening was topped when, with a low rumble of
thunder, it began to rain. Tipping his head toward the
sky, he allowed the drops to splash his face until he
thought he'd regained a semblance of sobriety. Then,
still wavering, he turned around and headed for the stables.

When the postboy had the spanking-new curricle and
pair readied, Bland leapt into the driver's seat, spurs
jangling. Without a backward glance or a coin to the
lad, he slashed the white beauties on their rumps and
raced off down the muddy road, laughing at the colorful obscenities the postboy screamed after him.

Fortunately, for the road was very slippery, he was a
crack whip, a member of the Four-Horse Club. Despite
his drunkenness, his driving skills came to the fore rapidly, more than once saving him from sliding into the
ditch at the side of the road. Keeping one bloodshot eye
trained on the ever-darkening sky, he contemplated his
next move.

He had four choices. He could return to Merryfield,
his estate just outside Carlisle, and wait for his creditors
to come for him and throw him into debtors' prison; he
could flee the country and never see his beloved London again; he could take up a position as a fashion con-
sultant; or he could go to Lady Fanny and demand she
make things right.

It wasn't a hard choice to make.

Perhaps if Lady Fanny were present, he thought, he
would be able to prove to Lord MacDonald that the chit
really did want to marry him. And if she did not agree
to make things right . . . well, he'd cross that bridge
when he came to it.

With an unpleasant smile he brought his whip down
even more sharply against the horses' flanks, making
them whinny in pain. The sound brought him a sharp,
almost erotic pleasure, and he wielded the whip again
for the pure enjoyment of it. With luck, he thought as
the terrified horses doubled their already frantic pace,
he'd reach Merryfield in an hour or two. He'd get a few

hours' sleep, and then he'd call upon Lady Fanny at dawn to demand she fulfill her promise to marry him.

It was not necessary, he found when he arrived at his estate, to return to Carlisle Cottage after all. A note, waiting on his dressing table from that same lady, subserviently informed him that she had heard of her father's rudeness and requested the baronet meet her in Dumfries, Scotland, where they would be married without delay.

Apparently the incident with Lord MacDonald, that old fool, had indeed been an unfortunate mistake. He sighed happily. How could the earl ever have doubted that Lady Fanny wanted the illustrious Sir Blanden Fitch for her husband?

Calling Forbes, he ordered the valet to pack.

5

Fanny sat on her bed, chewing a slice of toast dripping with butter and hot raspberry jam and sipping a mug of creamed chocolate while she flipped through the pages of the most recent *La Belle Assemblée*. The sun had long since gone down. Since her maid, Bessie, was in the habit of leaving clean linens in a trunk at the foot of the canopied bed, it had been a simple thing for Fanny to remove six long, creamy silk sheets, twist and tie them into a makeshift rope, and hide it beneath her pillow.

Although she had hoped to simply open her door, walk down the hall, and quietly leave the house by the front door, she didn't see anything wrong with having a backup escape plan as well. In truth, she couldn't take sole credit for the rope idea; Argyll was the one who'd pointed out that, since her father was so insistent she marry the duke, the earl would likely have someone posted outside her door in case his daughter decided to take a midnight journey.

She sighed. If only it weren't necessary to leave Dagmar. Reaching down, she ran her fingers through the dog's rough gray fur. At almost two years old, the wolfhound took up nearly the entire mattress except where her mistress sat, scrunched into a ball. Dagmar raised her enormous head, and her dark eyes sparkled as she gazed adoringly at Fanny. As soon as she arrived in Dumfries, Fanny decided abruptly, she would demand that her father send the dog to MacDonald Manor.

A sick lump settled in her stomach as she wondered if Lord MacDonald would be too angry to comply.

There must be some way to take Dagmar along! But for now, she'd best send the dog to the stables so the beast wouldn't give away her escape plans by howling when, if necessary, she left her room by way of the window.

Suddenly Fanny realized Bessie was looking at her curiously. "Did you say something?"

"Aye. I asked if 'ee wanted to wear yer pearls or yer crucifix tomorrow." Bessie grinned. "But I guess 'ee didna 'ear me. Got a spot of weddin' nerves, 'ave 'ee?"

Fanny took a deep breath. "I most certainly do not. I'd like you to leave now. I want to go to bed. Oh, and please have a footman take Dagmar to the stables tonight. I think her stomach is bothering her."

Bessie eyed the sleepy dog doubtfully. "She looks a'roit to me."

Fanny frowned. "I think I understand my own dog better than you do, Bessie. Do as I say at once. As I said, I'd like to go to bed."

The maid sighed and nodded, then giggled intimately, unable to keep mum. "Yes, me lady. Ye'd best get to bed. Ye'll be needin' all the rest 'ee can get, 'cause if the duke's 'alf the man me Johnnie is, yer goin' ta need it!"

Johnnie was second footman at Carlisle Cottage. Bessie had been hoping for a proposal for nearly three years but had finally accepted the fact that it wasn't coming and settled down to enjoy what she could get.

Fanny glared at the maid, who, giggling boisterously, grasped the wolfhound's leather collar, dragged the grumbling dog off the bed, and left the room.

No sooner had Bessie disappeared than Fanny leapt from the mattress and raced toward the door. Noiselessly she turned the handle and pushed the door ajar. She froze. Not five paces away a footman in red, black, and yellow plaid livery in the MacDonald tartan dozed in semi-vigilant guard against the corridor wall. With a dark scowl she closed the door and pushed the inside bolt home.

Scurrying to the bed, she moved her pillow to one side and retrieved the sheet-rope. Then, reaching beneath the bed, she pulled out a large carpetbag. She tossed it beside the rope on her sumptuous burgundy velvet comforter. Next she hurried to her bureau, bent to the bottom drawer, and pulled out her traveling outfit.

When she had donned the sturdy kerseymere gown, warm woolen stockings, and ankle boots and gloves of soft leather, Fanny strode to the armoire and removed several more gowns and their accessories, undergarments, stockings, and a heavy, rather nondescript pelisse of thick braided wool.

Thrusting these items deep into the cavernous carpetbag, she moved back toward the bureau, reached behind it, and pulled out a smaller satchel in which she'd already packed a hairbrush, a toothbrush, tooth powder, and a small black velvet sack of coins, the remains of her quarterly allowance. All these objects followed her clothing into the carpetbag.

Suddenly she paused, frowning, and glanced back at the bed. Returning to the armoire, she removed another bundle of gowns. Pushing the rope and the packed carpetbag from the mattress to the floor, she arranged the gowns in a large, human-shaped lump beneath the comforter, pulling the cover over the top of her pillow as if the person in the bed were sleeping soundly.

Satisfied that anyone who glanced into the room would notice nothing amiss, she smiled. Turning, she walked to the window and looked out at the darkness beyond, then glanced back to her rope on the floor. She retrieved it and, tugging at its knots, wondered if it would hold her or if she would plummet to her death in the middle of the gravel drive.

Hesitating, she swung the rope absently from side to side as she gazed about the room. Then, turning quickly, she climbed up onto her enormous bed, flung the rope over the mahogany canopy frame, and secured it to the cross-post.

Gripping the rope with a determined grimace, she rested her toes on the edge of the bed, allowing the main part of her body to hang over the edge of the mattress until all her weight was suspended from the silk cord. For a moment everything seemed destined for success. Then, just as she'd made up her mind the rope would indeed be a useful escape tool, the fine silk knots slipped apart as if they'd been buttered.

With a thud she landed, buttocks first, on the carpeted floor. "Oooff!" she grunted as she rolled backward in a heap of disarranged petticoats. Rubbing her backside, she climbed to her feet and glared at the useless rope. Apparently silk, while delightful to sleep on, had its drawbacks.

However, the fact remained that the following morning was her wedding day, and she still had to get out of the house undetected. Relieved she had had the foresight to test the rope before entrusting herself to its strength, she dismissed the incident with a shrug and turned her mind to coming up with another plan.

After a moment, she smiled. "Of course!"

Swiftly she moved back to the open window. Leaning out of it, she studied the outer wall of the manor. Just beyond the wide marble windowsill, a large climbing rose meandered lazily up a wooden trellis. That should serve perfectly.

But did she have the nerve to try such an acrobatic escape? There wasn't time for contemplation. For, once again, a more pressing issue rose in her mind: Did she have any choice?

Somewhere far below in the darkness, the duke waited for her. If she didn't get down there soon, she thought glumly, he might even go to her father and tell the earl of her plans.

Pushing the window as wide as it would go, she picked up the heavy carpetbag and shoved it over the windowsill and out into the darkness. A loud grunt led her to wonder at her aim. She peered cautiously over the sill, then frowned. The devil! She couldn't see a damned thing. The night was pitch-black. Even the moon, although nearly full, was covered by fluffy clouds.

She froze as a footman in Carlisle livery stepped into view, holding aloft a lantern. But, rather than looking up at her, the man hung the lamp on the hook beside the front door. How odd. Although many estate houses lit their doorsteps, Fanny's father had always spoken against this practice, deeming it a fire hazard. The footman disappeared into the house.

Well, at least now she could see what she was doing. Not that that was necessarily a boon. Swallowing the lump that had taken up lodging in her throat as she assessed the vast distance between window and ground, Fanny took a deep, sustaining breath, gripped the windowsill between her trembling fingers and, without giving herself time to think, swung her legs out the window.

Turning so that her breasts pressed against the stone wall, she eased herself down over the ledge until her legs dangled in the air. For a second she flailed madly. Then the sturdy toes of her boots slipped between the trellis slats, and she breathed a sigh of relief.

Carefully putting her weight on the trellis, she clung to the windowsill in case the wooden structure gave way. Then, taking another deep breath, she released her hold on the sill and began moving down the wall, gripping the wooden rungs with fear-stiffened fingers. Bit by bit she inched closer to the ground.

As some flying night creature flitted past her face, she bit back a scream. The trellis gave an aching creak as she twisted violently to one side to avoid the bat. For a terrifying moment her heart stopped beating. Had the wooden slats ripped free from their moorings? No. After spending several moments reassuring herself that she wasn't going to plummet to her death—at least not yet—she resumed her downward journey.

She had not gone far, however, when she realized with dismay that the rose was insistently clinging to her skirts with its razor claws. As a thorn stabbed her palm, she cried out in pain and bit back tears.

Why hadn't she thought to wear her gloves instead of packing them away in her carpetbag for later use? Feeling foolish and hoping no one had heard her exclamation, she attempted the descent again, only to have another thorn attack her tender flesh. "Damnation!" she gasped, shaking her fingers sharply.

Her concern about the thorns piercing her flesh was

only momentary, however, since at that instant a quiet chuckle drifted up to her. Simultaneously she realized that her skirt was caught by the briars. She tugged at the kerseymere gown, but it only became more deeply embedded among the thorns. Worse, she now realized her hem had caught at waist level, leaving her stockinged legs and lace-covered buttocks hanging uncovered in midair! She could only hope the lamplight wasn't casting an embarrassingly illuminating glow on her scantily clad backside.

Inasmuch as she couldn't pry her skirts loose, she would have to climb back up to disentangle herself. Lifting a leg, she prepared to re-ascend, only to find to her unbounded chagrin that now her petticoat and chemise had joined her skirts in their thorny prison. What now? She couldn't go up, and she couldn't go down. Closing her eyes, she leaned into the wall, praying fervently that some guardian angel—preferably one who did not resemble the Duke of Argyll—would swoop down from heaven to disengage her trapped clothing.

What should she do? For what seemed an eternity she hung like a fly in a web, pinned to the trellis, unable to think of any solution save one. At last she sighed. The only thing she could do was let herself drop like a ripe fig, tearing her skirts from their thorny prison. Hopefully, she thought grimly, she would be ripped free and not left hanging from the vine like a fish on a hook.

So wrapped up in these thoughts was she that at first she did not hear the quietly spoken words from below. Finally, though, the phrase penetrated her haze of consternation and fear.

"Lady Fanny, let go."

The duke! Surely he didn't expect her to trust him, a bloody Campbell! And yet, what was it her father had said about trust? That without it there was no relationship? That was absurd. She didn't have a relationship with this disreputable rake, and she didn't want one.

Again the words came, more firmly this time. "Let go. I will catch you!"

"No!" she hissed. "You'd drop me out of spite!" She heard an exasperated chuckle.

"You must. You have my word I shan't let you fall. Let go! Now!"

"Your word?" she retorted. "What good is the word of a Campbell? And stop giving me orders."

"Let go! Now, Lady Fanny!"

The words held an unmistakable timbre of command, and, to her astonishment, she found herself obeying. Opening her stiffened fingers, she dropped like a stone, praying he would catch her rather than let her crash to her death on the gravel. Her tangled skirts gave a loud ripping sound, and in an instant the duke's strong fingers were sliding up her calves as she descended, over her knees, and surrounding her slender thighs. Some bemused part of her mind realized she must have been closer to the ground than she thought as she found herself suspended in the duke's arms, one of his hands still under her skirts, cradling her buttocks.

"There. You're safe now." He smiled. "I told you you could trust me."

Fanny sniffed. "I'm sure the only reason you saved me was because you mistakenly think I'll agree to marry you out of gratitude. Well, I won't. As for being safe"—she glanced pointedly at his arms—"I was probably more secure suspended in midair than in the arms of a rogue like you! Put me down!"

Setting her carefully on her feet, the duke grimaced and rubbed his forehead. "Did you have to throw that bag at me? What do you have in there, anyway, a fire iron?"

Fanny chuckled nastily. "If I'd thought of it, I'd surely have brought one to protect myself from you. And if I was sorry about hitting you in the head, I'd say so. But I'm not. You deserved it. Your escape idea almost killed me." She looked thoughtful. "But what can one expect from a Campbell? Maybe that's exactly what you wanted to happen to me."

"I'd have caught you just as easily if you'd fallen all the way from your windowsill," he replied confidently.

Heaving the heavy carpetbag over one shoulder as though it were a feather, he moved away.

Fanny followed quickly so as not to lose him in the dark as he set out across the grounds at a good clip. She noted that he had exchanged his kilt for leather breeches, a white linen shirt, a jacket of soft wool, and gleaming black Wellingtons. Surprised at the fineness of his attire, she realized with a start that he would undoubtedly be as much at home in a London salon as he would in the hills of Scotland. Except for that unfashionably long hair and beard, of course.

He didn't pause until they stood hidden in the woods near the main road. Gasping to catch her breath, Fanny tugged at his sleeve. "Wait a minute. I've left behind something very important."

The duke looked at her curiously. "I thought the important thing was getting away without being discovered."

"It is, but this is also important."

He tipped his head to one side. "What is it?"

"My dog. I left her in the stables."

He blinked. "Your dog?"

"I can't leave her. If I do, my father might refuse to send her to Scotland when I get there."

"Would that be such a tragedy?"

"Yes. I'll not leave without her."

"Then you'll marry me in the morning, for you'd certainly be caught if you went back for your dog. And I cannot get her for you, because she doesn't know me and would probably wake the house with her barking."

Fanny considered her options. Although it pained her, she had to admit he was right. If she went back for Dagmar, there was a good chance she'd be discovered. The duke had been quite honorable in reminding her of that, she thought in surprise, for she'd have assumed he'd want her caught and taken back to her room. She really couldn't understand why he was helping her. Didn't he realize she might foil his plan to trick her into marrying him?

At last she nodded, hiding the sheen of the tears filling her eyes. "All right. We'll go on."

With a wry chuckle, the duke shook his head. "I knew the threat of marrying me would make you move. God forbid you should suffer such a fate."

Since she could only agree, Fanny didn't answer. When they reached the edge of the estate they stopped again. The duke seemed to be looking for something, tipping his head this way and that. A stiff wind had risen and whipped the branches of trees and shrubs in a frenzied dance.

Fanny put a hand to her chignon to better secure its pins, but she found that most of them had been dislodged by her adventures with the rose thorns and the duke's arms. Freed, her hair curled wildly over her shoulders, swirling in the wind.

At that moment the gibbous waxing moon slid from behind the clouds, and a soft ray of light penetrated the shifting branches high above, illuminating the duke's face. Narrowing her eyes, Fanny stared at him as he dropped the carpetbag and turned toward her with the predatory grace of a panther.

His teeth gleamed as his lips parted in a smile. "I think I deserve a kiss for coming to your rescue so gallantly. We have a few moments. Come here."

There wasn't time to react. One iron hand moved swiftly to trap her wrist, and Fanny felt herself being pulled toward him. Good God, she must have been mad to follow this man into the forest! He was a Campbell, for God's sake, an acknowledged womanizer. And he had seen her in a state of near undress!

Her heart caught in her throat as she saw his face descending toward her own, his lips parting in another strangely stirring smile. His breath was sweet on her face as his mouth covered hers, muffling her gasp of outrage.

Struggling fiercely, Fanny fought to escape but was crushed against the duke's hard chest for her efforts. With her one free hand she struck the side of his face with all her might. He froze. Slowly he lifted his mouth from hers and wrapped a hand in her thick mane. His eyes, pools of mystery in the night, imprisoned hers.

His lips, moistened by her own, curved up slightly. Fanny felt an odd shaft of excitement rush through her.

"Kiss me, Fanny."

She felt his chest rise in a satisfied sigh as, to her astonishment, her treacherous body moved toward him of its own volition. His lips reclaimed hers. He kissed her hard, demandingly, relentlessly. He clutched her tightly, until her hips ground intimately against his loins and her lush breasts flattened against his chest.

Fanny bent like a willow as the wind rushed around them, feeling herself meld to the duke as if they were two pieces from the same puzzle. He smelled of musk and maleness, leather and tobacco. Fanny felt his whiskers tickle her face and somewhere in the back of her mind it registered that they were remarkably soft.

The kiss might have deepened into something more had not Fanny suddenly remembered precisely who she was embracing. As the duke's mouth parted her lips, she forced herself to relax in his embrace and grant his silken tongue entrance—for just as long as it took her teeth to open and bite down.

6

With a confounded chuckle the duke pulled away, touching his tongue. "Damn, wench! You bit me!"

Vibrating with unfamiliar longings that made her want to throw herself back into his arms, or at the very least touch his soft lips and brush the silky curls of his beard with her fingertips, the devil take the consequences, Fanny panted for control. "Yes, I did," she gasped. "And I'll do worse than that if you try to take such liberties again. I told you you could escort me to Dumfries, not fondle me anytime you felt like it."

Even to her own ears her tremulous voice didn't sound very convincing. The duke's chuckles deepened to delighted laughter, and Fanny tried to ignore the rich, velvety maleness of the sound. "I'm glad you find it so amusing, Your Grace," she said flatly. "However, while you stand here enjoying yourself, the hours till morning pass. If we don't get out of here, my father will discover my disappearance and call out a search party."

"Well then, we should be on our way." Still grinning, the duke picked up the carpetbag and, waving for her to lead, moved after her in the direction of the Great North Road to Scotland.

Not much time had passed before Fanny got the distinct impression that they were being followed, an impression confirmed by the duke's constant searching of the shadows. Hesitating, she turned and looked back.

A low cry rose in her throat as a short, hideous figure lurched out of the darkness and onto the road not thirty paces behind. It loomed toward them, and it was not until the figure was almost upon them that Fanny realized it was the duke's manservant, whom she'd seen wandering about the courtyard at Carlisle Cottage that afternoon. Her legs shook with relief.

"I brung yer bag, sir," the little man wheezed breathlessly. "Sorry I'm late." Showing the large duffle to the duke, he put it over his shoulder and turned toward Fanny. "Me lady. A pleasure, I'm sure."

Turning on the duke, Fanny bristled. "Is there anyone else you told of our venture, Your Grace? You're certain you don't need a cook, or perhaps a footman or two to tend to your needs?"

Frowning, the duke blinked at her. "I couldn't very well leave Gordy to live with your father, madam. He's has been with me since the war. He lives in Inveraray, not England. What would you have me do? Turn him out simply because you don't want him to accompany us?"

Flushing, Fanny shook her head. "I'm sorry. I'm just nervous. Of course you cannot leave him here. He startled me, that's all." Turning toward the short man, she nodded politely. "Forgive me. I didn't mean to be rude."

Gordy smiled, exposing a wide, toothless gap. " 'Tis all right, yer ladyship. I understand that 'is Grace can be a bit aggravatin' and pushy now and again. There be lots o' things I dinna like aboot 'im. That beard, fer example," he added confidingly. "I've tried tae tell 'im it does nothin' for 'im save make 'im look like an 'uge bear, but 'e insists on keepin' it. I'm 'opin' ye'll be able tae talk 'im into shavin' it off."

Flashing the little man a surprised glance, Fanny laughed, remembering her comment to the same effect in the Egyptian room at Carlisle Cottage. "On second thought, I'm very pleased to make your acquaintance, Mr. Gordy. It seems we think alike. At least about His Grace's beard." She didn't feel it necessary to add that she wouldn't be around long enough to influence Argyll's personal habits. She hid her grin as the duke frowned and rubbed his chin self-consciously.

The manservant's head bobbed up and down. "Oh, me name's only Gordy, ma'am. Well, it's really Gordon

Campbell, but me friends call me Gordy. And I 'ope ye will consider me a friend."

Watching this exchange with a faint smile, the duke countered, "I don't think I'd have told Lady Fanny your surname if I were you, Gordy. Now you'll have to sleep with your eyes open so that she doesn't cut your throat out of pure malice."

Oddly, Fanny didn't feel even a twinge of contempt for the little man. Perhaps it was because she felt sorry for him. His face was quite disfigured, as if someone had sliced the left half away with a large blade. He was, quite probably, the ugliest individual she had ever seen. Looking at the duke, she said hastily, "I do not mean Gordy any harm, or yourself either, Your Grace. Just so long as you keep your end of our bargain. You escort me as far as Dumfries, and then you leave me alone."

Shooting his master an astonished glance, Gordy opened his mouth. As if to keep his servant from speaking, the duke hurriedly filled the silence. "Of course, my lady. I always keep my bargains."

"Not quite always," Fanny quipped, reminding him of his broken vow years before. Turning away, she moved off down the road.

"Lady Fanny, wait a moment."

She turned around. "What now?" The duke still stood where Gordy had joined them.

"I'm going back for my horses. I took a sword in the thigh during the war, and although I thought it wouldn't bother me, the damned leg hurts abominably. I wanted to be sure Gordy was with you before I left, though, so you wouldn't be unprotected."

Fanny gazed at him for a long moment. What was he up to now? "Why didn't you ask Gordy to bring them? For that matter, why didn't you bring them yourself?"

"I thought either would look too obvious. After all, why would a bridegroom need his horses saddled and prepared for travel the night before his wedding? And why would his servant do so, unless he were bent on theft?"

"And you think returning in the middle of the night will fail to cause comment?"

"I won't get caught. I had extensive espionage experience in the war against Napoleon and thought I could slip in and out more easily than Gordy."

Fanny narrowed her eyes. She hadn't noticed him limping, which, if he really had been injured, he surely would have. Still, she agreed silently, it would be nice to ride rather than walk. Already her feet felt as if they'd been trampled by elephants. "All right. How long will you be?"

The duke grinned. "Are you going to miss me?"

Fanny glared. "No. I just wanted to know how long I will be able to enjoy your absence."

"*Touché*, madam." Having skillfully evaded her questions, he extended an arm in a flamboyant bow and moved back in the direction they had come.

"Wait!" She ran after him. Putting a hand on his elbow, she gazed up at him imploringly. "My dog. Could you perhaps . . ." Her voice trailed off.

"After that remark? I think not." His eyes gleamed. "But for another kiss I might consider it."

"Absolutely not."

Shrugging, the duke moved off into the shadows.

Actually, Malen's failure to bring his livestock had not been an accident but a ruse to allow him to return to Carlisle Cottage to explain matters to Lord MacDonald. Now, comfortably ensconced in a large leather armchair, feet stretched out before him near a crackling fire, a full glass of brandy in one hand and a blueberry tart in the other, the duke cast a relaxed glance at the earl. "So far so good, my lord," he murmured. He proceeded to tell Lord Mac-Donald about the night's escapade.

By the end of the tale, the earl was laughing heartily. "By God, Argyll, if I had any doubts left that you were the man for my Fanny, I have them no more. I must admit I wasn't too sure about the wisdom of your helping Fanny 'escape' from here, but you have dictated her every move correctly." He shook his head and looked at his hands. After a moment he looked up. "Your Grace, there is something I must know."

Malen nodded. Seeing how much the earl adored his

only child, he anticipated what the question would be. "You wish to know, besides the possible truce between our clans, if there is some other reason I want to marry Lady Fanny badly enough to trick her into it."

The earl looked surprised. "Precisely. I remember you weren't exactly thrilled by my idea of posting the banns without telling her, so this new plan to help her 'escape' to Scotland and marry her there came as quite a surprise. I'd also like to hear exactly how you plan to make her your wife. I must tell you that the girl's mother doesn't like the notion of Fanny traveling all over Scotland with a man not her husband. Nor do I."

Looking his hereditary foe directly in the eye, Malen responded earnestly. "Very well, MacDonald. I'll tell you. I not only agree with you that I am the man for your daughter, but I also believe Lady Fanny is the woman for me. I have believed so from the moment I met her."

Since he didn't know whether or not Fanny had told anyone of her promise to wait for him years earlier, he did not feel it necessary to add that he had met Lord MacDonald's daughter much earlier than yesterday afternoon in the Egyptian room. "By helping her escape *from* me, I hope to make her want to stay *with* me. And to love me, if possible. If there is one thing I learned during the war, it is that adventure draws people closer together. This will be Fanny's great adventure—with me to rescue her from every peril. Not that I intend to let her fall into any danger. But I can think of nothing more romantic to the female sex than being rescued by a knight in shining armor. That is what I hope to be to your daughter by the end of this journey."

Lord MacDonald shook his head. "You seem to understand Fanny's venturesome nature perfectly. One would almost think you'd known her for years."

Malen grinned, then composed his features back into a serious expression. "Rest assured that unless I were certain the only way to win your daughter's regard was through this deception, I'd never have agreed to her harebrained scheme. But there was little else I could do when she told me of her intention to go to Scotland to marry this Fitch person."

He laughed. "Tell me, sir, have you ever been able to talk Lady Fanny out of something once she made her mind up to do it?"

Lord MacDonald chuckled. "Not a chance."

Malen threw his companion a rueful smile. "I thought not. But perhaps that's what makes her so interesting."

The earl gazed at his young companion with new respect. "You're an insightful young man, Argyll. I am relieved to hear you want better than just a marriage of convenience. I've always wanted more than that for Fanny. Her mother and I married for love and have never had an unhappy day."

He smiled softly, then looked the duke in the eye. "I feel compelled to tell you that, had your reasons been solely political, I'd have stopped the match myself, even with all that has transpired. My heart has been raw from having to deal so harshly with Fanny." He frowned. "She's my only child, after all. I trust you will understand my concern, and my questions, and not be offended."

Malen inclined his head. "I would have expected no less."

The earl nodded, then looked thoughtful. "What of the wedding ceremony? Where do you plan to marry? And how do you expect to gain Fanny's compliance?"

Malen grinned. "I've not worked that part out completely, but I have a plan."

"Do you not mean to marry her before a priest?" The earl looked scandalized.

"Not right away. If all goes well, she'll become my bride through the Scottish law of consent. Over the anvil, as it's called. Tonight."

Lord MacDonald frowned again. "You mean you'll trick her into declaring herself your wife before witnesses, like elopers at Gretna Green? By God, man, I don't even know if that is legal anymore."

"It is. And it's really still quite common. Besides, to protect your daughter's respectability, I'd do almost anything to make her my wife, MacDonald. You have my word on it. You also have my promise that by the time you meet with us at Inveraray Castle in two weeks for a proper wedding, your daughter will be happy to be my duchess."

Lord MacDonald looked doubtful. "So you want our party to attend you at Inveraray Castle two weeks from today. I hope Fanny will comply. It would be a disaster if we arrived to find she had locked herself in her chamber or a tower. My clansmen would feel obligated to 'rescue' her."

Seeing his prospective father-in-law's uncertainty, Malen set his glass down on the table beside his chair and leaned forward, elbows resting on his knees. He gazed sincerely into Lord MacDonald's face. "Everything will work out. I know it will. You honor me by entrusting your daughter into my care, and I will not betray that trust. I promise you she will be both safe and happy by the time you arrive."

Lord MacDonald nodded. "God be with you. You'll need all the help you can get to prod the chit to the altar, and I'll not question your methods further. 'Twill be interesting to see if you can bring her to heel in two weeks. In the event you cannot, we will have to think of something else to bring peace to our people."

Malen nodded his agreement and rose to his feet. "Thank you, sir. And now, since Fanny is in my care, I should be off. Gordy is watching over her, so there is no need to fear, but I would feel better if I were there also. If my horses are ready, I'll be on my way.

"Oh," he added suddenly. "Speaking of heeling, there is the matter of a dog Fanny asked me to bring along."

Lord MacDonald let out a whoop of laughter. "Dagmar?" When his laughter had subsided, he wiped his streaming eyes and looked at the duke. "Did she tell you what this dog looks like, Your Grace?"

Malen frowned. "No. Why do I get the impression this isn't going to be as easy as I thought?"

Shaking his head, the earl laughed again. "Come now, Argyll. Would you expect a woman like my Fanny to have a common lap dog? No, sir, indeed not. This is a horse! Thing weighs near six stone and has teeth the size of daggers! God protect you if you take this dog along and then try to get close to the chit! No, Your Grace, if you mean to win my daughter over in two weeks, you'd best leave the animal here. I will bring it to Inveraray with me."

Malen grinned. "Sounds like an interesting beast. I must say I had visions of a useless ball of fluff. Personally, I've never seen the attraction of little dogs. Why have a canine at all if it is not of some benefit to you? Tell me, what breed is it?"

The earl eyed his companion skeptically. "An Irish wolfhound."

This time it was Malen's face that cracked into a smile as he remembered the dog Fanny had had years ago. A fine beast that had been, and it had liked him as much as he'd liked it. "You don't say. Wolfhounds are rare in Britain these days."

"Yes. My father raised the animals, and Fanny inherited his love of them." Lord MacDonald shook his head and sighed. "Do you know that one of the reasons she was determined to marry this completely unsuitable Fitch fellow was so that she could live in Scotland and breed the beasts? She never wanted to come to England in the first place."

"Is that right?" Malen asked interestedly, thinking of Fanny's alleged betrothal. "Is she that serious about the creatures, then?"

The earl nodded. "Without a doubt. You'd best know that before you marry her."

"I foresee no problem in her owning as many wolfhounds as she likes. Inveraray Castle is large enough for a veritable army of dogs. Now that you mention it, I believe some of the castle tapestries have wolfhounds depicted on them." Then he paused, thinking of the earl's former comment. Could it be possible that Fanny was not only the most desirable woman in the world, but that she also shared his own feelings about the useless frivolity of Town life? Although he recalled hearing her tell her grandfather some such so many years before, he'd not dared hope she'd still feel that way.

Holding his breath, he asked hesitantly, "When you

say she wanted to stay in Scotland, do you imply that
Lady Fanny won't wish to spend every Season in London? That's unusual for a female."

The earl glanced at him worriedly. "Yes. I hope that
won't be problem. I'm sure you'll be able to talk her
into going to Town once in a while if you enjoy the
place, but I must tell you she'd be happiest if she never
set foot in England again."

With difficulty, Malen kept from shouting for joy.
"That won't be a problem. Now, back to the matter of
Dagmar," he said. He chuckled. "I doubt your daughter
would let me survive the night if I showed up without
her dog. So, even though I may not live through this ex-
pedition if Dagmar takes exception to me, I suppose I'd
best get under way. The sooner I get started, the sooner
your daughter will have a husband."

Lord MacDonald watched his prospective son-in-law
knowingly, a pleased smile on his lips. "Gets under
your skin, does she, lad?"

"Aye, that she does," Malen said softly, his Scotch
burr making an appearance as it always did at deeply
emotional moments.

As Lord MacDonald left the room to arrange for the
livestock, Malen moved to gaze out the window. He'd
been here far too long already. He'd have to hurry if he
were to catch Fanny and Gordy before they reached the
Anvil, the inn where he'd planned to stop. Still, as unkind as letting her walk so long seemed, unless she was
exhausted, Fanny was likely to see through the plot
he'd concocted.

Thinking of Fanny's warm body against his, he
sighed impatiently, eager to be with her again. In his
pocket, the luckenbooth brooch had become a leaden
weight. He could not wait to pin it over her warm
bosom.

7

The moment he saw Gordy standing outside the Anvil with an anxious look on his face, Malen knew something was wrong. Kicking Pagan sharply in the flanks, he rode posthaste toward the inn. "Gordy!" he shouted when he was near enough to be heard. "What are you doing out here? Where is Lady Fanny?"

Gordy looked wildly relieved to see his master. "She's givin' that innkeeper what fer, that's where she is. 'E says 'e don't take such as 'er, and *she* says, 'What do ye mean, the likes o' me?' So 'e says, 'I mean the kind o' woman who walks the 'ighways lookin' fer a bit o' action.' So *she* flies off the 'andle and looks like she means tae belt 'im one. That's when I come back out 'ere tae watch fer ye, Yer Grace!"

In a single fluid motion, Malen leapt off his stallion's back. "Damnation. I'd hoped to reach you before you got here."

" 'Er ladyship is a fast walker. Me legs is killin' me." Gordy's eyes widened as the huge silver dog leashed by two metres of rope to Pagan's pommel growled menacingly. "What the devil is that?"

"It's a wolfhound. You'd better hope Lady Fanny is all right, my man, for *I'll* kill you if anything has happened to her! Good God, man, why didn't you stay inside to protect her? Here," he snapped as he thrust the horses' reins toward the batman. "Hold the horses while I see what's happening."

Looking askance, Gordy took the reins from his master, carefully moving as far from the wolfhound as possible. "Protect 'er? Believe me, sir, that lass doesna need protection. I felt sorry fer the poor innkeeper. Speakin' o' protection," he said loudly as Malen moved away, "who's goin' tae protect me from this monstrous beast whilst yer gone?"

Rushing toward the door, Malen thrust it aside and stepped into the brightly lit common room. A few guests, scattered around the tables as they waited for coach passage either back to Carlisle or on to Dumfries, looked up as he stepped into the inn. Some of these, whom the duke recognized as his own clansmen, smiled their welcome.

Near the door, a young man and woman turned sharply as if they expected someone else. Elopers, no doubt. And hadn't yet tied the knot, by the look of their nerves. Dismissing them, Malen turned toward a familiar voice echoing angrily through the small room. As he took in the scene, his face split into a wide grin.

"How dare you? How dare you speak to me like that you—you mealy-headed ape!" Fanny cried, brandishing a chunk of kindling she had apparently picked up from the stack near the huge fireplace as she chased the white-haired innkeeper around a large oak table.

Malen let out a bark of laughter.

As a blow glanced off the innkeeper's snowy pate, the man covered his head with his arms. "Ouch! Lass! Please! 'Tis sorry I am if I've made a mistake! Aye! That's it, a mistake! Please, lass! I apologize heartily!"

Fanny didn't look fatigued, Malen noted with a chuckle. In fact, for one who'd just walked for hours, she looked remarkably spry. Content for the moment to watch the unfolding drama, he leaned back against doorjamb, ready to stop Fanny if she got too close to the innkeeper again.

The old man's scrawny arms fluttered over his head protectively as he ran to the opposite side of the table from Fanny. He let out a terrified squeak and slid beneath the table as she clambered up on top of it and scooted toward him, waving her weapon menacingly.

The makeshift club missed his head.

"Come out, you coward!" she called. "You lily-livered pudding-heart! You whey-faced milksop!"

Still on the floor, the cowering innkeeper scrambled

to the other end of the long table. Hot on his trail, Fanny pulled her skirts up out of the way, exposing shapely ankles and shins as she hopped gracefully over dishes and mugs. Malen grinned appreciatively.

"Stop running and hold still, you poltroonish lack-bottom!"

Heartily enjoying the ruckus, Malen laughed merrily until he noticed he was not the only man enjoying the view of well-formed limbs. Several grimy country bumpkins, obviously half-seas over, leered and shouted lewd encouragements, which Fanny, in her rage, didn't seem to hear.

The duke stopped laughing. Moving quickly, he stepped behind Fanny and, reaching past her rounded buttocks, which protruded pleasantly as she bent over the edge of the table trying to reach the innkeeper, swept her into his arms. Fanny gasped in outrage and turned on him with the kindling stick. Malen's eyes flew to her club. "Stop!" he cried. "You've already inflicted bodily damage on me once today!"

Fanny froze in mid-swing as she found herself face-to-face with the Duke of Argyll. He grinned, teeth white against his swarthy beard. Waving their tankards of ale in salute, the drunken patrons cheered wildly. Even the young couple managed nervous smiles at the stunned expression on Fanny's face.

"Is this how you treat me, woman? Leaving me at the altar just before our wedding?" Malen cried, hoping Fanny would stumble into following his lead. Could marrying her possibly be this simple? Could he be so lucky? Here at the Anvil, many elopers came to tie the knot, but he'd not thought his bride-to-be would fall into his arms so easily. He gazed into Fanny's eyes, hoping she was more tired than she looked—too tired to notice what he was attempting.

Fanny glared at the duke in shocked outrage. "Put me down this instant!" To her dismay, her eyes filled with exhausted tears. Until his appearance, she'd actually believed he'd decided to let her go to Scotland with only his servant as protection. And she'd been mortified to discover that she was almost disappointed!

"Be still, lass," Malen said breathlessly as the girl in his arms twisted furiously but weakly. Good, he thought with intense satisfaction. She was near to dropping in her tracks. "I promise I'll put you down if you promise not to run away again. We could both use a good night's sleep." He eyed her meaningfully, and Fanny's wild thrashing came to an abrupt halt.

"In a real bed?" she whispered hopefully, gazing at the staircase against the north wall. People had been disappearing up the stairs since her arrival, and she was sure they led to the sleeping apartments. The innkeeper had refused her a room, but Argyll seemed to suggest *he* could obtain one. Could she trust the duke to keep his distance? Probably not. But she was too tired to argue. If he could convince this obstinate innkeeper to give her a place to sleep, she'd almost marry him willingly. Almost, but not quite. Her grip tightened on the club. Just let him try anything.

"Aye, lass. You must be exhausted," Malen whispered back, not allowing the pang of remorse he suddenly felt for allowing her to walk forever while he nibbled tarts and sipped brandy to show on his face. He frowned, not liking the unfamiliar sensation of guilt. Mercilessly he pushed it away, unwilling to lose this opportunity to make Fanny his wife.

Fanny fought to keep the tears of fatigue from streaming down her face. She nodded.

Malen continued speaking so softly that the rest of the inn's occupants could not hear. "It is with me or not at all, my girl. Believe me, I know this innkeeper personally. Even if you hadn't assaulted him, he would never have given a woman of tarnished reputation— which, from your heated comments, I suppose him to have suggested you were—leave to sleep under his roof."

Fanny hesitated. Half of her was shocked that she would even consider spending the night in the same bedchamber with a man not her husband. A man who wanted to trap her into marriage. The other half was too drained to care. She realized, too, with a surprised jolt, that, despite her distrust of this Campbell duke, if he gave his word, she believed he'd keep it. She couldn't have said why she thought he'd behave honorably, but for some inexplicable reason, she almost trusted him. Was she mad?

Malen nodded. "To sleep."

"Your word?"

He hesitated. This was one vow he didn't know if he could keep. After all, he'd promised himself that she'd pleasure him immediately after their marriage, to make up for the loss of his three mistresses. And even at the thought of possessing her, his body tingled hopefully.

"Do you promise all we'll do is sleep, Your Grace?" Pinning him with her gaze, Fanny searched his face.

Malen sighed. If she became his wife this night, he would, against all his instincts, keep his hands to himself. "I promise."

Looking at him for a long moment to be certain he meant it, Fanny nodded. "All right."

The duke moved toward the stairs. As he reached their base he turned back toward the innkeeper, who, seeing that the dangerous wench had been taken in hand, climbed out from under the table. His eyes widened as he recognized his esteemed patron.

"Which room, good sir?" Malen asked politely. Since he had often stayed at this inn, he was well aware the old man was a prude and would most definitely not allow a man, even a duke, and woman not properly wed—Malen was sure all had heard him say that Fanny had run out on him *before* they'd gotten to the altar—to spend the night together at the Anvil. At least, he hoped the old man wouldn't be too obsequious to fulfill his part in the plan.

The innkeeper chewed his lips uncertainly, as if battling with himself.

Malen nodded encouragingly. "Satisfy yourself, my good man," he said softly. He watched as the old man gave a relieved smile and began the ancient marriage ceremony. Now then, if only Fanny wouldn't realize what was happening until after they had given their vows.

"Er . . . are ye truly this woman's husband, Yer Grace?"

The duke smiled slowly. Turning to meet the gaze of the inn patrons, he said in a loud, solemn voice, "I, Malen Campbell, Duke of Argyll, am her husband."

"And ye have no other wife?"

Returning his gaze to the innkeeper, Malen spoke quietly but in a voice that left no question that he was deadly serious. "I say again, this is my wife, my only wife. There is no other but she. Today, tomorrow, and forever." He turned full circle, challenging anyone present to debate the issue.

The men who had recognized the duke stared in open shock. Each was obviously committing the momentous occasion to memory to share it with his grandchildren.

"Have ye a ring?" the innkeeper asked.

"I have no ring. But I have this." All eyes were upon Malen as he shifted Fanny in his arms, reached into the pocket of his jacket, and removed the luckenbooth.

The thistle-carved amethyst cabochon gleamed in the center of the brooch as, with great satisfaction, the duke set Fanny on her feet and swiftly pinned the brooch to the fabric over the rounded swell of her left breast. Taking her hand, he turned her so that all could see his mark upon her. He stopped so that she faced the innkeeper.

Frowning, the old man looked at Fanny. "What is yer name, lass?"

Cocking her head to one side, Fanny stared at him in bewilderment. What was going on? And what did her name have to do with anything? Did every guest who stopped at the Anvil undergo such scrutiny? It seemed dashed suspicious. "Fanny. Lady Fanny MacDonald."

A muffled gasp went up from the Campbell clan members scattered around the common room.

The innkeeper waited expectantly. When Fanny didn't say anything, he smiled and prompted her. "Lady Fanny MacDonald, ye must assure me that ye are His Grace's wife."

Malen hid his smile. It looked as if this was going to be even easier than he'd hoped. For a moment the girl beside him hesitated, then looked questioningly up at him, clearly wondering if this was what it would take to assure her of a bed to sleep in. She gazed at him for a long moment, and, suddenly, to Malen's dismay, Fanny's eyes narrowed in comprehension. Whirling about, she pierced the innkeeper with her sharp gaze. Her voice was filled with disbelieving rage.

"I most certainly will—" She gasped as the duke grabbed her elbow and spun her into his arms.

Praying the innkeeper would think him merely an overeager bridegroom, Malen plastered his lips to Fanny's, kissing her so solidly that she couldn't get a word out. Without removing his lips, he peered up at the innkeeper. To his intense satisfaction, the old man grinned and turned to the other occupants of the room. "Is there any among ye who questions the legality o' this union?"

The response was a resounding, if incredulous, "Nay!"

The innkeeper nodded. "Well then, Yer Grace, if ye can tear yerself away from yer duchess for a moment, I'll tell ye what God joins together, let no man put asunder. Ye are now man and wife. I'd tell ye tae kiss the bride, but ye're already doin' a fine job o' that."

With his mouth still fused to Fanny's lips, Malen waggled his eyebrows toward the stairs in an unspoken question. The innkeeper chuckled. "The second chamber on yer right at the top o' the stairs, ye randy lad. I regret my nuptial chamber is already bespoke, but I think ye'll find the bed in yer chamber tae yer likin'. If ye can make it that far."

Clutching Fanny to his chest and taking the stairs three at a time, Malen raced to the upper landing. Another great cheer broke out from below, and someone took up playing his bagpipes in a rousing Scottish love song. Malen felt a surge of relief. When he'd seen them seated around the tables, he'd wondered if his clansmen would balk as Fanny stated her name.

From the top of the steep staircase Malen saw that Gordy had just entered the inn and was rapidly being apprised of the situation by his astonished fellow

Campbells. Grinning broadly, the servant picked up Fanny's bag and thumped his way up the stairs. Malen rushed his unwilling bride down the hall and stepped into the dark room the innkeeper had indicated. Finally lifting his lips from hers, he set her on her feet.

Without meeting his eyes, she jerked out of his arms and walked in a huff to the window on the opposite side of the room.

Gordy stepped in to put the bag on the floor. "The 'orses and t' other beast are all settled in the stable, Yer Grace. I'll 'ave the 'orses saddled early, since I imagine ye'll be wantin' tae leave wi' the dawn."

Malen nodded hastily. "Yes, I will. That will be all, Gordy. Thank you. I'll speak with you in the morning."

Gordy, though accustomed to his master's commanding ways, stood his ground, obviously waiting for an opportunity to congratulate his new duchess. "Sir? Are ye sure that I canna do anythin' else fer ye?" He bobbed his head toward the girl standing with her back to them.

Malen made a face at him. "Positive, Gordy. You may go."

The little batman didn't budge.

Growling softly, Malen took the servant's elbow and propelled him out into the hall. "I said that would be all." Once outside the room, he whispered so that Fanny wouldn't hear. "For God's sake, stop gawking like the village idiot. You'll speak with Her Grace as soon as she accepts her new position. Just now I think she would as soon kill you as thank you for your good wishes. Now get out of here and get yourself a room."

The batman threw his master an affronted glance. Giving a sniff, he pulled his elbow free. "Thankee, sir, but if it's all the same tae ye, I'll be takin' me pipes downstairs and joinin' in the party. At least there I'll be appreciated."

Malen grinned. "As you are decidedly *not* here. Good night, Gordy."

With a disgusted grunt, the batman turned and hobbled down the stairs without giving his master a backward glance.

Stepping back into the room, Malen closed the door behind him. Moving surely in the darkness, he lit the candle sitting on a small table. The flame sputtered fitfully, then flared, filling the chamber with a soft glow as, from the common room below, the skirl of bagpipes penetrated the floor.

Fanny's entire body trembled with rage. Her mind reeled with the realization that she was now, according to ancient Scottish law, the Duchess of Argyll. Whirling, she turned to face her new husband. Her voice was hostile, outraged, and, she noticed with chagrin, somewhat tremulous. "How dare you? How dare you, you bastard! You planned this, didn't you?"

Malen appeared to consider the question. He tipped his head back and gazed at her through slightly lowered lids, his mouth pursed, his brow creased. Then he grinned. "Aye. Although I didn't plan your handy altercation with the innkeeper. I'd planned to be back at your side before you reached the Anvil, but my errand took a bit longer than I'd expected."

Annoyed by the matter-of-fact tone of his voice and the victorious sparkle in his eyes, Fanny snapped, "Well, we will get an annulment as soon as we reach a place civilized enough to start the proceedings. You can't expect me to stay married to you."

Delighted with the way the evening had turned out, Malen was more than willing to be magnanimous. Now that they were wed, there was plenty of time to convince Fanny that she belonged with him. "As you wish, my lady. We will discuss it."

Fanny blinked at his easy acquiescence. "And," she continued nervously, hoping he wouldn't insist on claiming his conjugal rights, "you will not kiss me again. Or anything else."

Malen experienced a surge of unpleasant emotion at the frightened expression on Fanny's face. His cheeks felt tight and hot. It occurred to him that, once again, the sensation he was experiencing felt remarkably like guilt, only this time it was much stronger. He frowned. He didn't like the feeling one bit. "I promise I will not kiss you again unless you ask me."

Fanny nodded shakily, not quite satisfied with his response but too befuddled to argue further. "Good. Now if you will please leave, I'd like to go to bed."

Malen reached out and placed a hand on Fanny's shoulder. Her bones felt delicate and feminine. His stomach flip-flopped at the warmth seeping through her gown. "Leave? I cannot leave you unprotected. Didn't you notice the disreputable-looking fellows downstairs? Every one seemed more than a little under the hatches. No, if I walked out of this room, I have no doubt that at least one of them would be convinced you were precisely the kind of woman the innkeeper intimated, and he would force his way in here to sample your wares," he improvised.

Suddenly too weary to think a moment longer, Fanny pulled away from him and sank down on the edge of the bed. "You . . . you are the most obstinate, irritating, infuriating man I've ever met."

An unexpected surge of tenderness rushed through Malen, and he frowned at his sudden longing to comfort her. "You're right. And I'm sorry if you're overset, Fanny. Please understand I don't want to hurt you. I know you won't believe me, but I have your best interests at heart, as well as our clans'."

Fanny sighed wearily. "That's debatable, but I'm too tired to argue anymore. I give up. I quit. You may stay. Or go. I don't really care what you do, Your Grace, just so long as I can lie down and close my eyes for a while. But," she said warningly, "you keep your hands to yourself. You gave me your word, and this is your chance to prove you are capable of keeping a vow."

"Wonderful," Malen said happily. Rubbing his hands together, he started eagerly toward the bed. "Shall we to bed, then, madam?"

Fanny's feet froze to the oak floor. Her face went rigid. Her fingers, stiff and cold, clutched at her dusty woolen gown. Was he truly suggesting that they . . . that she . . . Oh! How *dare* he? How like a Campbell to say one thing, only to attempt another! Especially this Campbell. He had no more honor than a hangman!

Malen gazed at his new bride. Her expression

couldn't be more agonized if she were on her way to the gallows. Glancing at her and then at the inviting mattress, he sighed. It would be so pleasant to spend his wedding night in Fanny's bed, instead of a hard chair, but he knew if he did, he'd be unable to keep his promise.

He was quite certain he could make her respond, but it would be still be a form of force. And although he admitted he had always been known as a womanizer, he was not a scoundrel—despite what Fanny so obviously thought. "I will borrow one of your blankets to sleep over there," he said, pointing to the chair opposite the bed.

Fanny stared into his eyes. "I must be crazy to let you stay here." The duke didn't answer, and at last she shrugged and turned away. Trying to ignore him, she reached for her carpetbag and pulled out the small satchel containing her toothbrush and powder. After completing her toilet, somewhat self-conscious but too tired to truly care, she replaced the items in the satchel, pulled out a brush for her hair, and proceeded to smooth the knots from her tangled mane.

Eyes glittering, Malen watched the rosewood-handled brush rise and descend, stroking the silky curls, brushing away the dust of the road and making Fanny's fiery hair shimmer in the candlelight. Stretched by her upraised arm, her bodice strained against her full bosom. Drawing a steadying breath, he cleared his throat and tried for humor to hide his sudden flare of desire. "I don't suppose you'd let me borrow that toothbrush?"

Fanny laughed and put the toiletries and satchel back in her carpetbag. "When hell freezes over."

He threw her an affronted glance. "It never hurts to ask."

Out of the corner of her eye, Fanny studied the duke thoughtfully. What kind of man trapped a woman into marriage one minute and asked to borrow her toilet items the next? What kind of man agreed to let his new bride sleep in peace rather than assert his husbandly rights? And why was she so certain he would keep his vow? Why did she trust this man whom, of all the men in the world, she had the most reason to distrust?

She sighed. Eager to shove these disturbing thoughts to the back of her mind, she put forward a question that had been troubling her since the moment Gordy had appeared outside the grounds of Carlisle Cottage. "What happened to your servant? I noticed his face is terribly disfigured."

"We were in Spain. He was my batman. I had just rounded a copse of trees when a French soldier jumped me, brandishing his sword. He thrust it through my thigh, here," he said, pointing to a place just above his knee. "I would not be alive today if Gordy had not leapt between us."

Fanny looked abashed. "I thought you were lying when you said you wanted to go after your horses because of your leg. I thought you were up to something."

Malen smiled morosely, wondering if he should come clean and tell her about his meeting with her father. He decided not to. Sometimes being too honest could be more destructive than lying. "I guess I haven't given you much reason to trust me, have I?"

Shocked by his admission, Fanny gasped at her new husband. Once again the duke had astounded her.

Malen resumed his story. "Unfortunately," he continued, "when my leg was pierced, I fell, and Gordy tripped over me just in time to intercept the soldier's next blow—with his face. The sword severed part of his ear, an eyebrow, the tip of his nose, and part of his upper lip. I rolled away, grabbed my sword, and thrust it through the Frenchman's gut before he could finish Gordy off. What's truly amazing is that Gordy's never blamed me for his misfortune, which many another man might have done. In fact, he's probably the best friend I've ever had."

Her features dark with compassion, Fanny put a hand on Malen's arm. "I am sorry, for both of you." To her astonishment, she found that the words were true. She was silent for a moment, trying to understand why she was sympathizing with rather than plotting to murder this man for getting her into her present situation.

She must be more exhausted than she'd realized. Noticing his gaze was still trained on her face, she asked quickly, "Does your leg still hurt much?"

Malen laughed. "Only when I walk for hours at a time."

Fanny nearly smiled. "Well, I'd say I was sorry about that, too, but you know if you hadn't insisted on escorting me, your leg wouldn't hurt at all. Nor would we now find ourselves faced with seeking an annulment." Not that she expected him to give her an annulment so easily. She wasn't a fool.

Unwilling to break the fragile feeling of companionship that had sprung up between them so unexpectedly, Malen said nothing. What could he say that would ease her mind? Nothing but an act of God would make him release her now.

Reaching up, Fanny fingered the silver brooch Malen had pinned to her dress during the strange marriage ceremony. "My grandfather used to tell me about the MacDonald luckenbooth." She flushed. "It was stolen during the Glencoe massacre. Grandfather always said there could be no peace between our clans until the brooch was returned. But then, I guess he didn't foresee a Campbell duke stealing the MacDonald heir away and marrying her." She laughed dryly. "At any rate, this brooch is very lovely."

"Yes, I thought so," Malen said carefully.

"A crown, thistle, leaves, and a heart," Fanny mused aloud, gazing down at the pin. "I wonder what the symbols mean."

"Tradition says the heart means the giver promises to love the recipient for eternity." Malen watched a flush steal over Fanny's high-boned cheeks. "The thistle, of course, has been a national symbol for Scotland for over two thousand years."

Fanny nodded.

"The thistle also represents constancy and fidelity, and the crown means the woman who receives the brooch is queen of her man's heart. After the couple is blessed with a child, the brooch might be pinned to the baby's blanket as an amulet against evil spirits."

Sighing, Fanny wondered if any man would ever have given her such a tribute of his own free will. It wasn't likely she'd ever have the chance to know. Even once the duke gave her an annulment from this politically inspired union, Sir Blanden Fitch would be waiting in Dumfries, ready to press her to marry him for personal gain. If only she hadn't acted so hastily in writing to Bland.

Stifling her regrets, Fanny unpinned the brooch and began to hand it to the duke. "Well, I suppose you'll want this back now, since you only used it for your charade downstairs."

Refastening it on her bodice, Malen said smoothly, "Why don't you wear it? It is far prettier and less likely to be lost pinned on your bodice than loose in my pocket." Without looking back to see if she agreed, he turned away and began to undress for bed.

Feeling Fanny's eyes on him, Malen stripped slowly. Surely there could be no harm in making her see his attractions. Smiling faintly, he lifted his fingers to the laces at the neck of his white dolman-sleeved shirt and lazily untied them. The shirt fell silently to the floor, a blaze of white in a pool of moonbeams. Bending slowly, he picked it up and draped it over the chair where he intended to sleep. Stretching mightily and feigning a yawn, he turned toward Fanny and for a long moment stood still before her, allowing her to look her fill at the thick blue-black curls covering his naked chest. He was delighted with the flare of her nostrils and the slight parting of her full, rose-red lips.

A low murmur escaped Fanny's throat as she watched the duke. He was so deliciously, dangerously masculine. It was all she could do to maintain the shred of control that kept her from moving toward him to touch those curls on his tanned chest. Would they be as soft as they looked? She gasped as his hands began moving again, sliding down his muscled, washboard-flat belly toward the waist of his leather breeches.

Fanny's own hands flew to her burning cheeks, and she whirled around. She must be mad! This wasn't just any man; this was a Campbell. And an extremely devious one at that. She had not forgotten his statement that he wouldn't kiss her again unless she asked him to, and she had come dangerously close to doing just that! He was deliberately trying to get her to fall into his arms and make love with him so that it would be impossible to get an annulment!

Malen laughed softly as he stepped out of his tight breeches. Wrapping the blanket around his waist, he glanced at Fanny's stiff shoulders. Grinning, he said carelessly, "You can turn around now. I'm decent."

Ever so slowly, Fanny turned. It was a mistake. Was this his idea of decent? He was practically naked! Why, beneath that blanket, he *was* naked! Her breath caught in her chest as he smiled at her. He was so incredibly, excruciatingly male. Oh, God, she should have risked being accosted by drunks rather than sleep in the same room with Argyll!

Malen watched as Fanny's pink tongue flicked out to lick her lips. It was an indescribably sensuous motion.

Fanny felt as if something inside her were trying to get out. Her skin was suddenly much too hot. Her eyes fluttered to his chest, where silky-looking curls curved up to touch his collarbone, then tapered down in a V that disappeared beneath the blanket. Her breath came in short, shallow gulps as she wondered how tightly the blanket was secured.

When he saw where she was looking, Malen was nearly undone. His hands clutched the blanket wrapped around his narrow hips as he noticed her labored breathing and her nipples hardening to points through the stuff of her gown.

As the blood began to surge into that part of himself he wanted to bury deep within his exquisite bride, Malen remembered with a rush of disappointment that he had given his vow and would keep it if it killed him! Turning regretfully, he broke the spell that had settled about them like a sparkling mist.

Fanny's hand flew to cover her mouth as she realized she'd been gaping at him like a man-hungry demimondaine. What must he think? Spinning on her heels, she stumbled to the window overlooking the small courtyard and did not turn around until she heard the duke settle himself in the chair, tip it back with a grinding creak, and blow out the single candle, engulfing the room in darkness.

Hurriedly Fanny kicked off her boots. Loosening the top buttons of her gown, she moved to the bed and slid, exhausted but nervous, beneath the remaining blanket. It struck her suddenly that she still wore the luckenbooth with which the duke had marked her his duchess. Somehow it seemed to draw Malen closer to her, bonding them somehow. And even though her mind rebelled at the notion, before she could remove the brooch she drifted into sleep.

Malen smiled as he listened to her rustling movements. "Good night, sweet wife," he murmured. He was not surprised when he received no answer but a faint, ladylike snore.

8

It would have been hard to guess which of them was more startled when a crash resounded through the tiny chamber in the early-morning hours.

Terrified, Fanny leapt from the bed, then rushed to where the duke lay groaning on the floor. "Oh, dear! Are you all right?"

Malen's head had cracked sharply against the oak floor when his chair succumbed to the pressure of his shifting to find a comfortable sleeping position. Moving slowly, he raised a hand to his aching skull. He groaned again as Fanny's fingers pushed his out of the way and probed his injury.

A tiny bubble of laughter gurgled up from her throat, and she bit her lip to hold back a cascade of giggles at his irritated grunt. "Well, you're going to have quite a bump, but at least the skin isn't broken. I'm sorry to have to say this, but I think you'll live."

Glaring, Malen sat up slowly, cradling his head. "Thank you very much, Dr. Fanny," he said sarcastically. "You've no idea how much better that makes me feel. God but you're a bloodthirsty wench, laughing at my misfortune. What happened? Who were our attackers?"

Fighting another hysterical giggle, Fanny stammered, "I—I think it was your chair."

"My chair?" he grumbled in disgruntled disbelief.

"Yes," Fanny giggled, unable to control her mirth any longer. "Oh, I'm so sorry," she gasped. "I don't mean to laugh, honestly. But if you could just see yourself! And your chair! Look at it! It looks like a bunch of kindling!"

Malen directed his attention to the floor around him.

97

Indeed, shards of wood and nails lay scattered about. Finally the humor in the situation struck him, and he laughed with Fanny until they panted for air.

By the time they regained their composure several minutes later, Malen noticed, something incredible had happened. Until then Fanny had treated him with barely masked hostility. Now her eyes sparkled, and she smiled at him. He grinned at her in return. Then suddenly his eyes widened, and his breath caught.

Curious, Fanny looked down to where his eyes had settled. Uttering a horrified cry, she jumped back. The weight of the luckenbooth brooch had caused her unbuttoned gown to gape at the neck. Her underclothes had followed the gown, giving the duke an unimpeded view of her breasts and belly. Cheeks flaming, she continued backing away from him, scooting into the shadows on her bottom.

Drawing a trembling breath, Malen tried to rescue their tenuous bond of friendship. "Well," he said amiably, as though nothing untoward had taken place, "I suppose I sleep on the floor now."

Unable to meet his eyes and confused by a rush of disappointment at his detached observation, Fanny stood up and moved toward the bed. Apparently he had been unaffected by what he had seen. Obviously her virtue wasn't in as much jeopardy as she'd imagined. For some reason this vexed her severely.

Biting her lip, she looked back at him. "That isn't necessary. You are injured. You will share the mattress with me. However, I'll sleep under my blanket, and you will sleep on top of it and under yours."

Malen stared. Did she have any idea how difficult it would be for him to lie beside her without touching her sweet body? It would be near impossible! Summoning up his most roguish smile, he laughed suggestively and waggled his eyebrows in an overblown leer. "Well, 'tis not exactly as I'd like it, but I suppose it is better than bedding down on the floor. Besides," he lied, "you have nothing to fear from me tonight. Not with this enormous goose egg on my head."

Fanny padded back to the bed and slid under her

blanket. She lay stiffly, waiting to feel his weight beside her. When it came she was suffused with unexpected annoyance at the scratchy woolen blanket between them. What would it be like to touch him? To feel his body against hers?

Drawing a quiet breath, she inhaled his heady male scent and closed her eyes as unfamiliar sensations swept over her. For a long time she lay awake, breathing him in, acutely aware of the muscled shoulder and thigh pressing against her. Despite her exhaustion, it was suddenly impossible to sleep.

Malen lay completely still beneath the scratchy blanket until he heard Fanny's breathing deepen in slumber. She was so warm, so sweet, and she smelled of violets. Ever so slowly he leaned closer and lowered his face to her hair, drawing her perfume into his hungry nostrils.

God's blood, he cursed silently, *she's your wife, man. If you want her, take her!* But he could not. He had promised. To break that promise would ruin her trust in him forever. So he remained still, breathing in her sweetness and feeling her warmth penetrate the thin woolen blanket.

At last, as a compromise to his wounded male instincts, Malen shrugged of the blanket covering him and climbed carefully beneath Fanny's. At last, with her fully dressed body pressed to his bare skin, he drifted into frustrated sleep, not allowing himself to think of what would happen if she awakened.

Near morning Malen awoke to find his new bride had snuggled even closer. Her skirt was hitched high over one slender hip, and one shapely leg pinned both of his to the mattress. With a low groan Malen gripped her bare thigh and slid out from beneath her, pausing as she moaned softly. Trying to ignore the relentless pounding of his swollen manhood, he climbed back on top of her blanket, resenting the fabric barrier between them infinitely more than he had before feeling her warmth against his skin.

He retrieved his own cover from the floor, spread it over his lean hips, then cradled his MacDonald bride gently, as if she were the most precious thing in the world. Which, he found to his surprise, he had decided she was.

The sun was high in the sky when Malen finally awoke to find Fanny missing from the bed. With a scowl he rolled off the mattress, clasping his head with a groan as the night's mishap came back to him with painful clarity. Moving slowly so as not to jar his aching skull, he walked across the room and yanked open the bedchamber door. His voice echoed down the narrow hallway. "Gordy!"

As if he had been awaiting just such a summons, the batman appeared instantly. "Aye, Yer Grace?" He eyed the duke hopefully, raising his one remaining eyebrow in a leer.

Unable to stay grouchy with the little man gazing at him in such lurid expectancy, Malen laughed, then held his head as a new wave of pain throbbed through his skull. "Contrary to what you obviously hope, nothing happened last night. Where is the duchess?"

Gordy grunted disgustedly. "She be down at breakfast. Shall I be 'elpin' ye dress, then?"

"Aye." Malen hesitated as another thought occurred to him. Without giving himself time to question his motives, he added gruffly, "And I'll need a shave."

Gordy gaped. Then he bobbed his grizzled head with a blinding smile. "Yes, Yer Grace! At once!"

Twenty minutes later, washed, freshly shaved, and dressed in a clean set of clothes, Malen walked down the stairs to the inn's common room. His gaze glided over the company and came to rest on his bride. He smiled.

Fanny was delectable in a pale-peach corduroy traveling gown with a high waist and tight sleeves of white voile. The upper part of her bodice was white net gauze, but it revealed little, since she also wore a lacy chemise and petticoat underneath. The luckenbooth was pinned to her bodice and her glowing red curls flowed loose over her shoulders save for a slender apricot riband. She wore no hat. On her feet were boots of taupe leather, and on her hands, tan kidskin gloves.

She sat across from the same young woman he'd noticed the night before, half of the eloping couple who'd so obviously been waiting to be married. The two women were engrossed in quiet, serious conversation, but Fanny looked up as he strode toward the table.

"Your Grace!" she said with surprise. "You've shaved off your beard!"

Flushing, Malen bade Fanny's companion a good morn and settled himself beside the two women. Signaling a serving girl, he ordered a huge repast of kidneys, eggs, spinach soufflé, and fresh milk, and then turned back toward Fanny, placing a possessive hand over hers. "Yes. I was . . . er . . . tired of it." He cleared his throat self-consciously. "And I see you are wearing a fresh gown. You look lovely."

"Thank you. It's one of my favorites." Fanny blushed unexpectedly, catching her breath at the still-unfamiliar sensations that swept through her at his touch. "I'd have worn a riding habit, but I didn't bring one with me, since I didn't expect to be on horseback."

"I think your gown will suit." He frowned. "I had Gordy inquire about a carriage and pair, but he informs me the only horses available were borrowed yesterday morning. And even if the innkeeper has a carriage but no horses, I'd not like to use mine as beasts of burden. As for the coaches passing through, they are all filled for the next few days. Of course, we could stay here until space becomes available."

"Oh, no," Fanny replied hastily, realizing that if they stayed at the Anvil, they'd be expected to sleep together again, "you mustn't damage your horses on my account. I know my father always insists his prime bloods be used for nothing but riding. So ride we will. There's no need to await a coach. I'd really prefer we reached Dumfries before much longer. After all," she said quickly, "my other friend will be waiting for me. I assure you I'll be fine. I'll be happy simply not having to walk!" She watched as he frowned at the reference to her "friend," her betrothed.

From beneath the cover of her lashes, she examined him closely. Fawn leather breeches clung like a glove to his narrow hips and muscular thighs. His shoulder-length hair lay neatly against the nape of his neck, secured with a black satin riband. His shirt was again of fine lawn, this time in a delicate shade of blue. On anyone else, she surmised with grudging admiration, the shade might have looked less than virile, but on Argyll it merely emphasized his masculinity.

Now that she could see the shaven angles of his face, Fanny was astonished to discover the duke was an even more beautiful creature than she'd originally thought. He was, without a doubt, the most incredibly, inescapably handsome man she'd ever seen. Far more attractive, in a swarthy, dangerous way, than any of the London bucks with whom she'd been acquainted. Suddenly she realized he was still holding her hand. With an anxious tug, she tried to pull her fingers from his.

His grip tightened automatically, much as his legs tightened around Pagan when the stallion misbehaved. He smiled at the young woman seated opposite his bride, then focused his knowledgeable gaze on Fanny's flushed cheeks. "Please, my dear, don't pull away. I'm sure your companion understands why your new husband wants to hold your hand. Tell me, what were you lovely ladies discussing before I so rudely interrupted?"

Heat flooded Fanny's cheeks. "Oh, nothing of importance," she squeaked, cursing herself for the quaver in her voice.

Malen grinned. Obviously they'd been discussing their respective husbands—and very likely what had happened in each bedroom the night before. He chuckled as the other woman excused herself abruptly, her cheeks also flaming.

"I see," he said mischievously. "Nothing of importance. Did you not even compare sleeping accommodations?"

Fanny gasped. "No! Now let go. You have no right to paw me." More disturbed than annoyed, she finally managed to jerk her hand free.

Malen blinked. "Paw you? I beg your pardon, ma'am.

I merely wanted to hold your hand. After all, I won't be able to touch you much longer if you get your annulment."

"The word is *when*, not *if*, and don't you forget it!" Fanny retorted. "You promised we would get an annulment as soon as possible."

"What I *said* was that we would discuss it." His attention was diverted as a serving girl brought his breakfast.

Malen watched the wench's eyes widen in recognition, and he smiled. Many a night had he whiled away in Lucy's chamber abovestairs, away from the prudish innkeeper's sharp gaze. Glancing at Fanny to be certain she watched, he winked and thanked the serving girl profusely as, wiggling her hips suggestively, she bent low to lay the platter on the table in front of him.

Seeing the maid's prodigious charms almost tumbling out of her low-cut bodice, Fanny felt a sudden, violent wave of rage sweep over her. How dared that slut look at the duke that way? Had she no shame? And what of Argyll? Almost everyone here knew he was now her husband. What would they think if they saw him flirting with this hussy the morning after their wedding night?

As the buxom wench moved away, Malen gestured toward his filled breakfast platter, watching Fanny's expression closely. "Would you like to share my food? I have enough for two."

"No, thank you," Fanny replied irritably. Scowling, she watched as the duke shrugged and fell to with gusto.

"Perhaps you'd like something different? Some fruit, perhaps?" he asked solicitously as he patted his lips with a blindingly white napkin.

Glancing around, Fanny noticed that no one else in the room had been given a napkin. The harlot apparently knew His Grace's needs well and went out of her way to fill them. "No, thank you. I'm fine," she snapped.

Glancing up in mock surprise, Malen stifled the urge to grin. "Is something wrong?"

Flushing, Fanny shook her head. How could she tell him of her disappointment that he had not tried to kiss her at all last night? How could she tell him that her mind was whirling with confusion? She was supposed to hate him. And yet she couldn't seem to stop thinking about what it would be like to touch those silky black curls winding down his hard belly.

And how could she tell him that during the night she'd had a most troubling dream, in which he was holding her intimately? Or that she had enjoyed the dream excessively, and, had he awakened when she did, might have been more than willing to make the fantasy a reality? And there was no way she could tell him she took exception to his blatant encouragement of the serving wench's lewd behavior! He might think she actually cared.

Looking around, Fanny became aware that two pairs of eyes, belonging to two unwholesome-looking chaps seated in the shadows, stared at her appraisingly. She forced a luminous smile for them to her lips.

Gawking, the two men exchanged whispers. The larger of them began to rise, and Fanny felt a momentary rush of fear. Then the smaller man put a hand on the former's forearm, glanced at her, said something, and pulled his friend back down to the table. The larger man nodded, glanced at the duke, and then, settling his elbows on the table, continued watching her. Fanny wiped the smile from her lips and pointedly ignored them both, heartily relieved the bigger man's companion had stopped him from approaching her.

None of the scene escaped Malen's attention, either, although he appeared engrossed in his food. Without being obvious, he glanced at the two men in the corner. Out of the side of his mouth he said softly, "Do you always encourage strange men? 'Twill bring you grief one day, my girl. Take care not to look at them again." A flash of anger appeared in Fanny's brown eyes. Malen shook his head warningly. "Be still, Fanny."

"How dare you?" she whispered bitingly. "*You* are free to ogle any woman's breasts, but *I* cannot even smile at someone? Of all the outrageous—"

His hand shot forward to grip her wrist, tightening warningly. "I am a man, Fanny," Malen said quietly, looking casually from side to side to make certain they were not being observed. "I realize you like to think yourself above the usual rules for proper feminine behavior, but you will obey me in this matter. If you never do another thing I ask, obey me now. I am not being arrogant; I have only your safety in mind."

His eyes held Fanny's captive and, only when she nodded nervously, released them. He returned his attention to his breakfast. Still speaking softly, he explained, "Lucy, the serving maid, is an old friend of mine. You know neither of those vagrants. We can only hope they didn't take your smile as an invitation, or there will be the devil to pay."

Certain he was right, Fanny nodded but, unable to keep silent, hissed, "We are supposed to be newlyweds. How do you think it looks to everyone in this room that you take such a hearty interest in that young woman's charms?"

Ridiculously pleased at her response to his mild flirtation, Malen nevertheless also felt guilty. Again. What was it about Fanny that made him experience this uncomfortable sensation so often? Hadn't he decided he wouldn't let her curb his entertainments? Still, he supposed, ogling the serving wench had been more than a little childish. Fanny was within her rights for taking him to task. "You are right. I am sorry. I promise I will not embarrass you again."

"Thank you," Fanny said stiffly.

"You're welcome."

Neither spoke for several minutes, and the only sound was that of Malen's fork against his platter.

At last, unable to stand the uncomfortable silence, Fanny asked, "How is your head this morning? It isn't hurting too badly, I hope." Still somewhat annoyed, she raised a finger and deliberately poked the bump on his head, gratified when he let out a yelp. "Oh, I am sorry!"

Malen glared at Fanny's grin. "Impudent wretch. I said it before, and I'll say it again: You are, without a doubt, the most bloodthirsty woman I've ever met."

Fanny giggled, then turned serious. "Is it hurting very badly? Perhaps we should call for a doctor."

Malen shook his head, pleased by her concern. "That won't be necessary. I'll be fine after a day or so. Until then I'll just have a bit of a headache." He grinned ruefully. "As long as certain people keep their hands to themselves, that is."

Fanny laughed, and he continued gallantly, "Anyway, looking at you makes me feel infinitely better than looking at a medic." His eyes devoured her face, running over her loose copper curls, which, laced with a number of shiny peach-colored satin ribands, gleamed even in the subdued lighting of the common room.

Everything about her murmured luxurious, if innocent, sensuality: her smooth, long neck, the laciness of her pale-apricot bodice, her full breasts thrusting proudly beneath their covering as if begging to be touched.

Wrenching his gaze away from Fanny's bosom Malen closed his eyes and counted to ten. Then he counted ten more. At last, feeling his lust subside, he reopened them, careful not to look at her. Clearing his throat, he returned his attention to his meal. "You really should eat breakfast."

As her belly had been growling for the past hour, Fanny nodded. "You're right. I'll try."

This time, when the serving wench set Fanny's breakfast on the table, Malen studiously avoided looking at the girl, even though she bent indecently close to him. Her breasts were no more than an inch from his nose, and ignoring them took a great deal of determination, but the surge of pride he felt when Fanny smiled at him as the girl huffed away made the effort worthwhile.

When he and Fanny had almost finished their repast, Malen saw the two scruffy men Fanny had smiled at so invitingly rise and walk out the door. Fanny did not appear to notice their departure, but their lustful gazes didn't leave her face until the door had closed behind them. A warning tingle prickled the hairs on the back of Malen's neck, and he cursed silently, wishing he'd thought to bring more of an escort than Gordy.

9

Fanny felt much more the thing after eating a large breakfast under Argyll's watchful eye; even though it did entail chasing after her scampering heart each time the duke accidentally brushed her thigh with his. He, however, she noticed, devoted all his attention to consuming huge quantities of food as if he had a hollow leg, not sparing a glance for anything save the refills Lucy kept bringing him. Still, Fanny was forced to admit grudgingly, he kept his gaze off the maid's bosom.

But it disturbed her that his casual touches had affected *her* so badly. It had been all she could do to hold her fork steady enough to carry its loads to her trembling lips. What on earth was wrong with her? She didn't care for this man. Perhaps she had once, long ago, but not since he'd jilted her. Besides, she could not allow herself to care for him. It would go directly against the vow she'd made to her grandfather.

After finishing breakfast and fetching her carpetbag, Fanny stood outside the inn in the warm summer sunshine, waiting for Argyll and Gordy. When the duke emerged from the stables, she surprised herself by breaking into a happy smile and rushing forward to meet him.

Also surprised, Malen returned her greeting, barely able to resist sweeping her into his arms for a kiss. A fine thing that would be. Knowing his hotheaded Fanny, she would probably thump him over the head with that damned carpetbag, march back inside, and refuse to go anywhere with him. Then he would be forced to throw her over his saddle and carry her off against her will. For he certainly didn't intend to leave his new bride behind—any more than he intended to give her an annulment.

Suddenly he grinned. The thought of Fanny's attractively rounded rump aiming skyward as she bounced along on the front of his saddle was delectable. When his eyes settled on the luckenbooth brooch shining over her heart, his smile widened.

Misinterpreting his glance at the betrothal pin, Fanny raised an eyebrow. "Did you think I had lost it?" she asked wryly. "I thought you said it would be safer on my bodice than in your pocket. If you're worried, I'll gladly give it back." She felt unaccountably relieved when he shook his head.

Malen glanced at Fanny's gown assessingly. "Your skirt will be a trifle tight in the sidesaddle I borrowed from your father's stables. You may have to raise it slightly." At Fanny's uncertain glance, he teased with a roguish leer, "I promise I'll try not to ogle your ankles."

Unable to resist his playful banter, Fanny laughed.

Pleased by her good humor. Malen found himself wanting to make her laugh more. He managed a doubtful frown and, clapping a hand to his chest, spoke in the broad dialect of the north country. "But 'een ye prefer tae walk, I'll happ'ly carry her bag as fer as ye care tae go. Tae the ends o' the earth, me bonnie lassie, 'een that's wha' it takes tae win yer heart."

Fanny felt the bubble of laughter in her throat catch as the duke's eyes gleamed, turning to pools the color of shifting ocean waves. Her heart raced at the sensations his fiery gaze sent shooting through her body. After thus holding her prisoner for several moments, the duke smiled and turned his gaze away, effectively releasing her. She gasped for air and realized she'd been holding her breath.

"I have something that might interest you." The words had scarcely left Malen's mouth when a huge gray shape came hurtling out of the stable.

Her eyes shining, Fanny rushed to meet her dog. "Dagmar! Oh, Dagmar, it is good to see you!"

Malen grinned, suddenly extremely proud of himself.

"She's already eaten. Gordy tells me she had nearly an entire haunch of fresh beef this morning."

Ruffling the dog's fur, Fanny turned back to the duke, her eyes radiant with unshed tears. "Oh, thank you, Your Grace. Thank you!"

To his shock, at his glimpse of Fanny's tears Malen's heart seemed to swell to three times its size in his chest, pressing painfully against his ribs. What was this? He hadn't felt this way since he'd been nineteen years old and hiding behind the stone wall at MacDonald Manor!

Good Lord, was he actually falling back in love with the chit? Impossible! He was too old for such nonsense! It had been one thing to plan to make her want him, but he had had no intention of falling victim to Cupid's arrow himself.

Until now he had thought it was her body that consumed his attention. However, he was dumbfounded to find himself searching his mind for ways to keep the happy glow on her face.

Good God, he *was* in love with her!

Supremely dismayed, he managed to stammer, "No problem at all, I assure you. I would do anything to make you happy." To his further disconcertion, the words were true. Thoroughly horrified that the unthinkable had happened without his intention, Malen lowered his gaze and bent to retrieve the carpetbag Fanny had dropped upon seeing the wolfhound.

Similar sensations rushed through Fanny. Stunned to discover that the man she had, until now, believed to be a callous, uncaring knave was far more gentle and kind than she had ever thought possible, she stared at Malen—indeed, when had she stopped thinking of him as "the duke"?—as if seeing him for the first time.

His sleeves were rolled up to his elbows, and as she watched his bare arms ripple with strength, Fanny was nearly overcome with the desire to touch the bands of muscle. What, she wondered as an almost overwhelming longing flooded her body, would those cords of manly sinew feel like under her fingertips?

Then her face flamed as she pictured all his other muscles. For hadn't she seen him naked, but for the blanket around his narrow hips, only the night before? Longing changed to an odd heat, and fire licked over her breasts and belly. Trembling, Fanny raised the hand that had been stroking Dagmar's floppy ears to touch her own feverish cheek.

Malen, who not yet come to grips with his emotions but had at least managed to push them to the back of his mind, lifted his head to tell Fanny that the horses would be brought to the front of the inn momentarily. However, as his eyes rested on his bride's body, he caught his breath and forgot what he had intended to say.

Fanny stood with her back to the east. The sun was still low enough in the sky to be directly behind her, and it turned her loose, lustrous curls into a burnished halo of red and gold. Sunbeams streamed around her, making her figure easily discernible through the folds of her gown.

Her waist seemed unbelievably small, her breasts wondrously full and ripe. A tantalizing hint of shadow appeared at the juncture of her thighs.

Malen's temperature blazed, his nostrils flaring as his masculine parts throbbed demandingly. Good Lord, had he ever felt such hunger for any woman? And if he raised his eyes from her glowing body to her face, would he see there an answering thirst? Could she, too, feel the passion connecting them?

He could not raise his eyes. To look up at her and see her gaze at him in shocked disapproval would be too much to bear. Stunned at the revelation that he really was still in love with her, despite his previous belief that what he'd felt for Fanny so many years earlier had been naught but childish infatuation, he tried to make sense of his disordered thoughts and bring his passion under control.

All the years he had spent lusting after this female or that now seemed completely foolish, paling in comparison to the undeniable attraction pulling him inescapably toward this woman he had tricked into being his bride. Good God, *this* feeling was what had made him do the unthinkable and ask her to marry him with her grandfather dying in the mud not twenty paces away!

What had he done? Would she ever forgive him for first jilting her and then tricking her into marrying him? Until now he hadn't much cared, just so long as he was entitled to use her lush body each night. How could he have been so selfish? Surely when Fanny had accused him of being a bastard, she'd been right.

Fanny felt as though she were smothering. Her veins flowed with liquid fire, and her heart pounded as if she'd been running for her life. As she had, she thought suddenly. She had been running from Malen. He had made no secret of his desire to share her bed. And she had discovered to her chagrin that she wanted to experience the delights of his body as well. But now she wanted even more, and she found herself hoping he would come to like, if not love, her someday.

Until then, however, she realized abruptly, she would be happy to linger in his arms. To say anything else would be hypocritical. Malen turned her body to molten wax with a single touch, whereas the stylish attentions of Blanden Fitch had always left her cold. Lord! If Malen did give her the annulment she'd insisted upon, how would she ever endure Bland's clammy touch after experiencing Malen's masculine caress?

Considering the way the duke affected her, why was she so eager to get an annulment anyway? So she could marry Bland? That was absurd. Bland didn't love her, and he certainly didn't have the power over her that Malen had. She didn't want Bland; she never had. Marrying the baronet had merely seemed the easiest way to make her father pay for posting her betrothal banns without informing her. What was it her grandfather had said? That one day her father would ask too much and she would be forced to refuse?

Surely her father, who knew her temperament as well as anyone, had known she would balk at marrying the Campbell laird. But this marriage was important politically, so he'd posted the banns without her approval. And with the safety of their people at stake, could she really blame him?

She sighed. She supposed not. Had she been in his position, she might have done the same thing. At the same time, he had behaved badly, so she couldn't blame herself for refusing him.

Then and there she decided that the next time she saw Lord MacDonald, they were going to sit down and have a serious discussion on mutual respect.

And as far as her refusal went, why *had* she been so determined to avoid marrying the duke? Because of her grandfather. Yet surely if Ian MacDonald were alive now, as fiercely protective of his people as he was, he would undoubtedly realize this marriage would help the MacDonalds as well as the hated Campbells and grudgingly urge her to go through with it.

Besides, she thought suddenly, she'd never even met another Campbell before Malen and Gordy, so how could she hate them as much as she'd thought? Truthfully, she couldn't.

Finally acknowledging that she had nothing to lose by offering herself to Malen willingly, she lifted one foot and prepared to take that decisive step forward. When he spun away from her, Fanny was stung to the core. Catching the sob that rose unbidden to choke her, she rushed back into the inn. Giving Malen a look that could only be described as contemptuous, Dagmar trotted after her mistress.

Watching over his shoulder, Malen drew a deep breath and waited until Fanny had disappeared to turn around fully. The front of his breeches strained against his manhood, and the last thing he had needed was for her to see that. After a few more deep breaths, his body lost some of its swollen lust and he was able to return to the stable to see if Gordy was ready with their mounts.

The batman, leading the three horses, met the duke on his way. "Yer Grace! I'm 'opin' ye 'ad a pleasant breakfast."

Malen nodded gruffly. "Yes, thank you. Now I'd like to get on the road. We've wasted much of the morning already."

The smile did not leave Gordy's ruddy face. "Aye.

'Tis late, but I wouldna call it a waste. Both ye and 'er Grace seemed tae find it pleasant sitting doon tae breakfast."

Without replying, Malen spun on his heel and led the way to the front of the Anvil. Opening the inn's door, he leaned into the shadows. "Fanny? Let us be off!"

Keeping her gaze on her feet, Fanny hurried outside. She raised her eyes only when Malen reached out to help her mount. Then she allowed him to settle her on Arista, a small white mare from her father's stables, and hand her the reins. True to his word, she noticed pettishly, he didn't even glance at her stockinged legs when she was forced to hitch up her skirt and settle it around her knees.

After vaulting effortlessly into Pagan's saddle, Malen moved away from the inn. Dagmar took up a position at Fanny's side, loping along happily, while Gordy rode a gray gelding some distance behind them, puffing with tuneless eagerness on his bagpipes.

When they'd been riding for nearly an hour, the forest of Annan Glen rose around them. After passing through rolling hills, they were engulfed by a thick tent of dark-green firs. Before the three companions entered the forest, birds had been singing energetically, swooping through the sunbeams and rising to form elaborate circles high overhead. Now, however, not a sound stirred the gloomy wood.

It was much cooler here, Fanny noted with a slight shiver, and very dark. The mare she rode whickered nervously, sidestepping and making Fanny tug sharply on the reins. If Fanny narrowed her eyes and peered deeply into the shadowed distance, she could just barely see the outline of more trees fading into the murky glen. Possibly, she thought, the eerie silence was the result of the thick layers of pine needles blanketing the road, muffling the horse's hooves.

The only sounds breaking the stillness were the horses' nervous snorts, the clinking of their tack, and Malen's soft whistle as he urged Pagan on. But it seemed to Fanny that the horses' steps grew slower despite Malen's urgings or her nudging of Arista's flanks.

Suddenly Pagan tossed his head, whinnying in fright. While a lesser man would undoubtedly have been flung into the bushes, Malen clung to the saddle with ease, wrapping his leather-clad legs more tightly about the stallion's heaving sides.

Fanny could not help but admire his prowess or the way the muscles in his legs strained against the animal's flanks. As she watched, he leaned forward and stroked the great beast's neck softly, whispering words of encouragement. Pagan, she noticed nervously, did not look appeased. The stallion's eyes rolled in his head, whites glistening.

Even Gordy, who had been playing his bagpipes incessantly in an effort to fill the uncomfortable silence as the trio rode toward Dumfries, had let his pipes fall to hang on the side of his saddle. The servant's disfigured face wagged right and left edgily, eyes raking the forest. Neither he nor Malen spoke, although they exchanged a constant volley of troubled glances.

Careful that Fanny should not see, Malen leaned slowly to his right, tipping in the saddle so that his hand stroked his calf. With deceptive casualness he gripped his *skean dhu* by its braided leather handle and slid the small silver blade free of the thong that held it in place. Concealing it in his palm, he returned to an upright position in his saddle. Noting Fanny's questioning gaze, he explained softly, "An itch."

Like Gordy's, Fanny's eyes seemed drawn to the forest depths. A quick movement in the murky gloom made her stiffen. Something darted out in front of them, swooping past their noses. Stifling an outcry, Fanny sighed. A bird. The blue jay watched the group suspiciously from high in a fir. Fanny's eyes narrowed. Odd that a bird normally so raucous would be so silent.

Malen shifted his blade so it rested more comfortably in his palm. He felt a sudden desire to have his sword and bow in his lap. A quick glance at Gordy's scrupulous examination of the forest confirmed the impulse.

Malen cursed silently, wishing he'd had the foresight to bring a pistol. Still, hidden within the pack tied on Pagan's muscular haunches was a sword as well as a crossbow wrapped in chamois skins. Gordy was armed in like manner. The question was, how could they retrieve the weapons without frightening Fanny? And if he didn't risk scaring her, Malen thought darkly, would he live to regret it?

Somewhere deep in the forest an animal roared. Its cry was followed by a shrill scream of pain as some unlucky creature became the beast's dinner. Fanny jumped violently, startling her mount. With a high-pitched whinny, the mare reared up on her hind legs. With difficulty in the sidesaddle, Fanny eased the mare back to earth.

The air had gone from cool to cold now, and Fanny wished she'd thought to pull out the thick woolen pelisse in her carpetbag before leaving the Anvil. Shivering, she rubbed the goose bumps that had erupted on her slender arms. What was it about this place that seemed so evil?

Riding at her side, Malen shifted to pull a blanket from beneath the back of Pagan's saddle. Moving the stallion closer to the mare, he placed the blanket around Fanny's shoulders.

He knew Fanny was terrified. He could tell by the whiteness of her jaw. Her lips were drawn to a tight line, and her back felt like a wooden plank when he touched her. His spine tingled instinctively as Pagan gave another loud warning snort. "Easy, fellow," he whispered, patting the horse between the ears. The stallion's snorts became soft whickers under his master's comforting touch, but the beast was obviously still uneasy.

Fanny wrapped the blanket around her shoulders and dropped part of it to cover her legs. She stifled a cry of terror when Gordy inadvertently leaned against the bagpipes strapped to his gelding's side, making the instrument give an unearthly squeal.

The scents of pine and moss and wetness shrouded the forest. Faint wisps of fog rose from the moist earth, seeking the few sunlit spaces between the huge trees. Spiraling upward, they vanished through the heavy canopy of boughs high above. Still following them, the blue jay hopped from treetop to treetop, silent as death.

Suddenly Malen pulled Pagan to a halt and motioned for his companions to stop also. Raising one hand, he put two fingers to his lips. He tipped his head as if listening. Then his eyes narrowed, and he gestured to Gordy, who seemed to understand the unspoken command.

With a creak of leather the two men slid to the ground and rummaged in their packs. Fanny trembled when they withdrew claymores and crossbows. Opening her mouth to ask why they needed the weapons, she fell silent when Malen shook his head violently. The gesture loosened the black satin riband tying his hair at his neck, and it fell, forgotten, to the road at the duke's feet. Freed, his black curls swirling against his tanned, angular face gave him a feral, dangerous appearance. Remounting, he fit an arrow to his crossbow and laid the sword across his knees.

Even in her alarm, Fanny noticed that he looked superb. Seeing him with sword in hand also made her realize that he must have been a foe to be reckoned with during the war. She felt a sudden, surprising surge of pride that he was hers, even if only for a little while.

Some distance ahead, a circle of huge white stone slabs rose from the earth like great, jagged teeth. Long, narrow, flat slabs of the same white rock topped the megaliths. The road to Annan went right through the circle. The henge was remarkably lovely but somehow sinister, and Fanny noticed that each menhir was carved with strange runes.

When the group moved forward again, she did not miss Malen's muffled order to Gordy: "Watch the rocks." Although the directive had been given to the manservant, she, too, leaned forward in the saddle and eyed the great stones.

A low growl rolled from the depths of Dagmar's throat. Fangs bared, the dog snarled, turning her big head from side to side as if searching for a foe she could not see. Sniffing, she barked once, a deep, baying wail that echoed through the stillness.

They drew closer to the rocks and soon were passing through them. Sword raised, Malen rode Pagan in and out of the gaps. Finally his tense shoulders relaxed. Shaking his head, he jumped from the stallion's broad back and examined the area on foot. At last he turned back toward his companions and shrugged his broad shoulders.

Replacing his claymore in its chamois bandeau, he began putting away his bow and arrows. "I thought I heard something back there, but I guess my imagination got the best of—"

"Look out!" Fanny's scream frightened even herself. Her mare reared violently as the two rough, dirty men from the Anvil appeared as if from nowhere. Still holding an arrow in one hand, Malen whirled about and leapt to one side as the smaller of the two rogues reached out to grab him. With a violent motion the duke drove the arrow deep into the bandit's stomach. The fellow grunted, his face showing surprise disbelief, bent double, and sank wordlessly to the ground.

Brandishing a rock, the larger man rushed up behind Malen. With a great heave, he slammed the stone against the back of the duke's head. In dumb, fascinated horror, Fanny watched her husband crumple like a rag doll.

Leaping forward, Dagmar seized the highwayman's forearm in her razor-sharp teeth, clenching her jaws around him like a vise. Screaming, the man raised the rock and smashed it against the dog's skull once, twice, three times. Dagmar collapsed at Malen's side.

As the dog fell, Gordy leapt from his gelding and rushed into the fray. The tiny Scot fought violently, swinging his claymore, but the highwayman's rock was faster than the heavy broadsword. Gordy fell backward on the thick carpet of pine needles with a dull thud, and the bandit bashed Gordy's temple. The batman lay still.

Through it all Fanny sat atop her mare's back, mute with shock. When the bandit turned toward her with a satisfied grin, she felt the world begin spinning. Dizzy with fear and horror, she, too, landed on the road.

As the large man advanced toward her, Fanny was filled with a terror stronger than anything she had ever felt in her life. Scooting backward on her bottom, she came into contact with Malen's senseless body. The bandit's hamlike fist gripped her by one ankle so that she could go no farther, but Fanny tried to scrabble away from him. Grasping at the forest's undergrowth, her fingers closed on something. With no time to examine the object, she merely covered it instinctively with her hand and surreptitiously dropped it into her bodice.

Without sparing a glance for his dead compatriot, the man grinned again and yanked Fanny toward him. She was no match for his strength, even with his injuries from Dagmar's valiant assault. Pulling several thin strips of leather from his pocket, the bandit bound her wrists and ankles, then tied a blindfold around her eyes and stuffed a dirty gag between her lips. Picking her up like so much laundry, he flung her, belly-down, over Gordy's gelding's saddle. Then, leaping onto Pagan's back, he wrapped the reins around his wrist and brought his palm down savagely on the stallion's flanks.

Like an erupting volcano, Pagan began leaping and lurching through the air. Lifting all four hooves from the earth, he landed stiff-backed so that his rider came down hard in the saddle. Before the bandit could right himself, the stallion rose again in an even higher arch.

This time when the horse came to earth, the brigand sailed through the air. Pagan ran a small distance, dragging the bandit, whose wrist was still wrapped in the reins along behind. After some moments the bandit managed to free himself. Cursing violently, he clambered to his feet, picked up a large stone, and hurled it at Pagan, nicking his haunches so that the stallion reared and raced off through the trees.

Still cursing, the bandit grabbed Fanny's mare's reins and, after shoving the carpetbag to the ground, heaved his large body onto the sidesaddle. The dainty mare was so short that the tall man's legs nearly dragged on the ground, but he seemed to take no notice. Reaching behind, he took the gelding's reins and tied them to the mare's saddle.

As he kicked the little mare into a trot, lightning shattered the sky. In a moment, despite the thick cover of the trees, huge droplets of rain began spattering the ground. Glaring up at the sky and emitting another curse, the bandit slapped a hand viciously across Arista's rump. The two horses shot through the trees.

The gelding's galloping strides made it difficult for Fanny to catch her breath. With each jolting step her mind closed a bit more, like an ever-narrowing tunnel. And soon there was nothing but a blackness even darker than that of the Annan Glen.

10

Fanny awoke with the acrid taste of dust in her mouth. She moved slightly and became aware that her head ached. A wave of panic rippled over her. Worse, everything was blackness. Was she blind? She squinted and went limp with momentary relief. No. Something was covering her eyes. A blindfold. The dusty taste came from a gag stuffed between her teeth.

It felt as if she were lying on a bed. Holding very still so that whoever had put her here would not know she was awake, she racked her throbbing brain and tried to recall what had happened. Then she remembered the bandits, and falling unconscious when the gelding's galloping made it impossible to catch her breath. She had passed out from lack of air. That would explain the heavy feeling in her head.

Covertly wiggling her fingers and toes, she discovered that her hands and feet were bound. The strangling odor of smoke burned her throat and nostrils. Then a faint sound off to her right made her hold very still. Footsteps neared.

"Ye dinna need tae pretend ye're still sleepin'," a crude voice rasped. "I seen ye movin'. B'sides, ye ain't been out cold more'n fifteen minutes at most. It ain't been longer'n that since we left yer man lyin' in the road. But 'e ain't dead. If 'e were, I couldna collect me ransom. Now, if ye'll promise not tae scream, I'll take that gag out'n yer mouth."

Fanny nodded her agreement, and the man plucked the gag from between her lips. After spitting out lint and dusty debris, she spoke in a voice that sounded much braver than she felt. "I would very much like to have this blindfold removed as well. I fail to understand why you put it on at all, since I've already seen you. I know I have. I recognize your voice."

The man snickered, a scratchy sound like shredding burlap. "Well, ye ain't so smart. Ye shouldna told me that, for I may 'ave let ye go if'n ye didna remember me face. As it is, ye won't be goin' anywhere. An' I gagged ye in case ye came tae and started screamin'. I didna want ye givin' me 'eart failure wi' a bloodcurdlin' cry. But enuf o' what *ye'd* like. Shall I be tellin' ye what *I'd* like now?" he demanded.

Ignoring his suggestive tone, Fanny tried to sit up. "Where am I?"

The bandit replied confidently. "In a cottage in the glen. I wanted tae go further, but it started rainin', and I 'ates rain. This place is used mostly by them as lives by their wits. Like me." His voice moved closer. "Now then. 'Ow 'bout you and me gettin' friendly while we wait fer yer 'usband tae fetch my money? Eh, lass? Or is the new Duchess of Argyll too grand tae be sharin' a bed wi' the likes o' me?"

Fanny screwed her mouth in distaste, and the cloth over her eyes scattered dust over her lips. Again she tried to sound confident. "If you've kidnapped me for a ransom from the Duke of Argyll, you've wasted your time. The duke hasn't the funds to pay a ransom, and even if he did, he wouldn't pay for me. I, on the other hand, have more than enough money to give you almost any sum you ask—if you release me, that is. If you'll just remove this disgusting blindfold, I'm sure we can have this misunderstanding cleared up in no time."

The bandit's voice was uncertain. " 'Ere, lass. I wasna born yesterday. I saw Argyll marry ye. I were there. An' ye canna tell me the duke wilna pay fer 'is own duchess. As fer 'im not 'avin' the funds tae pay, 'tis absurd. The swell cove must 'ave money if'n 'e's a duke. 'Sides, I've seen 'is 'ouse, and a grand 'ouse it is, too—not the 'ovel of a poor man like me."

Chuckling lewdly, he drew nearer still. "But tae the matter at 'and, ye needna deny that this mornin' ye were makin' eyes at me and dear departed Willie like 'is Grace didna satisfy ye the night before."

Her voice trembling slightly, Fanny repeated her request. "I really would like this blindfold removed."

The man snorted. "I guess it wilna matter. Ye ain't leavin' this place anyways. Even if yer 'usband does pay the ransom. An' if 'ee ain't got the blunt, I'll send a note tae yer fam'ly. Ye've already told me ye 'ave plenty o' rub. Once't I get me money, I'll jest rap ye in the noggin and dump ye in one o' the lochs 'ereabouts."

Fanny shuddered as the bandit's rough hands slipped the blindfold from her eyes and she got a look at his pox-pitted cheeks and blackened teeth. His breath smelled as if he'd been sucking on a dead cat. Hissing with disgust, she averted her face.

The man's hands, poised over her breasts like an eagle over two plump lambs, faltered. " 'Ere noo. Don't ye be actin' like that. Ye be nice tae me, and I'll be nice tae you. If ye ain't nice tae me, ye'll be sorry."

Forcing a smile to her lips, Fanny searched her mind for an answer that would put the man off. "It's just that you really are making a mistake. You see, the duke and I aren't staying married, so there's no reason for you to keep me here. And you don't know where to find my family, so unless you release me, you'll never see a penny."

"Ye ain't stayin' married, eh?" Giving her a disgusted grunt, the man turned away for a moment and then returned to stand beside the bed. He thrust a minute object the color of moonbeams touched with lavender stardust in front of her face. "This is the way a Scot brands 'is woman, lass. Wi' a luckenbooth. 'Tisna somethin' we do lightly. I took this off'n yer breast tae send back tae 'is Grace as proof I 'ave ye. I'm a Campbell meself, and I know 'is Grace ain't the kind o' man tae wed a woman and then discard 'er. I tell 'ee that if'n the duke didna mean tae keep ye, he'd not be puttin' 'is mark on ye."

"And I tell you you're mistaken!" Fanny snapped, growing increasingly anxious at the sight of the bulge ripening in the bandit's tattered trousers.

The man shrugged. Dropping the luckenbooth into his shirt pocket, he leered and raised a hand toward her breasts once again. "I don't see no reason I shouldna enjoy yer company, since ye ain't nivver goin' tae see 'is Grace again anyways. C'mon now, darlin'. Gi' me a bit o' love afore I send a note tae 'is Grace's castle."

Rough fingers caught at the fine lace lining the neck of her bodice, and Fanny suddenly remembered the object she had dropped between her breasts. Even as she fought to keep from swooning, her eyes widened as she wondered if it might be something that would help her escape.

Stalling for time, Fanny forced a tempting smile to her lips and simpered. "You know, you were correct about the duke failing to satisfy me last night. I'm certain you will do a much more thorough job. But, you know, if you'd remove my bonds, we'd probably both enjoy this more. Not to mention that it will be much easier for you, since one of your arms is injured. I'd be more than willing to do anything you required." For the first time in her life she cursed her inexperience in carnal matters and hoped she sounded convincing despite a voice quavering with horror.

The man looked at her wistfully but shook his head. "Nay. Ye'd try tae run away. An' I'll enjoy it anyhoo. If 'ee fight, 'twill just make it more excitin'."

Fanny tried to look hurt, not horrified, by this suggestion. "I certainly will not try to escape. Besides, you really ought to have someone look at that arm. I could wash and bandage it for you. If it gets infected you could lose it."

For a moment her captor hesitated. Then he leaned backward and shook his head. "Nay. I canna take the chance. But since yer eager, I'll try tae pleasure ye anyway." He looked thoughtful. "Perhaps if I just untied yer legs . . ." He chuckled suggestively. " 'Twould make it less difficult."

Fanny's answering laugh quavered. What had her big mouth gotten her into this time? With awkward fingers, the bandit untied the knot holding her ankles together.

Fanny wiggled her toes. "Will you let me have a moment to get my circulation back?" she pleaded sweetly.

The man dropped impatiently into a decrepit-looking rocking chair by the fireplace, where a tiny blaze sputtered fitfully, sending more smoke into the room than up the chimney.

Fanny's eyes searched the cottage for an escape route. This seemed to be the only room, and it was tiny and cramped. Malen would have to bend over to come through the door, it was so low. A pang shot through her. Was her husband dead? Or lying, maimed, in the dark of Annan Glen?

After a few minutes the bandit rose and began to move toward her. "Ye'll be ready now, I 'spect." He laughed, gesturing at the huge rise in his breeches. "Even if ye ain't, I am. An' I ain't waitin' any longer."

"I'm very thirsty," Fanny said rapidly. "Could you get me a drink first please? I'll also need some water so that I might look after your arm." She held her breath. If he would go outdoors, she could attempt her escape.

The bandit stared at her contemplatively and rubbed his mangled arm, grimacing as if it pained him enormously. After a moment he grunted and moved toward the door. He turned as he reached it. "Don't ye be tryin' nothin' funny whilst I'm gone." Then he stepped outside.

There was a thump as he dropped a beam through the rungs on the outside of the door. Apparently, Fanny thought grimly, this was not the first time this cottage had been used as a prison. She listened as his footsteps faded away. Then, jumping to her feet, she began leaping around the tiny room in a bizarre dance, bending and stomping, wriggling her hips and breasts, to dislodged the object in her bodice.

There was a metallic clink. Straining to see in the dark room, she bent toward the floor. Running her slippers back and forth, she searched with her toes. She felt something. Pushing the object with one foot, she maneuvered it into a tiny shaft of daylight shining through a hole in the thatched roof. Her heart leapt into her throat, thudding wildly. A knife! The one Malen kept at his stocking!

Dropping to her knees, Fanny ignored the dirt and grime and took the small dagger between her teeth, managing to dislodge it from its sheath. Moving toward the bed, she dropped the knife onto the mattress. Turning, she sat down with her back to the dagger. Then, grasping the *skean dhu* between her almost numb fingers, she sliced at the thongs that held her captive. The blade slid through the leather like a swan through water, and in a moment she was free.

Without taking time to rub the blood back into her hands, Fanny snatched up the dagger and rushed toward the door. In another moment she cut through the leather hasps, pushed the door aside, and, dropping the dagger into her bodice, ran pell-mell through the trees.

She did not remember she had left the luckenbooth with the bandit until she'd gone quite a distance. Her heart, which only a moment ago had leapt with relief at escaping, now sank to her feet. Malen had trusted her to keep it safe, and she had failed him.

It was not so much the chill rain as Pagan's persistent nudging that brought Malen back to his senses. Groaning, he turned on his side and blearily examined his surroundings.

He lay in a shallow ditch at the side of the road. Not far away a large wet gray lump lay in the same ditch. A wolfhound. It wasn't moving, although its chest rose and fell regularly. The dog made him remember something else. Fanny! His heart gave a wild lurch. Clothes dripping, he shivered and pushed himself to his feet, frantically searching the area. She was gone.

Gordy lay motionless in the middle of the road. The servant's face was very pale, and Malen couldn't tell if the batman was breathing. Moving swiftly, he felt for a pulse. The little man's heart beat steadily. Breathing a sigh of relief, Malen lifted the smaller man and placed him over Pagan's saddle. Then, moving to the wolfhound, he gathered her in his arms and returned to the stallion's side. The big horse stood quietly, awaiting his master's instructions.

For a moment Malen stared thoughtfully down the road. The rain was steadily growing harder. He had no idea where the bandit had taken Fanny, but he would have to get Gordy warm and dry before beginning his search for his lost duchess. Thankfully, at the rate the rain was coming down, he doubted that Fanny and her captor would travel far before seeking shelter themselves. Forcing his burning concern to the back of his mind, Malen returned his attention to Gordy. The jagged cut on the servant's head looked bad, and the batman's complexion was pasty. If he didn't get Gordy to shelter soon and tend to the wound, his old friend could possibly die. But where could he go?

Then his eyes brightened. Wasn't there an old cottage in the woods somewhere near here? He wrinkled his brow. Unless memory served him incorrectly, it should be about ten minutes' ride from the henge. With Gordy stretched over the saddle, and himself carrying Fanny's dropped carpetbag as well as the huge dog, that meant a trek of some twenty minutes.

Clicking his teeth in a signal for Pagan to follow, Malen began walking, trying not to think about Fanny and what the bandit might be doing to her at that very moment. But it was nearly impossible to keep his thoughts away from her. Where was she? Was she hurt? What did the men want? One was dead, of that Malen was certain, for the smaller bandit, who had taken his arrow in the belly, lay motionless in a pool of rainthinned blood. But the other, bigger man had gotten away. If he were angry enough over his friend's death, would he take his rage out on Fanny?

Malen drew a painful breath as his heart throbbed worriedly in his chest. He had brought her to this pass as surely as the sun would set that evening. He never should have agreed to this outrageous plan. If he hadn't, she would still be safely back at Carlisle Cottage. Most likely she'd have come around to agree that their marriage was the best solution to the clan troubles. But no, he'd been so sure helping her escape would be a romantic adventure that would make her fall madly in love with him, he'd risked her very life.

If they got out of this alive, he promised solemnly, he'd give Fanny anything she wanted. Even an annulment. He groaned. Was this the act of God he'd so caustically joked to himself would make him release her?

Gritting his teeth, he forced one foot to follow the other, trying to ignore the rain pounding on his aching head. With each passing step the dog and bag seemed to increase in weight. Only Malen's worry over Fanny and Gordy kept him going. Shifting his burden and wiping a hand over his face, he swept away the blinding raindrops, refusing to admit, even to himself, that mixed with them was an abundance of tears.

Then, suddenly, it was before him, a tiny cottage hunkered close to the ground. Its thatched roof was in much sorrier condition that Malen remembered, but he'd never been happier to see a place in his life. He made for the doorway.

The door hung at a curious angle, he noticed, almost as if it had been sliced off its hinges. Stepping inside, he dropped the carpetbag in the corner and lay the wolfhound on the floor near the fireplace. Dagmar thumped her tail a few times, then drifted back into senselessness.

Suddenly Malen's eyes narrowed. Holding a hand over the hearth, he could almost feel warmth. He shook his head. His imagination must be getting the better of him. Surely the cottage just seemed warm compared to the chill storm outside. Returning to Pagan's side, he lifted Gordy and carried the servant into the house, laying him across the dusty bed.

After making the batman as comfortable as possible, Malen went back outside to find shelter for Pagan. Taking the reins, he led the horse toward a natural paddock of vine-strangled trees he remembered from a visit here years ago. There he gave a start of surprise. Two horses already occupied the small shelter of scrub oaks. The mare and gelding! Pagan whinnied a greeting and trotted into the enclosure.

Then an arm gripped Malen's neck from behind. He

managed to utter a simple staccato cry before the bandit's huge hand effectively shut off the passageway to his lungs.

The downpour had lessened to a drizzle. Fanny leaned back against a slick boulder and chewed her thumbnail. Although the forest was bitter cold, her mind was so occupied that she hardly noticed the chill breeze riffling her soaked gown. Brushing a lock of damp hair away from her eyes, she waged a silent battle as she tried to decide where to look for Malen and Gordy. A part of her even longed to go back to the cottage to retrieve the brooch.

Then she sighed. She hadn't the first idea where she was even in comparison to the road. How could she possibly find Malen? And yet, if she went back to the cottage, how could she hope to overpower her huge kidnapper and retrieve the luckenbooth? Buffeted by indecision, she fought back a rush of panic as she realized that she might never find her way out of Annan Glen, much less save the lives of Gordy and the man she loved.

There. She had said it. She loved him. She'd loved him since the moment she'd first seen him skulking about the grounds of MacDonald Manor so many years ago, and she loved him now. So he was a Campbell. So he had failed to come back after promising he would. So he had tricked her into marriage. So what? She still loved him and would give anything if he would just be all right. Even herself.

Drawing a shaky breath, she forced herself to put thoughts of love out of her mind and think clearly. Obviously Malen had not been killed, or the kidnapper would not have been so certain of getting his ransom. She hoped. The big, brutish bandit hadn't seemed very bright. Anyway, Malen was most certainly wounded and in need of medical attention. But how to begin searching without getting hopelessly lost in the depths of Annan Glen?

But she did not have to search, for just as she had begun to look for the road, a shout echoed through the forest behind her. She froze.

"Malen!" Her mouth formed the name before she knew she had spoken, and then she was running through the trees, back the way she had come. She reached the cottage in minutes. Quickly she scanned the scene and, with a horrified gasp, saw Malen locked in mortal combat with the huge bandit.

Giving no thought to her own safety, Fanny streaked across the rain-soaked ground, slipping and sliding on the muddy path. The bastard was choking her husband! Consumed with rage, she reached into her bodice and raised her hand.

As Malen's eyes misted over, Fanny brought her hand down straight at the bandit's back. The razor-sharp blade of the *skean dhu* sank to its hilt between the kidnapper's shoulder blades. With a cry the man fell, face buried in the mud. He did not get up.

Fanny dropped to her knees beside Malen's gasping form. His face was nearly purple. Before realizing what she was about, she began raining kisses over his face, his neck, his hands. Her voice, ragged with sobs, broke as she murmured his name. "Malen? Darling? Can you speak? Oh, God, if you die because of me, I shall die also!"

Somewhere deep within the shrouding fog in his air-starved brain, Malen's mind registered the presence of the woman weeping over him. Although he understood none of her words, he opened his eyes and smiled up at her. "Duchess! My sweet duchess. I must be in heaven!"

With a cry of relief, Fanny bent to place a hand behind his back. Slowly and carefully she helped him to his feet. Malen grimaced but allowed her to lead him toward the cottage. Once inside the tiny building, Fanny managed to slide the prostrate Gordy to the far side of the mattress, then urged Malen to lie beside his servant.

It was then that she saw the wolfhound lying on the hearth. She hurried to Dagmar's side. Although dog's fur was matted with blood, the wound didn't look too serious, and her breathing was steady. Turning, Fanny threw a few sticks onto the hearth. The tiny fire had gone out during her flight, but after she blew heavily at the twigs, a few small flames burst into life. She added a log to the feeble blaze.

Satisfied that the dog would be as comfortable as possible until she had time to tend her, Fanny turned back to the bed. "Don't move," she said to the duke. "I'll be right back. I want to get some water to bathe your wounds."

Malen made a protesting sound, probably trying to forbid her to go near the dead bandit, but Fanny ignored him and headed outside. The kidnapper lay motionless in the mud where she had left him. She shuddered.

Where would she get water? As she stood racking her brain, she noticed a large battered pot filled to the brim with just that substance. Apparently the bandit had been carrying it back to her when he'd spotted Malen. With a relieved sigh she hurried over, heaved it up, and carried it into the cottage.

In no time the water steamed on the hearth. Now it only remained to find something clean with which to wash Malen and Gordy's wounds. She frowned. She couldn't use anything from her carpetbag, since the bandit had shoved it off the mare. Most likely, she thought with a shrug, her clothes and personal items were now strewn across the streaming road.

She could use her petticoat, but a thick layer of mud encrusted her skirts at least to the knee. There was really only one thing to do, she decided. Standing in the shadows, she pulled off her gown, divested herself of her petticoat and chemise, and replaced the apricot corduroy dress over her shivering body.

Teeth chattering, she took the petticoat between her chilled fingers and pulled. Pulled again. When a third attempt to rip the delicate fabric failed, she cursed softly and dropped into the decrepit rocking chair. Biting her lower lip, she studied the undergarments and wondered what to do now. Then her brow cleared.

She had to have the knife.

11

Stepping back outside, Fanny cautiously approached the prostrate form of the kidnapper and nudged him sharply with one toe. For a split second she wondered if she'd seen him breathe. Then, when she saw nothing more, she bent down and gripped the small *skean dhu* by its braided leather handle and, with a grimace, pulled it free. Then she whirled around, eager to be away from the body, and, holding the bloody knife at arm's length, hurried indoors.

After pouring boiling water over the blade, she proceeded to slit the cotton petticoat and chemise into strips of bandages, discarding the muddied sections. After sponging both men's wounds she discovered to her relief that Malen's head wound wasn't as serious as she had feared.

She could not keep a surge of concern for Gordy from rushing through her, though, for the servant's face was an odd shade of gray, and he seemed feverish. Clenching her teeth, she forced herself to scour the gash in his skull. Gordy had not regained consciousness by the time she finished but at least seemed to be sleeping a bit easier.

Adding to her relief, after Fanny had washed Dagmar's wounds, the big dog rolled onto her back, legs in the air, and seemed to sleep soundly. But the thing that brought Fanny the most happiness was that Malen was still alive. He'd come so close to death! Unable to help herself, she felt her eyes fill with relieved tears.

Malen lay still, gazing up at Fanny as she sponged his brow. Surge after surge of pain shuddered through

131

him as he looked at her lovely face and realized he must let her go. God, if only she loved him, he would be the happiest man on earth! Finally he knew he loved her more than life. But that didn't matter now. He'd given his oath to release her if she were all right. He nearly groaned with anguish at the thought.

His eyes narrowed as he watched Fanny's expression. She had been very quiet for quite some time now. Was she upset because of killing the bandit? Or had something far worse happened in the time she had been held prisoner?

As a single crystalline tear dripped down her smooth cheek, Malen felt his chill suspicion couple with the desire to take the giant kidnapper by the throat and crush the bastard's spine in two. Forcing his expression to remain calm, he lifted one hand. Taking Fanny's chin between his fingertips, he examined her face solemnly. She wouldn't meet his eyes, but neither did she pull away.

Damn. What if she had been ... He cursed softly as another tear joined its companion on the trail forged down her creamy cheek. That was it. It had to be. "Listen to me, Fanny," he murmured softly, careful not to startle her. "I don't want to upset you, but there is something I must know. Did the brigand ..." He drew a trembling breath. "Did the bastard ... hurt you?"

Flushing violently, Fanny shook her head and brushed roughly at her tears. Shame rushed through her as she remembered the bandit's rough fingers hovering at her breasts. She looked away. "No. He was quite gentle. He removed my ... my blindfold when I asked him to and went to get me a drink of water and ... and ..." She hesitated, her cheeks glowing a deep-red. "And he untied my legs."

Malen's stomach knotted. "Yes, but did he ... touch you?"

Now Fanny shuddered at the memory of the man's lewd suggestions. "Yes, I told you, he—"

"Dear God." Malen's voice was heavy with pain, sorrow, and the agonized realization that he had brought this upon her. He'd had to accept responsibility for her kidnapping, and now he knew her rape was on his head as well. Still, even though he couldn't give back her virginity, there was one thing he *could* give her. The annulment she wanted. Even though losing her would almost kill him.

Then he paused. But suppose she was with child? Throwing her out into the world, pregnant and unmarried, would be unthinkable. Surely it would be best to wait and see.

He was amazed to find himself almost hoping she was carrying the kidnapper's child, just so he would be unable to give her the annulment she wanted. Never in his wildest dreams had he expected he would care so deeply for a woman as to be willing to raise another man's by-blow. Yet he did.

Thoroughly overwrought by her shame at appearing to cooperate with the loathsome kidnapper, her overwhelming relief at Malen's safety, and the possible futility of her love for the duke, Fanny sobbed and made as if to rise. Malen's hand on her wrist pulled her back to her place in the rocking chair beside the bed. Scalding tears rolled down her cheeks as he stroked her hand awkwardly. Was he too filled with disgust to speak? Horrified that she had allowed the kidnapper to touch her? The very gentleness of his caress made her tears fall faster. Although revolted, he was still too kind to rebuke her. Her tears quickened to a torrent.

Unable to bear seeing Fanny in such pain, Malen rose from the bed, lifted her in his arms, and sat down in the rocking chair. With her head cradled securely beneath his chin, he began to rock back and forth, crooning soft Gaelic words she probably didn't understand. One of his hands repeatedly caressed her back, while the other cupped her head, softly brushing her disarranged curls away from her forehead. His voice deepened to an emotional burr. "Easy, lass. 'Tis all right. Rest, love. Everythin' will be all right. Ye'll see. Everythin' will be fine. I will *make* everythin' fine for ye, darlin'."

Fanny pressed her face into Malen's chest. Her cheek rested on the open neck of his mud-stained linen shirt, but even the mud did not detract from the softly curling hairs that tickled her face or the sweet, musky scent of his body. His chest was warm and hard. His deep voice and the hand that ran up and down her spine soothed her, and slowly her tears stopped falling. Snuggling closer, she slept.

It was with great difficulty, when he felt her breathing deepen to slumber, that Malen refrained from dropping the hand brushing her violet-scented curls to the ripe mounds of her breasts where they pressed against his side. Cursing his ill-timed lust, he shifted the sleeping girl away from his swollen manhood. She smelled so sweet, felt so soft. Since she had removed her petticoat and chemise to make bandages, the hollow between her breasts was easily visible beneath her gauzy net bodice.

Malen clenched his teeth until his jaw ached. Oh, if only he felt free to wake her, to take her in his arms and teach her the sweet side of the horror she had been through. That was the one good thing he'd learned from his years of debauchery, he thought dully: He knew well how to pleasure a woman. And if Fanny would let him, he'd devote the rest of his life to pleasing her. He sighed and did not wake her. Instead, rigidly ignoring his clamoring senses, he rose and carefully set his duchess back in the chair.

Fanny's head lolled back, her lashes appearing thicker and darker than before against her pale, tear-streaked cheeks. Her lovely red hair hung in tangled disarray over her breasts, and Malen couldn't help thinking that, even in her pain, she was the most beautiful creature he'd ever seen.

His heart gave a sharp wrench. Was there any way to return a woman's sense of honor once she had been violated? And, since he had brought her to this, was he really any better than her kidnapper? On that disturbing thought, Malen turned abruptly and walked out the door into the fresh, rain-washed air.

The afternoon shadows had deepened to night when Fanny awoke. A rich, tantalizing smell filled the tiny cottage, and she sniffed appreciatively. Lifting her head from the back of the rocking chair, she glanced around the room. The leather hasps on the door had been mended. The door hung open slightly. Gordy lay quietly on the bed, and Malen stooped over a pot hanging from a hook over the fire. The flames had died to a bed of glowing red coals, and smoke no longer filled the room.

"What smells so good?" she asked groggily.

Malen looked up with a smile. "Rabbit stew. I made it myself, using herbs, rainwater, and one unfortunate rabbit that I ran to earth."

He looked so proud of himself that Fanny refused to allow the thought of the furry woodland creature simmering in the pot to bother her. Besides, she *was* starved. "Mmm. Is it almost done? I'm famished."

Malen, who had been watching her with veiled concern, felt the bands squeezing his heart loosen considerably. A hearty appetite was a sure sign of returning health, emotional as well as physical. "Just about. Give it another fifteen minutes or so for the burdock root to soften through."

Trying to restore some semblance of order to her ravaged coiffure, Fanny ran her fingers through her tangled curls. Her eyes felt hot and swollen, as if someone had sprinkled sand into them while she slept. "What is burdock?"

Busily stirring the contents of the pot with a freshly skinned willow branch, Malen answered without raising his head. "It's a plant that grows wild hereabouts. Its root closely resembles potatoes."

"Hmm. Does it taste good?"

Malen looked up with a crooked grin that didn't quite reach his eyes. His shoulder-length black hair had been tied back once again with a bit of fabric from her chemise. To Fanny, the lacy string only emphasized his masculinity.

"Wait and see."

"Are you sure you used the right plant? How do you know you didn't put some kind of poisonous plant in there?"

Malen glanced back into the pot. "I used the leaves for medicinal purposes and the roots for victuals many times during the war when there was nothing else available. The leaves are huge, shaped like hearts or elephant ears. You can't mistake them for anything else. I also put in some wild onions and sage."

Fanny's mouth watered. "If it tastes half as good as it smells, I may eat the whole pot. I don't know if I can make it another fifteen minutes," she replied honestly.

As Malen raised his face to hers once again, Fanny's heart gave a painful throb. She recognized the emotion etched on his angular features: guilt. He looked as if he were being eaten alive by it. Until tonight he had seemed invincible, proud, supremely confident. Now, however, he was clearly suffering. Obviously he felt responsible for her kidnapping. What could she say to lessen his sense of blame?

Perhaps the best thing to do was pretend she hadn't seen his agony and concentrate on diverting his attention. She glanced at the bed. "How is Gordy? He seemed to have lost a lot of blood."

Malen frowned. "Yes. Head wounds often bleed profusely and can be very dangerous. He hasn't awakened yet. But you did a superb job of doctoring him. If he doesn't wake by morning, we'll have to try to get some broth down his throat anyway. I want to get him to Dumfries as soon as possible, so we'll need to leave here at the crack of dawn." He flushed and looked away. "If you're able, that is."

Fanny looked at him, surprised. Why wouldn't she be able? "Of course. But can we make it to Dumfries in one day? I know it's possible by coach, but on horseback?"

"If we hurry. There's one problem, though." He looked into her eyes.

Fanny smiled. "Well, tell me! After everything else, I think I can take it."

Malen flinched, then cleared his throat. "We only have two mounts. When I arrived here and put Pagan in the small grove of scrub oaks by the house, I found your mare and the gelding already stabled there. About an hour ago, when I finished gathering foodstuffs, I returned to the cottage to find both the gelding and the bandit gone."

Fanny felt the blood drain from her face. "Gone? But he was dead! I killed him!"

Malen shook his head. "Apparently not. He was alive enough to ride. I had meant to bury him before you woke up, but I didn't bargain for his ability to get up and walk away. When I returned after looking for food, I was worried sick that the bastard might have returned to the cottage and made off with you again."

Barely able to control her trembling, Fanny replied, "I can't help but wish he *were* dead. Suppose he comes back?"

"With his wounds, I doubt if he's in any condition to try anything else."

"Let's hope you're right." Then something occurred to her. "How did you find this cottage, anyway?"

"I stayed here several years ago. Most people who travel this area know its whereabouts, since it's a good place to take shelter in an emergency." He glanced around the room. "It's in much worse shape than when I was here last. Still, I am glad of it. It may save Gordy's life. We've already lost far too much," he said grimly.

Lowering her hands to her lap, Fanny stared at them, unable to meet the duke's gaze. "There is something I must tell you . . ."

Malen's heart leapt into his throat. Was she going to tell him of her rape? When he caught up with the kidnapper, he thought savagely, the man was as good as dead. His hands clenched into fists. "You can tell me anything, Fanny. I will never betray you." The thought that their acquaintance had been a web of betrayal since their first meeting flashed guiltily through his mind. He quickly banished it.

"It's the luckenbooth. The kidnapper stole it. Oh, Malen, I'm so sorry. I know you trusted me with it."

He stared at her dumbly. "The brooch?" He shook his head with a relieved smile. "Your life is far more important than any jewel!"

Gratefully returning his smile, Fanny said quickly, "Nevertheless, I am sorry I lost it. I would offer to get another one, but I realize I cannot possibly replace your family heirloom."

Again guilt swept through Malen. But, placing a finger under Fanny's chin, he forced her to look into his eyes. "I repeat, the brooch is nothing. You have been so brave through all this. I want you to know I hold myself fully responsible, and if it takes the rest of my life, I swear I will make it up to you." Gazing at her pale face, he found himself desperately wishing she would give him that chance. But there was no way he could force her to give him another opportunity, considering his record thus far. "The stew is almost done."

Then he noticed Fanny shiver in the breeze wafting through the partially open door. Closing it, he gestured at an object in a shadowy corner of the room. "I brought your carpetbag from the road earlier. Fortunately everything inside was still moderately dry. Why don't you put on something warmer than that gown? You don't want to catch cold."

Fanny gave a cry of pleasure. "Oh, thank you. I was afraid it was lost for good."

After watching her hurry toward the bag, Malen turned his eyes away from her lush body. He almost hated to see her cover it with something that would obstruct his view.

Suddenly Fanny let out a cry. He spun around.

Evidently she had noticed for the first time how transparent the fabric covering her bosom was. Cheeks flaming, she ripped open the trunk and pulled out the first gown she could find, a thick blue wool, then seized a clean, dry petticoat and a fresh chemise.

Holding them in front of her, she turned on Malen, her eyes blazing. "You could have told me I was half naked!"

Confused, he moved toward her, only to have her back up, spitting like a wet cat. "Don't touch me! How could you have let me sit there practically naked and not told me!"

"But it didn't seem to matter at the—"

"Oh, didn't it! You are as bad as the kidnapper!"

He blanched.

"I heard you were a womanizer and a rogue, but I didn't expect you to be so dishonorable as to sit there watching me make a fool of myself," she raged. "It's just as I told my father. No woman is safe with you!"

Turning away, Malen smiled bitterly. "I promise you are completely safe from my disgusting attentions."

Seeing how stricken he looked, Fanny felt a tide of remorse wash over her. Reaching out, she placed her fingers on his forearm. "I didn't mean that. Truly I didn't. I must just be more unnerved than I thought," she said honestly.

He shrugged her off.

Fanny's throat tightened. "Malen? Please forgive me."

Turning around, the duke stared at her, his eyes like twin blue-green flames. Suddenly heat streamed through Fanny's belly and over her thighs as sudden longing swept over her. Never in her life had she wanted anything so much as to hurl herself into this man's arms. Frightened by the overpowering urgency of her desire, she stepped back.

The moment she retreated, Malen sighed as if all the life were drained out of him. "Why are you afraid of me? Do you really think me capable of hurting you? Do you truly think me no better than the bandit? I'd prove otherwise, if you'd let me." His voice broke.

Suddenly more concerned with the agony in his voice than with her own confusion, Fanny rushed forward and took his arm again. "Oh, Malen," she said in a whisper. "I will let you prove it to me."

He didn't dare respond. He knew that if he did, he'd grab hold of her and never let her go. And letting her go was the only way he could make amends to her for her trials. But this longing to hold her was nearly unbearable. It was almost ripping him in two. When he spoke, his voice was gravelly with reined-in emotion. "When we reach Dumfries, I will look into an annulment."

Horror flooded Fanny, turning her inner heart to ice. This was not what she wanted! Not anymore! Didn't he understand that? "Malen," she repeated in a trembling voice. "You could never disgust me. Never. Why, you are everything a woman could want. I know you would never hurt me. You are too good, too kind."

When he said nothing, her heart lurched, and she swallowed a fresh bout of tears. She gazed longingly at his stiff profile. Obviously even though he would not condemn her for allowing the bandit to touch her, he no longer wanted her for his wife. Not that she should be surprised. No man wanted a woman who'd been touched by another man. That was, to the best of her knowledge, the one requirement every gentleman had.

And then there was the matter of her earlier behavior. She had been immature and selfish, when she should have been considering their clan members. In her heart she'd known her father and Malen were correct about this marriage bringing peace to the clans, but she had been too determined to prove she was her own mistress to listen to common sense. And now she would pay the price.

At last Malen spoke, his voice a rough whisper. "But you are afraid of me, aren't you, Fanny? I've caused you too much hurt for you *not* to fear me."

Fanny drew a quivering breath and searched her mind for the right thing to say. She dared not profess her love, when he so obviously didn't want it. But she could still be near him, even if it would tear her apart. She was determined to try, if only for their clans. It was the least she could do. Tipping her chin up, she smiled bravely. "No, I am not afraid of you. I know you would never willingly hurt me. You are my friend."

The bands surrounding Malen's heart closed again. Friend? She thought of him as a *friend?* Then he cursed silently. Well, what else could she think? Hadn't he just promised her the thing she wanted most? An annulment. His jaw clenched. She could keep her friendship, he thought savagely. He wanted her love or nothing at all.

For a fleeting moment Fanny was certain he was going to pull her into his arms. Then he pushed her hand away and strode out the door into the darkness, leaving her staring after him, bereft. Unchecked, tears coursed down her cheeks.

12

The moon had risen when Malen felt confident enough that he could control his hunger for Fanny to return to the cottage. He must have paced for hours in the cold and dark, unwilling to remain inside with her but refusing to leave the hovel unprotected. Now he stood on the doorstep, taking several deep breaths before entering the room.

Apparently Fanny had put another log on the fire. The flames sputtered and sparked as the breeze whooshed through the open door, and the room was comfortably warm. Fanny sat in the rocking chair, seemingly sound asleep. Nearby on the floor, a chipped crockery bowl held the remnants of a meal.

Through half-closed eyes Fanny watched Malen approach. His powerful shoulders drooped as though he'd lost his best friend. Although she'd managed to control her tears at last, she could not help the lump that rose in her throat. Somehow, she managed to speak past it. "Hello."

"I thought you were asleep."

"Just resting. Gordy woke up for a while, and I fed him some stew."

"Thank God. What about you? Have you eaten?"

"I . . . wasn't hungry."

Malen studied her pale features. She had to eat something. She'd been starving earlier. Although his own stomach roiled at the thought of food, he forced a grin and poured out two bowls of stew. "Well, you must be by now. I am. And you must keep your strength up. I don't think I could get two sick people to Dumfries."

He glanced at her dog. "What about Dagmar? Did you give her some stew?"

His smile made warmth trickle through Fanny's belly, thawing her frozen soul a bit. She nodded. "Yes. And she's fine now. It seems that her head is even harder than I used to think when I tried to train her and she refused to obey." She laughed shakily. "She liked your cooking."

"You will, too. Come on now, eat this for me."

Malen was pleased to note that, although she claimed not to be hungry, when Fanny finished her first serving and he spooned more into the cracked dish, she ate that as well. Satisfied, he managed to force down a few bites of his own portion.

As Fanny finished her second serving, he took the bowl from her chilled hands and rinsed and wiped it as he had his own. After placing the two dishes back on the hearth, he turned around and knelt beside the rocker. "Fanny, I know you are upset with me, but I am hoping we can put these feelings aside for the brief time we have together."

Fanny felt sick. Evidently he didn't like to see her mooning over him. Well, she'd do her best. After all, just because she was miserable didn't mean she had to make him unhappy, too. "You're right. Why don't we pretend nothing at all untoward has happened. We can worry about everything else when we get to Dumfries." She managed a weak smile.

Drawing a relieved breath, Malen relaxed a fraction. "Agreed. Now why don't you just stay there while I see what kind of sleeping arrangements I can put together." He turned away and studied the room. After a moment he moved toward a corner of the cottage and tore a loose plank from the ceiling.

Reaching up, he plucked some thatch from the hole he'd made and deposited it on the floor. "The straw underneath the thatch is quite dry," he said, looking up thoughtfully. "I don't think it got even slightly moist from the rain. I've often wondered why we don't thatch mansions rather than using tile. It's a much better insulator," he mumbled distractedly.

Fanny's eyes widened, and he threw her an apologetic glance. "I know you must disapprove of me for harming the cottage, but I intend to send someone back from Inveraray to mend it. It seems the least I can do, since the place is giving us much-needed shelter tonight."

"Oh," Fanny said quickly, "I'm not disapproving. I'm just impressed at your resourcefulness. I never would have thought of using the roof for a bed!"

Unaccountably pleased, Malen smiled and added more straw to the pile on the ground. "I learned to use all available resources during the war. When you sleep on the muddy ground a few times, you learn to use anything and everything to keep warm and dry. And when it's a matter of keeping your men warm and dry, you're even more resourceful. It's much like taking measures to keep one's tenants happy," he mused. "One can accomplish far more with the help of one's friends. Indeed, my tenants are largely responsible for the change in my finances. Without them, my properties would still be in disrepair. Every man, woman, and child pitched in to pull things back together. One hand always washes the other, and caring for them to the best of my ability is the least I can do to show my gratitude."

Fanny smiled. "It sounds as if they love you very much."

Malen looked thoughtful. "Well, they are mostly family, so I hope they love me as I love them. Little is more important than family ties." He winced. "They even led me to the idea of marrying the MacDonald heir. Blood being thicker than water, I reckoned that if the Campbell and MacDonald bloods were finally joined, there would be far less spillage." He sighed. "Now, however, I suppose I shall have to come up with another solution." He looked up from his labors. "But I talk too long. Your bed is ready," he said with a flourish.

The thatch was surprisingly soft and springy, Fanny noted as he helped her settle into it. She frowned as he quickly moved away. "But what about you? Gordy's bed is much too narrow for two. Besides, I think it would be best if you didn't awaken him by lying beside him."

Malen looked at her. He had intended to sleep with the batman, but now that Fanny mentioned it, undoubtedly it would be best if Gordy were allowed a good night's sleep. "I suppose I can sleep in the chair." He eyed the rocker doubtfully, remembering his accident at the inn.

Fanny shook her head vehemently. "Absolutely not. I will not allow it. You wouldn't get a moment's rest. And you need it. Remember, Gordy isn't the only one the bandit cracked on the skull. You made this bed. You will sleep here beside me."

No sooner was the invitation out of her mouth than an idea occurred to her. A shocking idea. A brilliant idea. She would seduce *him.* Then he wouldn't be *able* to get the annulment!

She frowned. It wouldn't be strictly honorable. But then, tricking her into marriage hadn't been honorable, either! Smiling sweetly, she moved to one side of the makeshift mattress. "Come, Malen. There's plenty of room."

Did she know what she was saying? Malen wondered. She couldn't possibly know what lying beside her would do to him. She was so trusting. No. He couldn't do it. To lie beside her, knowing this was their last night together, would be suicide. He'd never be able to keep his hands off her. "I really think I ought to sleep in the chair. I'd probably thrash around and keep you awake."

Fanny managed a lighthearted laugh. "You didn't keep me awake at the Anvil."

Oh, God, Malen groaned inwardly, remembering how her thigh had felt draped over his leg. Well, surely it wouldn't be so wrong just to hold her in his arms one last time. Nothing else would happen. He wouldn't let it.

After all, if he weakened and made love to her, even if she were *not* carrying the kidnapper's child inside her, he would never be able to let her go. And he had to release her, since she loathed the thought of being his duchess. Surely he could control himself; her happiness was at stake. He could do that much for her, after everything that had happened.

Seeing his uncertainty, Fanny rushed on. "Please, Malen. If you aren't willing to think of your own comfort, then think of mine. It will be much warmer with both of us sharing the thatch."

Unable to argue any longer, Malen nodded, hoping the fire in his loins wasn't blazing in his eyes. He cleared his throat uneasily. "All right. But don't say I didn't warn you if you can't sleep."

Sighing with satisfaction, Fanny patted the blanket at her side. "Come. It's late."

Swallowing, Malen lowered himself beside her and sank deep into the thick straw, only to discover an unforeseen problem. It was impossible to lie on the edge of the pile without falling off and onto the cold floor. The only other option was falling toward the middle, which meant pressing close to Fanny.

With a sigh he allowed himself to sink toward the center. Carefully positioning his body so that it barely touched Fanny's, he lay stiffly, staring up at the ceiling and expelling his breath from between clenched teeth.

Fanny frowned. How did one go about seducing a man of the world? "Comfortable?" she asked lamely.

"Quite. Go to sleep," he growled.

"Suddenly I'm not really sleepy. Let's talk a while."

"You said you weren't hungry, too, but you ate two bowls of stew. Go to sleep."

"It was delicious. You're a good cook."

"Thank you. *Go to sleep*." His nostrils flared. Dear Lord. He could smell violets!

Fuming quietly, Fanny racked her brain. For a long while she lay still. Then she smiled. Opening her mouth in a huge yawn, she raised her arms above her head. Lowering them, she "accidentally" slid one behind Malen's neck. He drew in his breath sharply, and she froze.

"Fanny?"

She pretended she was asleep. Encouraged when he

didn't pull away, she made a soft purring noise and curved toward him until her head lay on his chest and her body pressed against his hard, masculine length. Lifting her other arm to meet the one around his neck, she interlaced her fingers so that she held him in a feather-soft clasp.

Malen shuddered with suppressed desire. Slowly he shifted until he lay a slight distance away, but he rolled off the hay for his efforts, taking Fanny with him. She landed full length on his chest, her legs cradled between his. He could feel the heat of her female center against his rigid manhood, and he cursed the pounding hunger that threatened to consume him.

Moving carefully, he shifted himself back onto the straw, carefully bringing Fanny's limp body with him and settling her back where she'd been before the mishap. Tugging at her fingers, he tried to remove them from around his neck, but they seemed glued together. Sighing, he surrendered himself to her disconcerting touch and attempted to sleep.

It was no use. Sparks of desire effervesced over his skin where Fanny held him. *Lord*, he groaned silently. If he made it through this night without going mad, it would be a miracle. He shifted his body away from hers. A moment later Fanny pressed near again as if seeking his warmth, and this time her pillow-soft breasts touched his ribs. His groin throbbed. Using intense self-control, he kept from raising his hands to touch the enticing mounds.

"Oh," Fanny moaned softly, as if dreaming. Lifting one eyelid slightly, she peeped up at Malen's face. His gaze was fixed on the ceiling, and his jaw was set as if he were in agony. He looked almost enraged. Pinching her eyes shut again, she bit her lip. What was she doing wrong?

Perhaps, Malen thought, he should just put his arms around her, since she was apparently feeling cold. He raised his arms and curled them around her shoulders. She nestled into the circle of his embrace as if designed for it.

His skin was like fire, Fanny thought fervently. Moaning again, this time unconsciously, she "accidentally" slid one leg over his. She could feel the solidity of his muscles, the iron sinews of his arms and legs, beneath his fine lawn shirt and leather breeches. Her breasts throbbed where they met the corded strength of his chest.

Almost mad with desire, Malen tried to think of something—anything—besides the sharp points of Fanny's nipples thrusting against his ribs. Lowering his head with a soft groan, he touched his lips to her copper curls in a chaste caress. It was a mistake. Breathing in her delicate scent, feeling her silky hair brush his chin, he shivered hungrily.

Certain he couldn't see her face, Fanny opened her eyes and examined the black curls peeking out of the V of his shirt. Her fingertips itched to touch them, to trail experimentally through the thick mat. Unable to help herself, she slid one hand lower to rest gently against his warm flesh and tempting curls. Malen gasped beneath her touch, and she whimpered with innocent desire, gazing at him through passion-hazed eyes.

Malen started violently. "Fanny! You're awake!"

Fanny trembled with desire. "Yes," she said. "Malen?" she ventured in a whisper.

"Yes? What is it?"

"You—you once said you'd kiss me if I asked. Well," she faltered, "would you kiss me good-night, Your Grace?"

"Oh, Fanny," he whispered. Reaching for her, he rolled her onto her back, leaned over her, and claimed her lips with a victorious groan.

Fanny's world spun out of control. Instinctively she clung to her duke, her hands sliding over his chest and down his belly, stroking, pressing, lifting his cotton shirt to touch the curls on his chest. She was thrilled to discover that his nipples were as hard as hers.

Beneath her touch, Malen battled with his sense of honor. And lost. She wanted him. He wanted her. She was his wife, dammit! With an agonizing groan he crushed her to him, sliding his tongue between her parted lips as she cried out his name. His manhood hammered with the desire to be buried deep inside her silken female sheath. He quickly parted the pearl buttons at the neck of her gown until the tops of her curving breasts were exposed to his ravenous gaze. Lowering his mouth, he rained torrid kisses over the rounded flesh. She tasted sweeter than honey. Hurriedly, he finished unbuttoning her bodice. His fingers trembled as he pushed the folds wide and gazed at her bosom, which was now covered only by a fine white gauze chemise. The neckline of the undergarment was laced with a pale-pink satin riband, tied in a bow nestled enticingly between her breasts.

By now his fingers were shaking so severely he could scarcely grasp the riband's ends to free the delectable twin mounds, but at last her lovely flushed skin lay bared to his gaze. Malen buried his face in the sweet-smelling valley, inhaling her violet scent. "Fanny. Dear, sweet Fanny," he breathed. "You are so beautiful."

Fanny gasped as his tongue trailed over one mound and pulled its peak into his mouth. Never had she known such delicious torment. An odd urgency thrumming inside her, she clasped the back of his head, and her fingers found the cotton string holding back his hair. As she tugged it free, he raised his head to look at her, and his black curls fell in an unruly tangle around his angular cheeks covered with a shadow of beard. Once again she thought how much he resembled a pirate. Her pirate. And she wanted to feel his lips and tongue on her again. She arched her back and clutched the folds of his shirt. "Oh, Malen!" she whispered. "Love me! Please love me!"

Malen abruptly jerked back to reality. What the devil was he doing? He had no right! Doubtless Fanny was only behaving in this amorous fashion because she was so sleepy. To continue making love to her would be the height of dishonor. He had dishonored her enough by allowing her to be kidnapped and raped just because he'd thought bringing her out here rather than marrying her in her father's house in Carlisle was such a romantic idea.

Thrusting her away, he lurched to his feet, turning

swiftly to hide his arousal. "Cover yourself," he commanded gruffly as he ran a trembling hand through his hair. "You see now why I must sleep in the rocking chair."

Fanny felt as if she'd been slapped. He didn't want her. She rolled away and pulled her bodice closed. Without speaking, she lay her head on the straw, her heart too sore even to allow tears. As if a leaden weight pressed her into the floor, she listened silently as Malen settled himself in the rocker behind her.

It was all Malen could do not to go to Fanny and kiss away her confusion. Poor darling, she must be so bewildered. First she was kidnapped, then raped, and now attacked by him. He sighed heavily. It would be best if Gordy could accompany her to Dumfries and her waiting betrothed and leave Malen to go as far away from her as possible. But Gordy was injured. God, what a mess.

After a long time, Fanny dozed. Malen, on the other hand, watched her slumbering form long into the night.

13

It was obvious to Fanny the following morning that Malen was as eager as she to pretend nothing had happened.

In no time they were packed up and ready to depart. Gordy had awakened with a terrific headache but was able to stay on Fanny's mare without aid. Fanny had bandaged his wound with another length of petticoat and, with the lace strapped to his pate, the little man looked almost comical, rather like a very ugly, bewhiskered, overgrown baby. If her heart hadn't been crackling with sadness, she might have laughed.

From her position on a pallet strung behind the stallion, Dagmar looked up as her mistress came out of the cottage. Her tail thumped softly, and her limpid black eyes glowed with devotion. Deeply touched by Malen's kindness to her dog, Fanny looked at him gratefully, hoping her longing didn't show in her eyes. As long as she didn't touch him, she thought optimistically, she might yet get to Dumfries without shaming herself totally.

Realizing there was nothing to do but ride pillion, Malen took Fanny's carpetbag from her and, after strapping it behind Gordy to the mare's saddle, leapt nimbly onto Pagan's back and held out his hand. Fanny stared at his fingers but didn't move.

Malen's heart plummeted. "Would you prefer I walk?" he asked softly, avoiding her gaze. Her unwillingness to touch him was like a dagger twisting in his heart. "I'd prefer to ride, since we need to reach Dumfries by nightfall." He grimaced suddenly as he realized that here was another example of his foolish no-

tions getting them into untenable circumstances. "If I'd
been thinking, I'd have insisted we wait at the Anvil for
the next coach. But I wasn't, and I can only apologize.
As it is, I don't want us to spend another night on the
road, but if you would be more comfortable with me
walking while you ride Pagan, I'm willing."

Fanny felt her cheeks suffuse with color. Doubtless
what he *meant* was he didn't want to spend another
night avoiding her hurling herself at him. "No. I'll ride
with you. It won't make me uncomfortable at all," she
lied. "Besides, you shouldn't feel bad about the coach. I
doubt they'd have allowed Dagmar on, and I'd not
have wanted her to run alongside. Coaches go too fast
for her to have kept up for long."

Malen didn't answer, but he felt a rush of gratitude
that she forgave him for their travel difficulties, too.
What a superb woman she was. Any other female of his
acquaintance would have succumbed to vapors long
ago. If only she thought him half as wonderful as he
thought her, he'd be the happiest man in the world.

Scrupulously keeping her eyes glued to Pagan's saddle, Fanny stepped forward, placed her foot in the stir-
rup, and let the duke swing her up behind. There was
a momentary lurch as Pagan became accustomed to
carrying two people and pulling the pallet behind simultaneously. Tucking her nose beneath her tail,
Dagmar settled down and went to sleep.

Although it was obvious to Malen that Fanny was
doing her best to keep her distance, he quickly realized
there was not enough space on the saddle to prevent
her breasts from brushing his shoulder blades with each
of the stallion's steps. He couldn't help but relish the
sensation. After all, unless she happened to be carrying
the kidnapper's child, it might be the last chance he had
to enjoy such personal contact. Ruthlessly thrusting
away any thoughts to the contrary, he leaned back
slightly with each of Pagan's long strides.

Fanny was ashamed of herself for leaning forward
with each of the stallion's steps, but her body cried out
to be touched by the man she loved. Surely it couldn't
be so wrong to take what little pleasure she could get.

After all, soon she would belong to another. Her heart sank as she wondered if Bland was already waiting at MacDonald Manor, eager to make her his bride.

When Malen could stand the sweet torment no longer, he kicked the stallion into trot. "Put your arms around my waist," he said stiffly, expecting the constant jolts of excitement to stop once she was pressed against him. Unfortunately, the new intimacy required only served to make him more conscious of Fanny's ripe bosom.

Fanny gripped Malen's waist tightly, pressing herself against him almost wantonly despite the sinking certainty that he had spurred the stallion on just to get to Dumfries—and away from her—sooner. How could she let him go? How could she settle for spending the rest of her life with Sir Blanden Fitch after experiencing such passion with her duke?

Hours of such emotional upheaval finally exhausted her, and her cheek dropped against Malen's back.

When he felt Fanny's breathing deepen, Malen clasped her arms firmly about his waist. Her skin felt like velvet, and he stroked her wrists absently as he racked his brain for a way to keep this woman, who had, in the last few days, become vital to his happiness.

He also noticed that Gordy was in pain, although the little man remained silent. Malen eyed the servant's pallid complexion worriedly but knew he couldn't offer to slow their pace, for it was vital that the batman get medical aid as soon as possible. Therefore they rode steadily until they reached the Scottish town of Dumfries just as the sun was going down. They made their weary way to MacDonald Manor, where all three of them went directly to bed.

Fanny was up and dressed even before the sun had topped the horizon. After fetching a cup of tea and a piece of toast from the kitchen, where the cook and the scullery maids were still yawning, Fanny told Phipps she was going for a walk. Having known his mistress as a child, the old butler didn't try to hide his disapproval at the thought of her venturing out without a companion, but Fanny grinned and soothed him by promising not to walk farther than the estate gardens.

The cobbled path felt sweetly familiar beneath her feet as she moved away from the old gray stone mansion and crossed the lawns to the special place where she and her grandfather had spent so many afternoons. Green apples barely flushed with pink speckled the old tree, and a mild breeze fanned her cheeks. Sniffing appreciatively, she sat down on the narrow stone bench. The air smelled wonderful, faintly moist and sweet, as if some unseen farmer were harvesting his first crop.

Had it really been so long ago since she'd last sat here with Ian MacDonald? If only she could speak to him, if only she could explain that she had discovered that all Campbells weren't the bloodthirsty scoundrels he'd believed them to be.

After a time, she sighed. Perhaps it was best that she couldn't speak to him. Perhaps he would never understand how she could love a heathen Campbell. Marry one for the good of the clan, perhaps, but love one? Never. With a restive movement she rose and turned back toward the house. As a figure surged up in front of her on the path, her hand flew to her mouth to stifle a cry.

"Well, it's about time you got here. *I've* been here for three days, only that bastard of a butler of yours refused to give me a room. Said he hadn't been informed I was arriving. Honestly, my lady, the least you could have done was write him a note telling him to expect me."

Fanny's heart sank as Sir Blanden Fitch's peevish whine scraped the soft morning air. So he'd arrived.

The baronet continued petulantly. "As it is I've had to spend the last three nights sleeping in beds so dirty the linen could stand up by itself. I swear they don't wash it above three times a week. And the prices! Of course you'll pay my tab, since it's your fault I had to stay there at all. Honestly, what were you thinking of, running off before we'd had a chance to speak to your father about our marriage plans? As you must know, I had to speak to him alone the day before you wrote inviting me here, and I was treated like a snake with the pox for my efforts."

Unable to speak past the mountain of despair in her chest, Fanny merely stared at him. How could she ever have considered marrying such a boor?

"Cat got your tongue, or are you just ashamed of how you've treated your fiancé?" Bland sneered. "Well?" he demanded when she still did not reply. "Are you simply going to stand there with that stupid expression on your face? The least you could do is offer me breakfast. I haven't eaten yet, since that damned innkeeper doesn't serve anything but mutton and beans for breakfast, luncheon, and supper, even after I told him the very scent turned my delicate stomach. You'd think he'd have the decency to serve something more suitable to a lordly palate."

Bland smiled suddenly, a greasy, unpleasant simper. "Now that you have arrived, I might eat something worthy of me. Come. Let us go inside. I'm eager to hear you give that insolent butler a piece of your mind for treating me so rudely."

Still Fanny said nothing, and he threw her a scolding glance. "You must know you've been most remiss in not informing your household of my arrival and thus sparing me such miserable accommodations, but I'm willing to forgive and forget if you have learned your lesson. I know you must realize your fault in this matter and are eager to make amends. You may start by giving me breakfast."

Fanny felt as if she had turned to stone. At last she forced a tight smile. "It's good to see you, too, my lord. Have you missed me so much then?"

Bland frowned, gazing down the bridge of his incredibly thin nose. "Spare me trivialties. We both know why I have come. After eating, we shall invite the village priest, or whoever handles these matters, to attend us. Then we shall turn around and ride posthaste back to London."

He shuddered. "How anyone could willingly live in this godforsaken place is beyond my comprehension. I was never so happy in my life as the day my father died and I was able to remove to London and Carlisle. I declare there isn't a decent tailor within a hundred miles of here, and absolutely no entertainment!"

Fanny gawked at him. Her certainty that he wouldn't insist she sit in his pocket was, after all, the sole reason she had considered marrying him in the first place. "What do you mean, ride back to London? I plan to settle here. Of course I wouldn't mind if you wanted to live in London, but for myself, I wouldn't care if I never see Town again."

Aghast, Bland shook his head vehemently. "Good God, no! What would people think if I showed up in Town without you? I'll tell you what they'd think. They would say I had deserted you! Or, worse, that you had left me! My reputation would be ruined!" He scowled. "No, my lady, when we are wed we shall renovate my town house. I must tell you I'm glad you're wealthy," he added. "I know you are in love with me, and understandably so, but if your pockets had been to let, I'd have been forced to refuse your somewhat bold suit."

Fanny gasped. The pompous ass!

"Once the town house has been refurbished," he continued delightedly, "we shall live there. Of course, the place is not as large as your parents' Seasonal residence, but it is in a much more fashionable section of Town. Once we have settled in, I see no reason we'll ever need step one foot outside of London for the remainder of our lives."

As she watched him polish his gleaming nails against the sleeve of his sky-blue velvet jacket, Fanny was consumed with relief that she hadn't married him before discovering his plans. Wrinkling her nose, she took a step backward to avoid the cloud of scent unfurled by the movement of his arm.

Watching his preening, she was astonished by the myriad differences between him and the Duke of Argyll. Her father had been more correct about the baronet—and about Argyll—than she'd anticipated. Perhaps she had been too hard on the earl, she thought again. Still, even though he had been correct about Malen, that didn't make it right to treat her as a brainless female with more hair than wit. Yes, once she got out of this mess, they would definitely need to sit down and talk.

Absently, Fanny watched Bland run his palms over his carefully slicked, tightly curled blond hair. Alas, he had none of Malen's dark, dangerous, masculine good looks. The baronet looked rather like a poodle with a bad coiffure. She stifled a smile. She knew he tried very hard to contain his kinky curls, but even with his constant attention one or two wisps inevitably managed to break free from their oily prison, sticking out like antennae.

His skin was a sallow yellow, and his eyes—why had she never noticed that his eyes were such a watery, nondescript blue? Almost colorless, they were trained on the distant mountains in what he undoubtedly believed to be a Byronesque pose. Apparently he had noticed her scrutiny and taken it for admiring contemplation.

The lapels and cuffs of his blue jacket were thickly encrusted with shiny gold lace. Beneath this, a double-breasted waistcoat of jonquil satin embroidered with tiny purple forget-me-nots and faux diamond buttons partially hid a shirt of apple-green silk. His blindingly white cravat, tied in what she remembered he proudly called The Bland, threatened to poke out his eyes if he turned his head slightly this way or that, and on his chest reposed the usual conglomeration of fobs, ornaments, and eyepieces.

Padded unmentionables of ruby merino clung unforgivingly to his scarecrowish legs, and his feet and calves were covered by top boots, the bottom halves of which were an odd puce, the top folds, salmon-pink. The toe of each boot sported a shiny gold bow meant, she supposed, to match the lace on his jacket and bring the entire ensemble together. Gold spurs the size of teacups jangled raucously on his heels. She was jolted out of her study by his purring voice.

"Outstanding, isn't it?" the baronet said rapturously. Reaching into his breast pocket, he extracted a gold-plated hand mirror, in which he examined himself with a satisfied simper. "I designed this rig myself. You should feel most honored. I call it The Lady Fanny."

Stunned, Fanny nodded. "Er, yes. Quite. I'm flattered beyond words. Who *is* your tailor?"

Bland smirked. "I am afraid I cannot say. The merchants begged to remain nameless—probably afraid they'd be flooded with so many orders that they couldn't fill all of them. Not that I'd have told anyone their names, anyway. God forbid if someone should attempt to emulate my fashion flair. They couldn't help but fail, since no one of my acquaintance has my ability to match colors."

Returning the mirror to his pocket, he removed a small enameled snuffbox and, flicking it open, helped himself to a generous pinch. He snorted loudly like an irate gander, and Fanny bit her tongue to keep from laughing. Now that she'd decided not to marry this fop under any circumstances, she had relaxed considerably.

Tucking the box back into its hidey-hole, Bland looked her up and down, wrinkling his nose at her subdued green-and-white-striped kerseymere morning gown. "However, it is of no great concern that I am unable to tell you my tailor's name. One with as little fashion sense as yourself couldn't appreciate such matters anyway."

One rogue snicker escaped Fanny's lips. As the baronet glared repressively, she snapped her mouth shut.

"Madam," he continued, lowering his carefully plucked and painted brows in consternation, "when we are married, I hope you will learn to stifle your unbecoming excesses of levity. Perhaps you should be cupped. That might help. I find it most efficacious to be bled at least once a month."

Regaining her composure, Fanny shook her head. "I don't think that will be necessary. I'm fine now. Won't you come inside? You did say you were hungry, did you not?"

Nodding pompously, Bland folded his hands behind his back, tipped his nose haughtily toward the sky, and began walking, slowly and sedately, toward the house. Fanny watched him move away.

When she did not follow immediately, the baronet turned and stared questioningly down his nose. "Madam?"

"Yes. I'm coming," she said hastily. Moving swiftly, she managed to slip past him and out of the path of his unwashed, heavily perfumed body.

As they entered the breakfast room, Fanny smiled. Malen stood near the sideboard. This morning he was dressed casually but elegantly in unmentionables of soft tan wool, top boots of black and ivory, and a white lawn shirt with only a hint of lace at his neck. He wore no cravat.

Since he'd been expecting the baronet, Malen didn't look surprised to see a stranger in the breakfast room. His eyes, however, widened as they swept up and down Fitch's outlandish garb, and he nearly dropped the crystal pitcher he held in his right hand, recovering only when the juice slopped over the rim and onto the tiled floor. Setting the pitcher back on the sideboard, he bent and meticulously wiped up the spill with one of the napkins resting alongside the chafing dishes.

Without bothering to acknowledge the duke, whom he apparently took for a servant, Bland hurried to the buffet and helped himself to a huge portion of kippers, eggs, biscuits, bacon, and blueberry muffins. Seating himself at the long polished walnut table, he began stuffing food into his mouth so rapidly that some morsels fell back to his plate in nauseating clumps, which he hurriedly scooped up and pushed back through his puffy lips.

With a grunt of revulsion, Malen sat down at the table with a cup of coffee and fixed his attention on the face of his beloved. Fanny's beautiful curls were dressed atop her head and threaded with deep-green ribands. Tiny emerald earbobs adorned her delicate lobes. Her face looked fresh and rosy, her complexion like rich cream save for a faint flush across her cheekbones. His perusal came to a halt as she looked at him and spoke.

"Your Grace, may I introduce Sir Blanden Fitch. Sir Blanden, the Duke of Argyll. My husband."

14

A bite of half-chewed egg erupted from the baronet's mouth. One beringed hand flailed for his water glass, overturning a tureen of raspberry purée that ran like liquid rubies over the white lace tablecloth and overflowed onto the floor like a pool of blood. "Your what?" he gasped between coughs.

Fanny stared at him expressionlessly. "My husband."

His cheeks an unhealthy purple, the baronet managed to blurt, "But how can this be? You said you would marry me! You wrote asking me to attend you here!"

Fanny nodded. "Yes, so I did. But as you can see, that is impossible now."

Sudden, overwhelming joy rushed through Malen. She hadn't told her former fiancé about their proposed annulment! Did that mean there was hope for them?

Although obviously battling with his ire, Bland nodded stiffly. "I will not ask how this impropriety came about. You will simply obtain an annulment. You must keep your promise to me. My creditors will not wait forever."

Malen's eyes flashed. "Excuse me," he said abruptly. "Would you tell me, please, precisely what you mean by that?"

The baronet glared. "Even though I do not feel it necessary to enlighten *you* on the matter of my financial affairs, sir, I do not think it will hurt anything to tell you that when the lady promised to marry me, I posthaste purchased a new wardrobe, a new curricle, and a new pair. It was both right and fitting, since Lady Fanny is quite wealthy."

Malen's eyes glittered dangerously. "Do you mean

159

you spent her money before you were even wed? And now you hold her responsible for your debts?"

Bland looked surprised and annoyed. "But of course! Had she not said she'd marry me, I'd not have spent so much blunt I did not have! Any gentleman would have done the same."

Gritting his teeth to keep from striking the gaudy coxcomb, Malen managed to hold his hands clenched together in his lap. "I see. Are you in love with Lady Fanny?"

Flushing, Bland pushed away from the table. "Our personal feelings have nothing to do with you. You go too far, sirrah! Nevertheless, I inform you that, as befits our stations, both the lady and I would agree that ours will be a marriage of convenience. Not of"—he shuddered eloquently—"fleshly passions."

"Ah." Rising slowly, Malen turned to look at his duchess, curious to get her impression of the baronet's words. Fanny had flushed a brilliant scarlet. Her gaze was fixed on the floor. Then the baronet continued, and Malen turned his attention back to the speaker.

"Of course, even though ours will be a marriage in name only, we shall of necessity consummate our vows to legalize the union and to beget heirs. Therefore, it would be best, although not absolutely necessary, for the lady to be untouched."

Malen's temperature soared.

Apparently somewhat recovered from the shock of finding his betrothed wed to another, now that he had arrived upon the antidote, the baronet picked up a biscuit and buttered it lavishly. Taking a bite, he spoke through a crumbly mouthful. "She *is* still a virgin, is she not, Your Grace? Even though you stole my bride, I cannot imagine you would be so despicable as to steal her virtue as well. Not that I particularly mind," he mused, "so long as no one ever finds out, and so long as she is not carrying another man's child."

Although until recently Malen had shared the baronet's opinion on the value of an intact maidenhead, he now drew a trembling breath as an angry red haze suddenly blocked his vision. With a snarl he leapt to the baronet's side and, grasping Fitch by his carefully tied cravat, lifted the dandy from his chair. "I think," he said icily, "that I have heard enough."

Eyes blazing, Malen glared at Fanny as if daring her to interfere. Far from being so inclined, she scurried aside to let her husband dispatch his rival. While she had hoped he would remain silent on the annulment he intended to obtain, she hadn't expected the duke to go this far on her behalf. Following the two men, she arrived at the front door just in time to see Malen pause and throw his burden outside.

Bland bounced once and then lay still, gasping like a dying carp. "How dare you? How dare you!"

Stabbing a finger at the baronet, Malen snarled, "You are not to approach my wife ever again. If you happen to find yourself on the same street, you will not look at her. You will cross to the opposite side of the path. You will not speak to my wife, and, above all, you will not speak *of* her, or you will answer to me. Do I make myself clear?"

Bland scrambled to his feet. His face was tomato-red. "You have no right! She must marry *me*! If she does not, who will pay my creditors?"

Malen didn't try to hide his disgust. "How much?"

Bland's eyes sparkled greedily. "Ten thou—er—fifteen thousand pounds."

Turning to Fanny, Malen commanded curtly, "Bring me paper and pen."

Spinning on her toe, Fanny hurried down the hall and into the library, returning quickly with the desired items.

Without looking at either Bland or Fanny, Malen scrawled a promissory note. It would take another three years of hard work on his estates to make up the loss, but it would be worth every pound. Casting the note on the ground beside the baronet, he speared the fop with a gimlet stare.

When he spoke, his voice was like granite. "That should take care of your debts. Take the paper to my solicitor in London before the month is out, and he will see you get your money. But rest assured, if you so much as think about my wife again, I will know it, and I'll hold a match to that greased-up head of yours. Now get out of here before I beat you to a bloody pulp!"

Grunting, the dandy hurried down the steps and onto the drive. There he turned back and fixed a baleful gaze on Malen. "I will take your money because you owe it to me for stealing my fiancée. But I will not so easily disappear. This money will pay my bills, but it isn't nearly enough to keep me from coming back to see that Lady Fanny fulfills her duty." He glanced portentously at Fanny. "This I promise, madam: You will be my wife, or you will be no man's."

Malen lunged forward, and Bland took off at a run. After waiting a moment to be certain the baronet was truly leaving, the duke drew a deep breath and turned, prepared to withstand his duchess's ire for his violence toward her former betrothed.

Fanny's shoulders shook so hard she was forced to sit down on the step. She buried her face in her arms. "Oh, dear!" she whimpered.

With a heavy heart Malen watched as she trembled. "Fanny," he began, then closed his mouth when soothing words failed to come. He could not find it in his heart to be sorry for sending the revolting fop away, and he wouldn't lie about it. "Fanny, I realize you are upset, but I couldn't stand by and listen to him speak as though you were nothing but your bankbook. Why, even I, penniless as I am, had my solicitor write up a contract stating that I would never touch your fortune."

When she didn't respond, he continued lamely. "Please, Fanny, don't be so upset. I—"

"I've never seen anyone run so fast in my life!" Fanny interrupted breathlessly. Then she began giggling again, her entire body convulsing helplessly.

Malen gasped in astonishment. "You're laughing!" he said wonderingly. "You're laughing, not weeping. I don't understand. I thought you'd want my head on a platter. I thought you'd be furious at my presumptions."

At last Fanny managed to get her humor under control. Giving her streaming eyes a final swipe, she drew a shaky breath. "I know it's awful," she said tremulously, "to laugh at Bland like this, but I just can't help myself! I am so relieved!"

"Madam," Malen said forbiddingly, a touch of amusement in his voice, "I simply do not understand you. Did you or did you not at one time want to marry that man?"

Fanny grinned. "At one time I did think marrying Bland would be best. But that was before I realized what a pompous, pretentious, inflated Narcissus he was."

Malen raised an eyebrow. "I cannot imagine what compelled you to accept him in the first place."

As briefly as possible, Fanny explained the incident of the black velvet riband, and how Bland, taking her gift as a token of undying affection, had gone to Carlisle Cottage to ask Lord MacDonald for her hand, only to be summarily refused. She then admitted that because she had been furious with her father over the marriage banns, she had decided to save herself and punish Lord MacDonald by marrying Bland. Naturally, she realized now that the one who would have been truly punished was herself.

She ended by looking in Malen's eyes and pressing his hand with hers. "I thank you from the bottom of my heart for sending him on his way. I realize now that life with him would have been loveless and miserable. Naturally I will reimburse you for your note."

She suddenly felt dismayed. Malen's behavior wasn't any more loverlike than Bland's. In fact, if anything, it was less so. For while Bland had stated his intention to consummate their marriage, Malen had resisted her attempt to seduce him. No, surely the duke didn't really want her.

It took every drop of will in his body for Malen to keep from pulling his bride into his arms and begging her to stay with him. Instead, he smiled. "You are most welcome but I do not want your money. Now, madam, I suggest you gather you things so that we might be on our way to Inveraray."

Fanny's eyes widened. "Inveraray? But I thought I

was to stay here while you went to file for an annulment."

Malen frowned. Was she still so eager to be rid of him? "No. If it is all the same to you, I think it would be best if we continued to my home. There are . . . some papers I need there," he fibbed, rationalizing his lie with the fact that he couldn't let her go if she was, in fact, with child. And until he was absolutely certain she was not, he intended to keep her by his side.

Filled with relief, Fanny didn't argue.

Surprised she complied with such ease, Malen offered his arm, tucked her hand under his, and led her back up the steps and into MacDonald Manor.

While Fanny didn't allow her emotions to show during the trip to Malen's home in northern Scotland, she enjoyed every moment of the journey. Secretly she even wished he hadn't thought to obtain a mount for her from the stables at MacDonald Manor so that she might have ridden pillion with him.

Dagmar, who now seemed none the worse for her injury, was as perky as ever and had thrown such a fit at being left behind in the MacDonald stables to recuperate, that they'd been forced to take her along. She trotted happily alongside the horses.

They'd left Gordy in the capable hands of the local doctor, who assured them the batman would be on his feet within a few days and as good as new in no time. While she hoped his health would return quickly, it was impossible for Fanny to feel too sorry about Gordy's injury, since because of it she was able to travel alone across the lovely Scottish countryside with the man she loved.

The days passed with an almost mystical swiftness, days of idyllic warmth, sunshine, and peaceful companionship as she rode her small bay mare beside the duke. The highlands were breathtakingly beautiful. Fanny had no trouble imagining fairies and elves cavorting across grassy meadows and swimming in mirror-smooth lochs. When she said something to this effect, Malen grinned and hastened to tell her a number of tales of wandering souls who happened to meet the little folk.

The weather was perfect for sleeping under the stars—chastely, Fanny noted ruefully—only once breaking into a thundershower and that when the riders happened to be near enough a small farmhouse that they were able to seek shelter. The farmer's plump, rosy-cheeked wife was delighted to entertain the duke and his new duchess, offering them rich warm milk and fresh bread hot out of the oven, along with a large hambone for Dagmar.

Fanny enjoyed dandling the goodwife's fat, healthy baby on her knee, which Malen watched avidly, almost guiltily, causing the country woman to comment that there was nothing like newlyweds to make one smile. Hearing this, both flushed a deep scarlet.

Although Malen didn't say much during their last day of travel, he could barely keep his eyes off his duchess. Her lush figure was shown to advantage by the chocolate suede riding habit she'd brought from Dumfries. Her fiery mane, swept back into a braid as thick as a man's wrist, dangled down her slender back. His fingers itched to release the silken strands and bury his face in them.

Every so often a breeze carried him her scent of fresh spring violets. When this happened Malen breathed deeply, even though the perfume made him want to sweep Fanny off her horse and hungrily kiss every part of her.

As he gazed at her classic profile, Malen was caught up in the memory of Fanny holding the farm woman's baby. She had laughed and smiled and cuddled the babe as if it were the most precious thing in the world. He'd have given much to have had it be their child.

Fanny's heart felt heavy. If only they could continue riding forever. If only Malen would learn to love her. Surely he would if they had a few more days. Already he seemed to enjoy her company. If only— Suddenly she saw Malen stiffen in his saddle. She looked around but saw nothing odd. "What is it?"

He nodded toward a bend in the path ahead, where

the earth seemed to end abruptly as if it fell into oblivion. "Do you see the edge of that cliff? My home is not far now. We'll be at Inveraray Castle within fifteen minutes." He inhaled deeply of the fresh mountain air as they rode past the sheer drop. "Beautiful, isn't it?" he asked as he gazed down into the gorge. "Ah, 'tis always good to come home."

Watching his face, Fanny sighed inwardly. He needn't seem so happy about it. After all, it meant the end of their private time together. "Yes," she said dully, realizing that he would no doubt begin annulment proceedings the following day.

Frowning, Malen glanced at her out of the corner of his eye. He sighed. Was his home so distasteful to her? Then he remembered. Of course. It was the den of the Campbell clan. Tightening his lips, he said coolly, "Don't worry. I won't let anyone eat you." Clicking his teeth, he urged Pagan into a canter.

Staring at his departing back, Fanny realized with a start that she hadn't thought about the Campbells once during the journey from Dumfries. Nevertheless, riding into their stronghold did cause a sudden quiver of fear in the pit of her stomach. Without replying, she kicked the mare's ribs and moved glumly forward.

The remainder of the journey didn't take even the fifteen minutes he'd promised her, she thought morosely as they rode beneath a canopy of tall beeches and turned up the gravel drive toward Inveraray Castle. Even Dagmar seemed subdued, staying close to her mistress's side. But as they rounded a final bend and the house came into view, Fanny gasped, her fear forgotten. "Oh, my, it's the most beautiful place I've ever seen!"

The castle was breathtaking. Four conical towers punctuated each corner, and myriad windows and dormers graced the light-gray stone walls, newer construction having been built surrounding the ancient section. Colorful flags displaying the Campbell coat of arms fluttered at each of the towers. The building looked like nothing so much as a castle out of a fairy tale.

Huge trees dotted the extensive lawns, and as she

gazed at the enormous oaks and beeches, Fanny noticed a rope swing swaying lazily in the breeze, as if awaiting a youthful occupant. Were there children here?

Malen watched Fanny's face to gauge her reaction to his home. As she spotted the swing, he said quickly, "It used to be mine, but now the servants' and tenants' children love to play on it. Usually the lawn is crawling with them."

Fanny stared at him, surprised at his fondness for children. Wistfully, she found herself wishing *their* children would someday frolic on this lawn. As if the same thought had occurred to him, Malen gazed at her. Blushing, she looked away.

Not far from the swing a slow-moving brook meandered through the grass like a lazy snake taking a sunbath. A cobblestone path led from the front of the house down to the water's edge, and she could almost see a young Malen Campbell jumping off his swing and running lightheartedly toward the stream, fishing pole in hand.

Beyond the castle, mountains much like those they'd ridden through during the past week loomed lush and green. The manor looked so perfect nestled in this broad valley. Indeed, Fanny thought, Inveraray Castle was by far the most beautiful place she'd ever seen.

Malen smiled happily at her awed expression. "Now can you understand why I was so eager to get home?"

The smile vanished from Fanny's face as she lurched back to the present. No doubt Malen was glad to be back among his own kind and soon to be rid of her.

Malen groaned inwardly. The way Fanny was looking at him, widening her lovely velvet-brown eyes and wetting her lips with the tip of her pink tongue, was enough to drive a man mad. What did she think he was made of, iron? There wasn't a doubt in his mind that if they'd had to spend one more night under the stars, he'd not have been able to resist making Fanny his in every sense of the word. He'd amazed himself by his fortitude, but he didn't want to push his luck.

But it wasn't Fanny's innocently flirtatious manner alone that troubled him. It bothered him immeasurably that she didn't seem very traumatized by her rape. Surely any other woman wouldn't have so quickly gotten over being ravished. Gnawing doubts chewed at the back of Malen's mind, thoughts he didn't want to consider but couldn't avoid.

Suppose the incident with the kidnapper hadn't been Fanny's first time. Suppose his little spitfire had had numerous lovers. Could that be why she'd been so passionate in the cottage? He'd thought she'd been merely sleepy, but since then she'd continued to display inviting behavior. Those burning glances. Those hungry stares.

Could she realize, even now, that she might be pregnant, and wanted him to make love to her so that she could fool him into believing the child was his? The thought was almost too much to bear. She couldn't be so deceitful! But how could he be certain? He just didn't know, and it was fair to making him insane with jealousy. How in hell could she have recovered so quickly otherwise?

And if she were trying to fool him, did it make any difference in how he felt about her? Unfortunately, he thought grimly, it did not. He loved her. He was crazy for her. If he couldn't possess her soon, or get her away from him forever, he'd go mad!

15

Gritting his teeth as suspicions snaked through him, Malen kicked Pagan into a canter. "Hurry," he growled at Fanny. "I am eager to get inside and wash off the filth of the last week's travel."

Swallowing her tears at his revulsion at what had been the happiest week of her life, Fanny followed.

A groom came running as they neared the stable, and Malen dismounted. "Hello, Clem. Please see that Pagan and the lady's horse get an extra ration of oats, and the dog as much beef as she desires."

"Aye, Yer Grace," the boy said in awed tones as he stared worshipfully up at the duke. " 'Tis good tae have ye back safely, sir."

" 'Tis good to be back, lad." Moving to Fanny's side, he held out his arms to help her dismount. The tears sparkling in her eyes made him catch his breath, and suddenly he felt guilty for his unworthy thoughts. After all, she was far from home, in a strange place with people she thought hated her. Naturally she was terrified. And, after all, he didn't have any proof that she'd been deceitful. "Don't be afraid, lass. I won't let anyone harm you." As she slid to the ground, he put a finger under her chin and raised her face to meet his concerned gaze. "I'm sorry I was gruff. I'm just tired."

Shaking her head, Fanny cursed her weakness. "I'm not afraid. I must be tired also. Could you have someone show me to my room?"

"Of course. Come with me." Leading the way, Malen moved swiftly toward the manor house and climbed the steps. The door swung wide as if by magic, and a wizened face peered out at them. At the duke's appearance, the ancient visage cracked into a blazing smile.

"Your Grace! Welcome home, sir! 'Tis glad I am tae see ye!"

Malen smiled. "Weslo! It is good to see you also, my friend." He turned to Fanny and put a proprietary arm about her waist. "Fanny, I'd like you to meet the man who keeps things running smoothly in my absence and who kept me on the straight and narrow as a child. He smacked my backside more than once upon occasion, and I'm sure sometimes he'd like to even now. Weslo, I'd like you to meet my wife, the new Duchess of Argyll, Fanny MacDonald Campbell."

The smile on the old face faltered as Weslo gaped at Fanny, then glanced back at Malen as if to determine whether his master were joking. Doubt, mistrust, and confusion warred on his features. "MacDonald, Your Grace?"

Fanny watched the aged butler's blue eyes lock with the duke's. She felt faint. Her breath caught in her throat, and she could not speak. Why, oh, why had Malen told the butler she was the duchess? Why hadn't he simply introduced her as a guest or a relative, since they were soon to be parted? She looked up at him imploringly.

Malen frowned forbiddingly, suddenly every inch a duke. His formerly jovial tone became icy. "MacDonald *Campbell*, Weslo. And you are to see she is made welcome by the staff. I will be most displeased if she has any cause for complaint. Anyone who treats her with less respect than her position warrants will have me to deal with. Do you understand?"

Weslo smiled as he watched his master's arm tighten around Fanny's waist possessively, evidently pleased, despite the unorthodoxy of the situation, that his master was so taken with his new duchess. "I do indeed, sir." He turned toward Fanny. "Your Grace! 'Tis a pleasure, I'm sure. I place myself at your service whenever ye should require it. If ye need anythin' at all, feel free tae call upon me."

He bowed creakily, and Fanny could tell his greeting was genuine. "Thank you, Weslo."

Malen continued. "Her Grace is exhausted from our journey and would like nothing so much as to see her rooms."

The butler nodded. "Of course. If ye will follow me, Your Grace, I'll show ye to your chambers."

With an uncertain glance back at Malen, who nodded encouragingly, Fanny followed Weslo up the broad marble staircase in the center of the castle.

Her room was at the end of a long corridor. Thick Chinese rugs, resplendent with fire-breathing dragons, covered the floors. Fanny's feet sank into the softness as she struggled to keep up with the butler's rapid pace. Who'd have dreamed one so old could be so quick? When Weslo finally paused, she put a hand to her chest, panting.

"Here ye are, Your Grace," the butler said kindly, pushing open the double doors. "Again, if ye need anythin', call me. I'll have a footman bring up your belongings, and I'll be sendin' a lass tae help ye dress for dinner in a few hours." He hesitated. "That is, if ye dinna have your own maid."

"I don't," she said breathlessly. "Thank you."

Stepping into the room, she secured the doors behind her. Then she turned around to survey her new quarters.

The room was decorated in white, gold, and green. In the west corner, a huge bed sat atop a broad circular dais. It was sheltered by a luxurious canopy of emerald brocade fringed with gold. The bedposts were mahogany, and the coverlet was of ivory silk eyelet fringed with Brussels lace.

Layer after layer of ivory silk painted with tiny lime-green fleurs-de-lis hung from runners along the walls. Deep-green velvet cords pulled the lush fabric into swooping curves that fell in gleaming folds to brush the green-and-white marble floor graced by an enormous fern-patterned Aubusson carpet.

Two huge fireplaces, one on the north and one on the south, poured soothing warmth into the chamber. On their mantels sat countless bits of Dresden statuary, gilt snuffboxes, crystal candelabra, and a large ormolu clock. Oversized ivory armchairs and long viridian-and-gold sofas nestled invitingly around each hearth. On the east wall of the room rested a large dressing table, a trio of shining brass-and-ivory combs on its lace runner. A brush and hand mirror completed the set, and an assortment of bone-china cosmetic pots lay beside these.

Moving toward a tall mahogany armoire near the dressing table, Fanny pulled open the doors, curiously. For a moment she stared, dumfounded. Gowns of every color packed the stately cupboard, a profusion of reds and blues and greens, and small, heart-shaped lace pillows filled with potpourri hung from hooks amid the array. Picking up one of the hearts, she pressed the sweet-smelling pillow to her nose. Violets. How odd to discover another woman here who wore her own particular scent.

With a regretful sigh, she put the sachet back on its hook and turned to the two wide drawers beneath the armoire. In the top one, ribands and accessories of every color and description filled the drawer to overflowing, more potpourri bags nestling among them. In the lower, boxes of exquisite jewelry lay in luscious splendor. Fanny was impressed that Malen apparently trusted his servants so well that the jewelry was not locked away in a safe. Opposite the dressing table stood another armoire, and a quick inventory showed that it, too, held countless riches.

Shaking her head, Fanny wondered to whom all this luxury belonged. She sighed. It was a lovely room, exactly to her taste, almost as if everything in it had been made expressly for her. But surely the elegant chamber must belong to another woman.

As she was wondering if it would not be prudent to ring for Weslo so that he might show her to another chamber, she happened to glance back at the bed. She was so tired, her head had begun to pound. If she could just shut her eyes for a few minutes, she knew she'd feel better. A mass of emerald, gold, and white satin pillows lay on the coverlet, inviting her to lie down and forget her troubles for a while. More than happy to oblige, Fanny put her head on an ivory pillow and fell asleep almost instantly.

At a loud banging, Fanny sat up abruptly and stared at the double doors, horrified. How long had she been sleeping? Her situation came back with a rush, and she jumped off the bed, expecting the room's owner to burst in and complain loudly at Fanny's uninvited usage of her chamber. She hurried toward the doors, released the bolt, and pulled them open. To her intense relief, only a young maid carrying two enormous buckets of steaming water stood on the threshold. Eyes as big as saucers goggled at Fanny.

"Sorry tae disturb ye, Yer Grace, but Mr. Weslo says as 'ow I'm tae 'elp ye dress for dinner. I'm Pegeen."

The girl couldn't have been much above fifteen and looked so terrified that Fanny immediately felt sympathetic. "Is something troubling you, my dear?"

The maid looked as she would faint from fear. Several times she opened her mouth as if to speak, but no sound emerged.

At last Fanny laughed. "Come, Pegeen, I won't eat you. What has you so terrified?"

At last the maid took a deep breath and spoke so rapidly that Fanny had trouble following her. All too quickly, however, she grasped Pegeen's meaning, and her entire body went cold.

"They say belowstairs ye be the daughter o' the devil 'imself! They say ye've come tae kill us all in our beds tae take revenge for the Glencoe massacre! They say I'll noo doot be yer first victim, since although all us servants be fam'ly, we don't all 'ave the same last name. Since my name be Campbell, and ye 'ate all Campbells, they be sayin' ye'll kill me first!"

With this the girl set down her burden hastily, threw herself at Fanny's feet, and began to wail. "Please, mistress! Dinna kill me!"

Gazing at the maid in mute astonishment, Fanny dropped to her knees and placed a hand on the girl's shoulder. Her touch only seemed to make the girl sob more loudly. Fanny had to shout to be heard. "What nonsense is this? I have no intention of hurting you!" She repeated herself several times, until Pegeen's sobs became softer.

At last the maid's cries died to a whimper, and she peeped up at Fanny through tear-washed green eyes. "Ye don't?"

Fanny smiled gently. "Of course not."

The girl looked doubtful. "But why? Yer a Mac-Donald, aren't ye? The daughter o' the MacDonald laird?"

"Yes." Tears filled the maid's eyes again, and Fanny rushed on, eager to quell another outburst. "I am, but now I am also a Campbell like you." The thought occurred to her that she wouldn't be a Campbell much longer, but she doubted this observation would make Pegeen feel much better, so she didn't mention it. "They did tell you belowstairs that I am the duke's wife, did they not?"

Pegeen frowned. "Aye. They say ye've bewitched 'is Grace into bringin' ye 'ere."

Fanny laughed good-naturedly. "Well, I haven't. And since I am now a Campbell, it would be silly of me to harm a member of my own clan, wouldn't it?"

After staring at Fanny for a long moment, the maid nodded. "Aye. But e'en if ye don't, won't yer family still want tae kill us Campbells?"

Fanny looked thoughtful. "Well, I suppose that since *they* are my family, and *you* are my family, that would be the same thing as brothers and sisters trying to hurt each other."

Pegeen frowned. "Mebbe." For a long time she studied the new duchess, absorbing the enormity of what Fanny had said. At last she wiped her eyes with the edge of her apron and smiled. "Yer no' a monster, Yer Grace," she said as she got to her feet with an embarrassed grin. "In fact, I like ye."

"And I you, Pegeen." Returning the maid's smile, Fanny also stood, then nodded toward her carpetbag, which lay in the hall. Apparently a footman—too cowardly to face the MacDonald witch in her den, she thought wryly—had deserted it there. "My things are probably quite wrinkled, but I suppose we can find something that will serve for this evening."

Secure in her newfound confidence, Pegeen shook her head obstinately. "Nay, Yer Grace. 'Is Grace said that ye were tae wear sommat from th' armoires."

"There must be some mistake," Fanny said hastily. "The armoires are filled with clothes, but they aren't mine."

A stubborn expression crossed the maid's plain features. Folding her arms over her flat chest, Pegeen stared resolutely at her new mistress. "Nay, ma'am. 'E said sommat from the armoires, and sommat from the armoires it'll be. 'Is Grace would be verra upset if ye went down in sommat else."

Staring at the maid, Fanny quickly realized that although she and Pegeen had established a tenuous friendship, the young woman's allegiance was still firmly tied to the duke. Rather than engage in a battle of wills, she shrugged. "All right, but whoever those gowns belong to isn't going to like it. Since His Grace put you in charge, why don't you pick one?"

Overjoyed, the maid scurried to one cabinet and flung it wide. In a moment she pulled out an exquisite creation of teal-blue silk with tiny jet beads embroidered around its hem, its low-cut bodice, its high waist, and its tiny puffed sleeves. She reverently placed the gown on the bed. "I think this one, Yer Grace. The blue-green will complement yer red 'air tae perfection."

Fanny said nothing as the girl continued rummaging, this time removing stockings, matching shoes, long white gloves, and undergarments. Moments later Fanny found herself naked and seated in a long, steaming tub, which Pegeen had pulled in from the hallway and filled with violet-scented water. In another fifteen minutes she was wrapped in a soft-cotton towel, which the maid had warmed near one of the fires, and buffed dry.

She sighed with delight. "Pegeen, my dear girl, I must have been a fool to argue with you before. You are a treasure." In no time she was dressed in the luxurious gown, which she was dumfounded to find a perfect fit.

Seated in a gilt chair before the dressing table, Fanny watched as Pegeen completed her coiffure. The maid had pulled her long curls into a becoming mass atop her head, allowing a few curls to stray around her face and neck to soften the effect. Staring at herself in the glass, she had to admit that Pegeen's taste in clothing and her skill at hairdressing were unexcelled.

When the long white gloves had been pulled on, Pegeen stepped back, wrinkling her nose critically. "Sommat's missin'." Then her homely face lit up. "O' course," she crowed. Scurrying toward the drawers, the maid pulled out several long black velvet boxes. Moving swiftly, she laid them on the dressing table and motioned for her mistress to open them. "Pick sommat, Yer Grace."

They got no further than the first box. Both gasped as the lid rose. A choker-length necklace of large square-cut blue-green beryls and tiny diamonds glittered up at them from its white satin nest. A pair of matching earbobs and a wide bracelet completed the ensemble. Looking into the glass as Pegeen placed the bracelet over one long white glove, Fanny knew she had never looked finer. "Thank you, Pegeen," she murmured sincerely. "Your choices were perfect."

The maid beamed. "Yer Grace, 'tis most 'onored I am tae serve ye. A footman'll be 'ere soon tae escort ye downstairs."

Bobbing a curtsy, Pegeen left, and Fanny remained at the dressing table to wait. In mere minutes the footman arrived, quaking much as Pegeen had, although he managed not to sob with terror. Without speaking or lifting his gaze to hers, he led her along the long corridor, down the stairs, and at last came to a halt outside a drawing room. Another footman, posted at the door, opened it silently.

The duke was at her side in an instant. "Here you are at last," he said softly, gazing at her face with open admiration and lowering his gaze to encompass her lush figure encased in the blue silk. "You look even more lovely than I'd imagined. That color suits you. But then, I'm convinced anything would."

Suddenly Fanny felt overwhelmingly shy. "You may thank Pegeen for my appearance."

Malen's teeth gleamed. "And here I thought I had your parents to thank for that."

Fanny laughed. "You're absurd. As for my finery, I hope whomever these things belong to won't be too angry. I argued strenuously, but Pegeen insisted I choose an ensemble from those hanging in the two armoires in the chamber where I rested. I'm sure there's been some mistake and your butler showed me to another lady's apartment."

Malen shook his head. "I'm sure the lady to whom those things belong won't be too outraged." At Fanny's doubtful glance, he laughed. "They're yours. Remembering your coloring from the first time I saw you, I took the liberty of preparing a chamber and a new wardrobe for your arrival."

Fanny was stunned and deeply touched by his thoughtfulness and generosity. Then something occurred to her. "How did you know my size?"

Malen grinned.

Holding up a hand, she hurriedly amended, "No, don't tell me. I don't want to know. But what about the violet-scented potpourri? And the violet bath-oil? How did you remember it was my favorite scent?"

Malen smiled gently. "I remembered many things about you, Fanny, but was too foolish to follow my heart. I honestly thought you wouldn't want a penniless man, so I convinced myself that what I felt so many years ago was mere infatuation. I was wrong."

He didn't elaborate, but Fanny flushed as a wave of pleasure surged through her. Was he saying he still cared? That he had all along, only hadn't known it? She drew a tremulous breath as expectation swelled her heart. Could there be some hope for them after all? Could she possibly convince him to forego an annulment?

Malen held out his arm. "Shall we go in to dinner, Duchess? Everyone else is already seated and waiting for us."

Fanny placed her hand on his arm, reveling in the

rock-hard strength if offered. Then, realizing what he'd said, she looked up with frightened eyes. "Everyone? Who is 'everyone'?"

Malen squeezed her hand where it rested in the crook of his arm. He smiled reassuringly. "Word about our arrival apparently got out, and a few members of my family came to the castle posthaste. Don't worry, it is an informal gathering."

She stiffened. "All of them are Campbells?"

Malen's smile vanished. Would she refuse to meet them, thus offending his people beyond repair? He wouldn't be surprised. She hated anyone cursed with the surname of Campbell. Momentarily he thought of lying, but then he straightened his shoulders. "Aye."

Her hand trembled. "I see."

Eyes narrowing as he felt her quivering fingers, Malen reassessed his opinion of what was troubling her. He took her hand in his. "Are you afraid, lass?"

Fanny smiled falteringly. "A little."

Malen's expression softened with relief. So, she was every bit as afraid of them as they were of her. Not one of them hadn't approached him before she came down, asking if she would despise them or if she were as hateful as they'd heard all MacDonalds were. This might be simpler than he'd hoped. "There is no need. I'll let no one harm ye, lass. Just be your own sweet self, and they will love ye as much as—" He broke off abruptly as another footman opened the dining-room doors at the opposite end of the corridor.

Heart in her throat, Fanny shot him a curious glance, wondering what he'd been about to say and noting that his Scotch burr had deepened with his arrival home. "But Your Grace, there is one thing I do not understand. Why do you want me to meet them, since you intend to investigate an annulment?"

Malen stared at her for a long moment. "I am hoping I will not have to do that." Again, he was astounded to find himself hoping she was *enceinte*. "But we do not have time to discuss the matter now." Squeezing her fingers, he led her toward the dining room. "Smile, Duchess. Here we go."

Confused by his meaning but oddly joyful, Fanny let him propel her toward the dining room. As they stepped across the threshold, she gasped. The chamber buzzed with a hundred voices. When the group became aware of the duke and duchess's entrance, every person rose to stand at attention. "I thought you said a *few* members of your family!" she whispered desperately.

"I did." Malen grinned apologetically. "I have an extensive family. These are but a fragment of the total." Feeling her balk, he released her fingers and pressed his palm into the small of her back. "Onward, my love. We have a difficult battle ahead of us, to align your family with mine. Remember that your title is the highest in the land, save for those belonging to the royal family, and they aren't here. There isn't a person in the room who won't be eager to kowtow to you."

"Oh, God," Fanny whimpered. Drawing a deep breath, she called forth every ounce of courage she possessed, pinned a smile to her lips, and stepped toward the dining table.

16

As it happened, dinner was not the ordeal Fanny had expected. Although she felt overwhelmed for the first part of the evening, most of Malen's relations were charming, if somewhat reserved, and when she smiled and chatted easily with them, everyone seemed to soften toward her.

Malen acted the perfect host and the ideal husband, protective and attentive but not stifling. Instead of taking his honorary place at the opposite end of the enormous table, he chose to sit at Fanny's side throughout the meal, making certain everyone present knew they'd best behave respectfully toward his duchess unless they wished to incur the wrath of the powerful Duke of Argyll.

After the meal, in order to leave the men to their port and brandy, Fanny led the ladies to the drawing room where she'd met Malen before dinner. To her surprise, the Campbell ladies eagerly took her under their wing and explained the many wonders Inveraray and its castle had to offer a lucky guest, or in this case, a new duchess. There was hunting, both fox and stag, fishing, both freshwater and salt, hawking, sailing, kite flying, and an endless stream of other possibilities.

When Malen entered the room with the other men, he looked most pleased to see her sitting comfortably among the ladies. Fanny's heart tripped at the obvious pride in his gaze. If only she knew for certain what he'd been about to say before the footman had opened the dining-room door. Was she putting too much emphasis on what she *thought* he had intended to say? Was she doomed to disappointment?

With her mind and emotions in turmoil, Fanny battled between longing that he would come to her that night and the desire to marry him in a Christian ceremony before witnesses before ... well, before *that*.

She couldn't say precisely why it was important to her that she be married by a priest before consummating their marriage—if, that is, Malen didn't intend to seek an annulment—but it was. She only hoped it was also important to Malen. Still, she knew that if it were not, she would be more than willing to follow his lead. At the thought of his coming to claim his conjugal rights that night, her stomach tightened in anticipation, and she blushed violently.

An elderly dowager wearing a chartreuse satin evening frock complete with a huge gold turban saw the duchess glance at the duke and laughed heartily. Patting Fanny on the knee, she said softly, "It doesn't do to let a man know what power he has over you, my dear. Nor to let the entire company see how you feel about your husband."

Fanny's face flamed again. Was she so obvious? Her eyes darted to Malen's face to see if he'd noticed her silent worship. He was looking the other way. She breathed a sigh of relief and returned her attention to the dowager.

"Of course, if its any comfort," the woman continued, "His Grace has been hard-pressed to keep his eyes off you, as well. Oh, yes, he has, my dear." She nodded as Fanny's startled eyes flew back to Malen's face. "Ah, it is high time he chose a suitable wife."

Fanny tried to look interested as the old woman began elaborating on precisely why it was high time, but all she really wanted to do was gaze at Malen.

The duke leaned casually against the mantel near the huge marble fireplace, a wineglass dangling negligently from his long fingers. While the rest of his clansmen wore kilts in the Campbell tartan, he wore regular evening attire—a black coat of superfine wool, white silk waistcoat and shirt, pale-gray unmentionables, silk stockings, and flat-heeled dress slippers.

His only jewelry consisted of a large aquamarine—

nearly the same color as his lustrous eyes—nestled in the folds of his simply tied cravat, and smaller blue-green studs at his cuffs. His attire suited him. As did leather breeches and linen shirts. Or kilts. Fanny smiled. *Anything* looked splendid on her duke.

She sighed. If only he *were* hers. Forever.

Suddenly Malen glanced over at her, and her belly contracted as his glorious eyes blazed. Although aware the entire company had fallen silent as everyone noticed the intensity of their exchanged gaze, Fanny could not look away. Heat suffused her entire body, flooding her cheeks with color, and she found herself wishing their guests to perdition.

Just then the duke smiled slowly, raised his glass in a salute, and took a sip of wine. Fanny's hands flew to cover her burning cheeks. Taking a deep breath, she redirected her attention toward the dowager, who was beaming and doing her best to pretend she'd seen nothing. As the woman picked up the thread of her monologue, Fanny's eyes drifted back to Malen.

He was utterly spellbinding. His wavy black hair was tied back with a satin riband, and Fanny could not help a swell of satisfaction as she noticed he was by far the most handsome man present. Compared to him, his fellow clansmen looked almost dowdy. He was superb. A magnificent, sleek panther among house cats—and obviously their leader. She felt a rush of pride that he belonged to her, if only for a while, rather than to one of the female guests ogling him with blatant yearning. Once again she tore her gaze away and looked back at the old woman, who was still speaking.

"You know," the dowager said confidentially, "the duke used to bring all manner of improper women here before your marriage. None of us approved, of course, but men will be men, and one just doesn't tell a duke he's misbehaving." She laughed. "I must tell you, though, we were relieved, when you entered the dining room, to see you were so respectable and innocent. When we heard His Grace had married, we wondered if you would be yet another ... you know, one of *those* females."

Fanny felt a bolt of fury shoot through her veins at the thought of her glorious husband touching other women. Gritting her teeth, she tried to look calm.

The dowager waved a heavily ringed hand in dismissal. "But then, I suppose he needed the company. For the longest time after the old duke's death he did nothing but see to the upkeep of his estates. He was forced to do so, since they were in such an awful state, thanks to his ne'er-do-well grandfather. Now *there* was a rogue," she said with a girlish giggle. "His Grace is the spitting image of the old duke.

"And yet," she said suddenly, staring into space, "the boy behaved strangely for several years after inheriting the dukedom. Restive, you must know. Wouldn't have anything to do with any of the available young ladies hereabouts. We all wondered, when he took up with those women of ill repute some three years ago, if there weren't an unrequited love somewhere in his past. Such a round of debauchery he went on! It was disgraceful. But it was just as though he were trying to forget something—or someone—else."

Fanny gave a start. "Are you telling me he didn't have anything to do with *any* women until fairly recently?" Had he been pining for *her* all those years? Was it possible?

Now that she thought about it, even though she'd maligned Malen colorfully while arguing with her father, she didn't think she'd heard anything untoward about the duke's reputation until the last few years. Her heart thumped as she waited for the dowager's answer.

The old woman nodded. "Yes, and very strange we all thought it. We all tried our best to make him fall in love with one of our young women. Some lovely girls they were, too. But he wouldn't have any of them, and at last we gave up."

Fanny felt as though her heart would burst with joy. He'd been faithful to her until he'd given up hope of obtaining her. He hadn't just forgotten her. He really had loved her. The question now was, could he learn to love her as much again? Somehow she managed to keep her voice steady. "I see. That is most interesting."

The dowager smiled. "I am happy he has found you. Although many of us Campbells were uncertain of the wisdom of his choice, it would seem he was quite sagacious in choosing a MacDonald for his bride."

The other women murmured their agreement.

"I must confess," the dowager said dreamily, "the love that shines from His Grace's eyes when he looks at you is enough to warm my old heart." She sighed romantically, and the sound was echoed by the other ladies. "You're a charming gel, and I'd like to be among the first to welcome you to the family."

Fanny smiled. "Thank you very much. I'm happy to be here."

It was growing late. At Malen's signal Fanny thanked the ladies for coming to welcome her and got to her feet. Gathering their husbands, the women took their leave.

As she and Malen stood on the doorstep watching the lamps of the last carriage disappear down the drive, Fanny realized she was utterly exhausted. Still, she could not help a rush of disappointment when Malen deposited her at her bedchamber door, kissed her cheek, and disappeared into his own adjoining room.

Ensconced in her bed, with Dagmar snoring on the floor beside her, she remembered the dowager's words, and her heart swelled with hope.

But if he did love her, she fretted, and if he really didn't intend to obtain an annulment, why had he left her to herself tonight? And what did he mean, he hoped it wouldn't be *necessary* to seek an annulment? What could possibly make an annulment necessary? Troubled, she lay awake long into the night, wondering what her future held.

The following morning, when Pegeen entered the room carrying a tray laden with fresh sliced peaches, toast, strawberry preserves, ham, rolls, a mug of steaming hot chocolate, and a large dish of bread and bacon gravy, Fanny laughed. "You surely don't expect me to eat all that!"

Pegeen grinned. "Not unless ye want tae. The bread

and gravy are for yer 'uge dog. I thought I'd best get on 'er good side whilst I 'ave the chance."

After setting the tray over Fanny's lap, the maid took the bowl of gravy-soaked bread and stepped toward the wolfhound, who lounged beside one of the hearths.

Dagmar's tail thumped as Pegeen set down the bowl, and though the girl hastily backed away, the wolfhound managed to stick out her lengthy tongue and swipe the maid across the face.

Pegeen laughed delightedly and wiped her cheek with her apron. Turning back toward Fanny, she glanced at the tray and said reassuringly, "I'll wager yer more 'ungry than ye 'spect after last night's merrymakin'. I 'ear ye were quite a success. Congratulations, Yer Grace, I knew they'd like ye." As she turned to leave the room, she paused and looked back uncertainly.

Fanny raised her eyebrows inquiringly.

"There be sommat I'd like tae ask ye, Yer Grace, but I dinna ken 'ow."

"Ask me anything, Pegeen. You needn't be afraid of me."

Pegeen smiled and shook her head. "Oh, I'm not, ma'am." After hemming and hawing for several moments, she finally drew a deep breath. "I want tae know if ye'll be keepin' me services as maid or if yer own maid from home will be comin'." Flushing furiously, she averted her gaze and plucked nervously at the hem of her white cotton apron.

Her smile deepening, Fanny said, "I don't know if Bessie will come or not. But unless I miss my guess, she's not going to be too eager to leave her sweetheart. If she doesn't, and if you'd like to stay on as my maid, I'd love to have you."

Beaming, Pegeen bobbed a curtsy. "Oh, that I would, Yer Grace. That I would indeed! Oh, ma'am, just wait'll I tell 'em downstairs!" With that she was gone in a flurry of petticoats, indecorously slamming the bed-chamber doors behind her.

With a contented sigh, Fanny smiled again and sniffed appreciatively as she eyed the appetizing break-

fast. Her stomach rumbled loudly. Hurriedly buttering a
roll and smothering it with fresh peaches, she bit into
the steaming, fluffy pastry and sighed again, sinking
back against the pillows in ecstasy.

In no time she had eaten everything on her plate and
pushed the tray aside, ready to seek out her husband
and insist he give her the grand tour of his home. As
she passed a window, however, a disturbance outside
drew her attention. Frowning, she pushed aside the
sheer voile underdrape and peered down into the courtyard below. Her blood turned to ice.

Moving as swiftly as possible, she yanked open one
of the armoires and, seizing a day dress of pale-green
muslin, pulled off her nightgown and threw a chemise,
petticoat, and the gown over her head. Tightly cinching
the gown's narrow waist, she hastily ran a brush
through her copper curls and then bolted, barefoot, for
the door.

Her headlong flight down the corridor and grand
staircase drew several curious stares from the footmen
stationed at each corner, but she ignored them,
sprinting across the tiled foyer and through the main
doors, which a footman barely managed to open as she
hurtled past him and out into the courtyard, Dagmar
hot on her heels. Barreling toward the small group gathered around a kneeling man, she screamed at the top of
her lungs. "Malen, stop! Stop, I beg of you!"

The man she knew as her sweet, gentle husband
gazed blindly toward her. High over his head he
grasped a claymore, ready to strike a death blow to his
hapless victim. Beside him, pale and drawn, Gordy
watched her approach.

"What on earth do you think you're doing?" Fanny
cried, incredulous. "And what is Gordy doing here?"

Cursing, Malen shoved the man with one foot and
dropped the sword to the ground. The prisoner stumbled and was steadied by Gordy, who then drew away
with an expression of disgust, as though he had
touched the lowest creature on earth. Groaning, the
man rolled to his side. A thick mat of whiskers made it

impossible to discern much of his face, but what Fanny could see was almost blue with terror.

"Stay there," Malen growled at the prisoner. "If you so much as move, I'll slowly carve you into a thousand pieces instead of granting you an easy death." Moving swiftly, he met Fanny halfway between the house and the group of men, catching her about the waist as she tried to rush past him.

Glaring at him with stricken eyes, Fanny struggled violently. "Let me go! What do you think you're doing? Are you mad?"

Grinning ironically, Malen said, "I should think what I'm doing obvious. I'm doing the world a service—disposing of loathsome vermin. This is no place for you, Duchess. Go inside at once."

Fanny stared at him, startled. "What are you talking about, 'doing the world a service'? It looked to me as if you were preparing to slice that poor man's head off!"

"I was."

Fanny's mouth fell open. "But why? What did he do that would require decapitating him?"

Malen paused, wondering if it would be too upsetting for Fanny to see her rapist again. At last, certain by the rebellious look on her face that she wasn't going to leave without a very good explanation, he moved to one side, keeping a firm grip on her arm. "Don't you recognize him? Take a good look. No, wait," he said suddenly, moving back in front of her. "Look at this instead." He held out his hand.

Fanny stared at the amulet of silver and amethyst nestled in the palm of Malen's hand. The luckenbooth gleamed and sparkled. After a moment she made a small, distressed sound. "He—he is the kidnapper?"

Watching her with concerned eyes, Malen nodded. "Aye. He showed up at MacDonald Manor inquiring if the owner of the house would be interested in purchasing the brooch—for a hefty price. Gordy's room overlooked the drive, and he recognized the man's voice and had him taken into custody. Then Gordy convinced the doctor to allow him to bring his prisoner to me."

Malen snorted. "Take a good look at him, Fanny, and

think carefully about what you tell me to do with him. If you have a reason to hate any Campbell, it's this one. He is exactly the kind of Campbell who took part in the Glencoe massacre. This is your chance to fulfill your oath to your grandfather, to punish the Campbells, once and for all."

With surprise Fanny realized she no longer felt the slightest inclination to follow her grandfather's credo of "The only good Campbell is a dead one." The important thing was to keep a man from dying. She shook her head. "I'm glad you've gotten the luckenbooth back, but I shouldn't think you'd need to kill the poor man now that it has been returned!" She hesitated. "Why was he trying to sell it to my family, anyway?"

"God's blood, woman!" Malen protested with rising anger. "Do you really think I'm willing to take a man's life because of a brooch? The brooch isn't even mine, for God's sake! It's yours."

Fanny stared at him blankly.

After glancing back at the prisoner to make certain he hadn't moved, Malen explained. "It's the MacDonald luckenbooth, Fanny. The one that was stolen from your family in 1692." He sighed. "I thought it would be a romantic touch to return it to you through a Scottish marriage ceremony. I found it among my grandfather's things when he died. I guess I should have handed it over when I first realized I had it. But I didn't, and the time never seemed quite right, after that fiasco of a wedding, to tell you it belonged to your family. Then, once it had been stolen, I didn't see how telling you its origin would relieve tensions between us, so I thought to keep silent unless it turned up again."

Gasping, Fanny took the luckenbooth from his hand and stared down at it, remembering the story her grandfather had repeated so often. Sudden tears pricked her eyes, and she wished her grandfather were able to see it back in MacDonald hands. "Thank you," she said brokenly. Then she looked up, confused. "But how did the kidnapper know it was our family heirloom?" she asked.

Malen smiled grimly. "Apparently you didn't examine the back of the brooch when you wore it." He took it from her, flipped it over, and held it up to her eyes. There, inscribed in tiny letters across the top of the crown, were the words *Duncan and Francesca Mac-Donald, 1689.*

Fanny gasped a second time. "My grandfather told me about the names carved in the back of the brooch! Oh, Malen," she said, her eyes shining, "thank you! And I think pinning it to my bodice is the most romantic thing I've ever heard of!" She flushed. "I always dreamed my future husband would do just that."

Malen bowed, gratified. "You're welcome. Now if you will go back to the house, I have something rather unpleasant to attend to."

Catching his arm as he turned back toward the prisoner, Fanny pulled the duke to a stop. "No!" she cried. "Stop it, Malen! Even though I'm delighted to have the luckenbooth back, I cannot allow you to be so base just because a thief stole a brooch! Killing a man needlessly is a far worse sin than stealing!"

Malen's eyes narrowed in suspicion. "I should think, madam, you'd want to inflict the death blow yourself." Unwilling to be squelched, the uncertainties that had insinuated themselves into his thoughts just before they'd arrived at Inveraray Castle rose in his mind.

Fanny stamped one bare foot. "Are you insane? Why would *I* want to kill the poor man now? I know he hurt you and Gordy and Dagmar, but does he deserve to be murdered for that now that he is helpless and can threaten no one?"

"Apparently not," Malen said grimly. Turning his face so she wouldn't see the agony her protective tone wrought in his heart, he strained to keep from rushing to dispatch the prisoner immediately. He lowered his voice so that his companions wouldn't overhear. "And what, precisely, would you have me do with him, Duchess? Shake his hand and invite him to stay so that he might share my wife's pleasures any time the notion takes his fancy?"

"Stay? Share your wife's pleasures? You're not making any sense," Fanny said exasperatedly. "If you hate the man so much, why do you not simply ban him from returning to your lands on pain of death? But to kill him without giving him a warning is despicable."

Malen stiffened. "Despicable, am I? For wanting to protect you?"

Fanny threw up her hands. "Protect me from what? Having my brooch stolen again? Will you let the man go if I promise to lock the luckenbooth in your safe? That seems odd, since there is so much valuable jewelry lying unprotected in my armoires, but if that will make you let that poor man go, so be it!"

"I don't give a damn about your brooch!" Malen roared. "I wanted merely to return some of your sense of honor so you wouldn't feel quite so soiled for the rest of your life."

"Honor? My sense of honor hasn't suffered. Granted, my kidnapping was quite terrifying, but I am nearly completely recovered, now. And I fail to see why I should feel 'soiled'."

Malen swallowed a snarl. It was all too clear now. There could be only one explanation for why his lovely duchess had recovered from her ravishment so rapidly. She had the morals of an alley cat.

17

Suddenly Malen felt a way he hadn't felt in years. Naïve. He should have known, from the way she tried to seduce him, that Fanny wasn't what she pretended to be. He remembered how skillfully wanton she had seemed for one supposedly innocent. But damnation, he still wanted her. He shook his head. "I know I must be the world's greatest fool, but I am willing to forget all the others if you will just promise me it will never happen again."

"All the others?" Fanny's eyes widened, then narrowed. "I don't have the faintest idea what you're talking about, Malen Campbell, but I don't think I want to hear any more. I can only assure you that if you kill that man, I leave for Carlisle in the morning." Sticking her nose in the air, she turned away.

Gripping her forearm tightly, Malen whirled her to face him. "Can you not even agree to that?" She tried to pull away, and he tightened his fingers painfully. "You will listen until I say otherwise. And you will go nowhere regardless of what I decide to do with him. Now, I'm going to ask you a question, and I want an answer. As honorably as I've behaved toward you, and as hard as it has been for me to resist making love to you— while it would seem countless others have sampled your delights—I deserve an answer, Duchess."

Fanny raised smoke-brown eyes in a baleful, smoldering stare. "What do you mean, 'countless others'?" she asked in a deathly quiet voice.

"Exactly that." He grimaced. "And don't try to tell me there haven't been any. There can be no other reason a woman raped wouldn't want her violator wiped off the face of the earth—only that there have been innumerable others before him. Your lack of morals would also explain why you tried to seduce me in the cottage. God, I've been gullible. So tell me, Duchess, how many others have there been?"

Fanny's hands turned to blocks of ice. "What do you mean, raped?"

Releasing her arm, Malen turned away as if he couldn't bear to look at her. "If I have to spell it out, I will. That man"—he nodded in the kidnapper's direction—"forced you to have carnal relations with him. And now you want him released. What, I beg you," he said bitterly, "am I to think, other than he gave you quite a memorable time?"

Fanny felt as though her chest were being crushed beneath a mountain of rage. As her fury rose, she stared at him silently. Several times she opened her mouth, but nothing came out. At last she managed a few words. "How dare you! Do you really think that just because you've led a debauched life, I have done the same? How *dare* you, sir!"

Malen gazed at her, eyebrows raised inquiringly, eyes glacial.

Unwilling to believe what was happening, Fanny drew a shaky breath. "Do you truly believe this infamous tale you are telling?" she gasped.

Malen thought for a moment. "What else am I to believe? You cried in my arms and admitted the man had touched you, but soon thereafter you were recovered enough to submit to my embrace."

Fanny was fuming. "Oh, I understand now. You, in all your masculine wisdom, decided that the only reason I would be crying was because I'd been violated. Of course, I never *said* the kidnapper had raped me. You asked if he had touched me and, since he had, I said yes. Then, in your noodle of a manly mind, since I said he had *touched* me, I meant I'd been *raped*. How typical of a man to jump to conclusions about a woman without bothering to *ask* her!"

Gazing at his stunning duchess, who stood glaring at him in unconcealed indignation, her magnificent red curls burning over her slender shoulders in wildly curling flames, Malen suddenly found himself wondering if he'd made a terrible mistake. A flicker of doubt settled in his belly.

Suddenly her eyes widened in comprehension. "No wonder you told me you wanted an annulment that night at the cottage. You weren't about to stay married to a fallen woman, were you?"

Malen glowered. "I said I'd look into the annulment because *you* wanted it. I merely decided to give you what you professed to want."

"Then why did you bring me here, if you intended to get an annulment?"

"Because I wanted to stay married to you, wench!" he cried. "Besides, I thought you might very well be with child. I couldn't make any permanent decision about our marriage until I knew for certain. So I brought you with me."

Fanny gawked at him. "With child?" Suddenly her face turned chalky white. "Oh, my God. *That's* what you meant when you said you hoped it wouldn't be necessary to get an annulment. You hoped I wasn't pregnant." Gritting her teeth, she tried to keep from sobbing as all her fondest dreams crumbled. "If I had been, no doubt you'd have gone posthaste to the proper authorities so you wouldn't be stuck with another man's by-blow. Oh!" she cried as another ghastly thought occurred to her. "And you pulled away from me in the cottage because you thought I wanted to seduce you so you'd think the child was yours. Didn't you? *Didn't you?*" she demanded fiercely.

Malen flushed. "What was I supposed to think, when you hadn't wanted anything to do with me until that moment, and then you were all over me?" he stammered.

Now Fanny flushed.

Malen continued. "And you've got it all backward. I told you, I thought *you* wanted the annulment. Or have you forgotten how vociferously you demanded one when you realized we were married?"

Suddenly his voice gentled, and he sighed. "No,

Fanny, I didn't want an annulment. That was the last thing I wanted. I'd have been happy to raise another man's child if it would keep you by my side. You see, I wanted to wait to discover if you were with child so I could refuse to let you go on ethical grounds."

Fanny's heart nearly stopped beating, and her flush deepened to crimson.

"You see, you also jump to conclusions. So now I repeat, if you are carrying the brigand's child," he said sincerely, "I'll still keep you and raise the babe as my own."

Fanny was flabbergasted. "Haven't you been listening to a word I've said?" she hissed furiously, carefully enunciating each word as if speaking to an imbecile. "I am not with child! I was not ravished!"

Malen looked perplexed. "Then why were you crying?"

Lifting her fingers, Fanny rubbed her temples, which had begun to throb. "Listen to me very carefully, because I'm only going to say this once. I was crying because I was struck with the realization that I loved you and couldn't live without you and the kidnapper had nearly killed you!"

One moment Malen felt as if he'd been hit in the head with a tree trunk. The next he felt as though he were soaring. Stunned, he gaped at her. "You ... you love me? You really love me? And you were crying because I was still alive? Even though you knew I was a Campbell? Oh, Fanny—"

As he moved to take her in his arms, Fanny slapped his ecstatic face as hard as she could. Anger so consuming it threatened to incinerate her poured through her veins at the thought he could actually have believed her capable of such depravity. "Don't you touch me, you bastard! How dare you suggest that I would welcome the intimate attentions of any man not my husband! How *dare* you think I would be so free with my favors! You know, between you and my father, it will be a wonder if I ever want anything to do with a man again. Both of you have treated me like a pawn you could push about as you pleased. As though I weren't an individual with my own mind. As though it were completely acceptable for you to use me for whatever you wanted, whenever you wanted. Neither of you ever asked me what *I* wanted. You simply took it for granted that you knew best.

"Admittedly, ofttimes I'm rather stubborn, and running away from MacDonald Manor out of spite was a childish thing to do, but being a female does not make me stupid. I might be impulsive, perhaps, but not stupid."

Malen opened his mouth, but she cut him off fiercely.

"First, there's my father, convinced he knew who was the man for me, and going to the extent of having the banns called in an effort to push me into marriage. And you! Thinking I'd been ravished, for goodness sake, but not having the common decency to ask, as though you would understand what had really happened far better than my poor, feeble female brain could! Then you conclude that I have recovered from my ravishment so swiftly because I am accustomed to carnality with countless strangers! And *then* you have the audacity to offer to *keep* me even if I am with child! Oh, how kind of you, sir!"

Malen shook his head. "Fanny, I didn't mean to offend you. I merely wanted you to know that I wouldn't desert you in your time of need."

"Need? I don't need you! Why would I need someone who jumps to conclusions without a whit of evidence other than the fact that he affects me more strongly than opium affects a Chinaman? Or who treats me as if I am nothing more than a piece of property, dragging me here, dragging me there, posting the banns for our marriage without even asking me, then tricking me into marrying him. And there's also the fact that one minute he wants me, but the next I'm a harlot for responding to him!"

"Fanny, I said I was sorry for tricking you."

"Sorry is not good enough! Obviously you give me no credit at all if you can honestly believe me to be both a brainless female and capable of the kind of immorality you've suggested! You impossible boor! I deserve

more respect than that from both you and my father!
Do you hear me? Respect! Both of you have taken me
for granted at every turn, and I've had it up to here"—
she made a slashing motion at her neck—"with both of
you!" With that she spun on her bare toes and ran back
to the castle, skirts flying.

Smiling, Malen let her go. She loved him! She really
loved him! And she was undoubtedly as pure as the
day she was born! There was no way she could have
faked that raging fury. Whistling, he moved lightly back
toward the small group of men, who, he noticed, were
all staring off into space as if they hadn't heard a word
of Fanny's ravings. Clearing his throat awkwardly, he
turned his attention to the kidnapper. "You have had a
lucky reprieve."

The kidnapper turned to look up at his captor. "Yer
Grace?" he whimpered hopefully.

"Get out of here, and never let me see your face
again. If I do, I'll kill you for kidnapping my wife. Consider your freedom her wedding gift to you. But you'll
be a dead man if you ever set foot on my lands again."
Moving behind the bandit, Malen sliced the ropes bind-
ing his hands. The man took off running without a
backward glance.

Turning to Gordy, Malen smiled. "How about some
breakfast? I'm famished."

Gordy frowned. "I confess I'm powerful 'ungry, 'avin'
ridden all night tae bring ye that varlet. But what about
'er Grace? She seemed in a powerful dither. Mayhap ye
should go tae 'er afore we break our fasts."

Glancing speculatively up at the castle to the window
he knew was hers, Malen watched the curtain flick
slightly as though someone had ducked out of sight. He
nodded and grinned. "She was rather upset, wasn't
she? But even though she was right about almost everything she said, I value my skull far too much to risk it
by attending her until she cools down." His grin widened. "You know, I don't know how I ever could have
been so foolish as to think what I felt for her years ago
was anything but love."

Gordy grunted. "Sounded more like war to me."

Malen laughed. "Aye, but what is love without a bit of war in it, my good man?"

Fanny remained in her room for the rest of the day, even going so far as to send Pegeen downstairs with a message that her mistress was suffering from the headache and would take a tray in her room.

Malen had not come up to her apartments to see if she was all right, and although she was miffed, she couldn't in all honesty say she blamed him. She had struck him very hard and castigated him severely and, she was forced to admit, perhaps a bit unfairly. So the hours passed with infinite slowness until it was time for bed.

After Pegeen helped Fanny dress in a luxurious nightgown of dream-fine silk with Brussels lace, the maid left Fanny's chamber to take Dagmar outside before bed. Fanny settled down with a volume of Byron and tried to make herself drowsy enough to sleep.

Some time later the ormolu clock on the mantel chimed ten o'clock, and Fanny realized Pegeen and Dagmar had been gone for nearly an hour. What was taking them so long? If they didn't return soon, she would have to send a footman looking for them.

But her mind was too occupied with other matters to worry about the maid and dog for long, and she frowned as her thoughts drifted back onto the same path they'd traveled all day. Had she been too hard on Malen? Perhaps he'd been telling the truth when he'd insisted he'd wanted the annulment only because he thought it would make her happy.

She doubted seriously that there was another man of her acquaintance who would have considered staying married to a woman ruined, especially if there was reason to believe her with child. Take those two girls who had disgraced themselves by running after the duke, for example. As far as she knew, they were still unwed.

Now that she thought on it, Malen had behaved quite honorably. And he was a gentle man. A caring man. As she thought of the way he had rocked her in the chair in the cottage, holding her close while she cried, her eyes filled with tears once again. Even if he *had* thought she'd been defiled, he'd still not told her to go to the devil, as many another man might have done. She smiled sadly. That wasn't the behavior of a heartless brute.

So he'd tricked her into marrying him. Maybe he'd been arrogant and pushy, but she had faults, too. Just look at her now, sitting in her room and pouting like a child. She'd acted immaturely too much of late, and it was time she grew up, for there were responsibilities to face. She was no longer a sixteen-year-old girl. No longer a child. She was a woman, and she wanted a man's love. Malen's love.

Also, there was still the matter of clan violence to consider. Although she didn't like having been used as a pawn, Fanny had to admit that Malen and her father were probably right; there was, beyond a doubt, no better way to soothe everyone's sensibilities than by a marriage between the two heads of state. How could she have spent so much time feeling sorry for herself when the lives of her clan members were at stake?

If she didn't resolve matters with the duke, what would become of the two clans? Would Malen be able to come up with another solution to the violence? Surely a man as intelligent as he could think of another answer if forced. But did she want to give him the opportunity? Suppose he decided he could handle the situation very well without her?

Then the thought occurred to her that even though she'd been furious most of the day, not once had she seriously considered leaving Inveraray. She smiled as she realized that the reason for this lay with Malen. Her home was wherever he was. Not MacDonald Manor or Carlisle Cottage, but with the man she loved, no matter how angry he made her.

Her smile deepened. She hoped Malen wasn't still upset about her outburst, but if he was, she would simply kiss his rage away. Blushing, she thought suddenly that even if he *wasn't* angry, she would kiss him. And pull the riband from his hair and run her fingers through his inky curls. And kiss him again. And . . . do whatever it was that married people did.

It was high time she and Malen started a family to secure their clans' future peace. Oh, heavens, she loved him! And she wanted his children. She smiled as she remembered her father's insistence that if she loved her husband, she would want his babies. How right he had been. At the thought of suckling Malen's babe at her breast, her entire body tingled with anticipation. Yes, she decided abruptly, she loved and wanted only him, and she would show him how much that very night. As soon as she heard him moving about in his chamber, she would go to him.

Suddenly a faint knock on her door made her jump, and Fanny's eyebrows rose as a face peeped around the jamb. It was that of a young woman, her hair hidden by a little white cap. Fanny didn't recall seeing her about the castle, and yet the girl looked familiar. Who was she?

The maid's expression was almost disdainful, and her voice undeniably curt. "Yer Grace?"

"Yes?" Fanny answered.

"There be a disturbance wi' yer dog outside, near the stables. They asked me tae tell ye tae go doon 't once."

Fanny's heart leapt into her throat. Oh, dear Lord, something must have happened to Pegeen and Dagmar to have kept them away so long. How could she have sat here mooning while they might be hurt? Stifling a cry of concern, she thrust her feet into sheepskin slippers, threw a white gauze peignoir over her lacy nightgown, and ran after the maid, who had already scurried away and was no longer in sight.

Within moments Fanny was outside, making her way toward the stables. A quick glance at the sky showed that thunderheads had covered the moon. The night was as black as a witch's cat, and the low mass of clouds swirled as if in a huge cast-iron cauldron.

She'd almost reached the long stable buildings when a muffled bark made her turn toward the woods instead. "Dagmar? Pegeen?" she shouted. "Are you there?" There was no reply. "Where are you?"

Another bark. Breaking into a run, Fanny hurried through the trees toward the sound. Where could they be? Another yelp, this time sounding as if the dog was in pain.

After running for nearly five minutes, Fanny drew to a halt, breathing heavily. There had been no more barks, and she knew she'd have to turn back unless she saw some sign of the dog and maid soon. But where was she? It was pitch-black in the forest, and she could barely see her hand before her face, much less find her way back to the castle.

That was when she heard it. An odd howling sound coming from the bushes up ahead. Moving swiftly, Fanny pushed through the trees—and came face-to-face with Sir Blanden Fitch.

Bowing low at the waist, the baronet smiled. "Well met, my lady." He laughed mirthlessly. "Woof . . . woof . . . woof."

18

Firelight danced across the crystal decanter as Malen poured himself a glass of brandy and moved to sit in a chair beside the hearth. Sipping slowly, he stared into the flames and wondered if Fanny's temper would have cooled by the time he finished his drink. She'd not come down for dinner, so she must still be upset. But even if she was, he thought purposefully, he'd kiss her until she wasn't.

Not that he didn't understand her anger. She'd been right about everything she'd said, save that he thought himself more intelligent than she because she was a woman. She was, by far, the most intelligent, logical person he'd ever met, male or female.

Still, he had been condescending, deigning to "keep" her if she were with child, despite what she wanted. And he should have taken her at her word and not read so much into her comments. But starting tonight, he intended to listen carefully when she spoke and ask her opinion before making choices concerning her.

Tossing off the last of the brandy, he got to his feet, adjusted his jade velvet dressing gown, and stepped toward the door joining their chambers. He knocked. No response. Was she asleep? Or just ignoring him? The latter thought made him grit his teeth in annoyance. He knocked harder. When there was still no answer, a knot of concern twisted his stomach. Frowning, he wiggled the door handle experimentally. It was locked. Locked? Surely she wouldn't have locked the door unless she was up to something. Damned vexatious chit, what new problem was she concocting?

Or was he too suspicious? Perhaps she was truly ill.

Without further ado he began pounding on the polished mahogany door with all his might. "Fanny! Are you all right? I understand if you are still annoyed with me, and if you are I'll leave you alone, but I am worried! Please call out if you are all right!"

Nothing. Drawing a deep breath, Malen braced himself and threw his weight against the door. The thick wood hardly bowed. Again he strove to break down the door. And again. Finally a tremendous splintering sound heralded the first vertical crack in the solid panel. After another thrust, the door split open. Reaching through the gaping hole, Malen unlocked the bolt from the opposite side, opened the door, and stepped into the room. "Fanny? Fanny! Where are you?"

His expression became grim. She was gone. Apparently he'd misjudged the depth of her rage. Not that it mattered. He had no intention of losing her again. He'd search the ends of the earth, if need be, to bring her back. Turning on his heel, he moved back into his chamber and drew on leather breeches and a wool coat, determined to find his troublesome bride and drag her back to his castle. Just as he finished dressing, the bedchamber door opened. Whirling, Malen swallowed an oath of disappointment as Gordy stepped into the room.

The batman's eyes widened. "What be ye doin', sir? I coulda sworn I 'ad ye all ready fer bed."

"Fanny's gone," he said flatly. "I'm going to find her." Pushing past his servant, he hurried into the hall and down the main staircase, quickly making his way outside. On the doorstep he paused, wondering where to start his search. Then he rushed toward the stables. If she'd run away, she'd have taken a horse.

Pushing open the stable doors, he stared in shocked dismay at the scene before him. In the center of the work area, where the men often played cards, half-empty mugs held cold chocolate. All twelve of the grooms and stablehands he employed lay on the floor around their chairs as if they'd fallen off during the game. Rushing toward the head groom, Malen grasped the man's shoulder and shook it frantically. No response. Snoring heartily, the man was dead to the world.

Stifling a curse, Malen lifted a mug to his nose and sniffed. Nothing. Sticking a finger into the liquid, he raised his hand to his lips and tasted. His eyes narrowed. During the war, when the doctor had sewn up his torn thigh, he had tasted something remarkably similar. It was, beyond a doubt, laudanum, barely masked by the rich chocolate.

It was doubtful that the grooms had even known what hit them. Most likely they'd all passed out around the same time. And once a sip or two of this potent mixture passed their lips, even if they'd seen their companions fall, it would have been too late to call for help.

Suddenly a muffled sound toward the back of the building drew his attention. Striding rapidly toward an empty stall, he peered over the door and cursed again. Pegeen lay curled in a circle on a pile of straw, snoring much like the stablehands.

Near her, looking none too happy, Dagmar stared wistfully at the closed door. When she recognized the duke, the wolfhound let out a deep bark and jumped up at the door to lick his face. Apparently she'd been drugged and locked in at the same time as Pegeen but had come to sooner. And even if she'd been barking for the last hour, Malen knew he'd not have heard her from the house.

Reaching down, he unlatched the stall and let the wolfhound into the hallway. Kneeling at her side, he looked the big dog straight in the eye. "Dagmar," he said firmly, "find Fanny. Where is Fanny?"

He didn't need to ask twice. The enormous dog let out a baying yelp, passed the stablehands snoring sonorously on the floor, and raced for the door. In seconds man and beast streaked across the lawns toward the small wood not far from the castle.

Fanny wrinkled her nose. The baronet reeked of stale whiskey and sour, nervous perspiration. His coat and shirt were muddy and torn, and his cravat had been ripped away altogether. At least three days' growth of beard covered his normally baby-soft cheeks. She fought the urge to step backward, instinctively knowing that to show her distaste and fear could be lethal. "What brings you out on such a foul night, my lord?" she asked in a quavering voice as thunder pealed overhead and the first few droplets of rain began pelting the trees.

The baronet's mouth turned up in a sneer. "Spare me the trivialities, my lady. You know why I'm here."

"Trivialities?" Fanny replied as calmly as she could. "I should think it a perfectly reasonable question, not trivial in the least. After all, you must admit it is odd, our chancing upon one another like this." She attempted a smile but was deeply disturbed by Bland's answering laugh.

"Odd, yes. Chance? I'm afraid not." Holding her gaze, he moved toward her.

"No? Well, perhaps you'd like to discuss what brings you here as we walk back home. It's rather chilly out here. It will be much more pleasant conversing before a warm fire instead of catching our deaths of cold in this rain." She tried to walk past him but shrank back as his scrawny fingers closed about her wrist. Unable to help herself, she jerked her arm out of his grasp.

Smiling faintly, as though he knew she couldn't escape unless he willed it, the baronet released her. "I do not want to go to the castle just now, my lady. I was thinking more along the lines of France or Italy. Somewhere your dear duke cannot find you until he has paid me the tidy sum of twenty thousand pounds." He smiled suddenly. "No, make that thirty thousand. After all, you have caused me a good bit of trouble."

Fanny shook her head. "Bland, I really must go home now. As you can see," she said, gesturing toward her nightclothes and then wishing she hadn't drawn attention to her scant attire, "I'm hardly dressed for travel. However, I'm sure if we speak to the duke, he will give you whatever sum you desire."

The baronet's mouth twisted. "Oh, please, spare me your witticisms. I haven't the time or the patience for them just now. I need money, and I need it fast. You see, after your husband threw me out of MacDonald Manor, I returned to England to settle with my creditors. They were most happy to receive His Grace's money, and I even had several hundred pounds left over. To celebrate, I went to White's."

His face darkened, and he took a predatory step toward Fanny. "As soon as I walked in the door, my so-called friends began mocking me about you. Saying you had thrown me over for the duke. Insisting you had better taste than to marry me. Me! The most fashionable man in London!" he shouted suddenly, his face a mask of rage.

An icy finger of fear traced Fanny's spine. Bland was quite, quite mad.

Slowly he regained his composure. "At any rate, I managed to fob off their mockery by placing yet another bet. Of course, it took the remainder of my money, but I think it was a good investment. Would you care to know the terms of this new wager, Lady Fanny?" he said, suddenly all politeness.

Her mouth as dry as the Sahara, Fanny nodded. "Certainly, if you'd like to tell me, Bland."

"I bet the fellows at White's that you were in the process of obtaining an annulment and that you were leaving Argyll to marry me. The unfortunate part of the tale is that, after I left the remainder of my money at White's, I was met at my town house by one of my haberdashers, who informed me that I had several outstanding bills." He snarled suddenly. "Damned insolent cit demanded I pay him immediately or he'd have me thrown into debtors' prison."

Bland shuddered. "Well, naturally, I refused and closed the door in his face. I mean, the man was absolutely impertinent! And then, if you can fathom it, he had the audacity to summon the Runners, who called upon me that same afternoon. I had to climb out my bedchamber window. I was chased like a rabbit to the Scottish border!" he bellowed.

"So you see, my lady, you must fulfill your promise and marry me. After all, I *was* your first choice." With that, he reached into his pocket and pulled out a tattered object. "And I have this to prove it!"

For a moment Fanny could not determine what he held. Then she recognized it as the riband she had given him at Lady Brannigan's house party the previous month. Chewing her lip, she thought rapidly. "Of course. You are absolutely right. And as soon as we get to Inveraray Castle, I will inform the duke that you and I are to be married. And—"

Stuffing the riband back into his pocket, Bland let out a roar of pure hatred. "Do you take me for such a fool, my lady, as to think I would trust you again? Not a chance!" Spittle dripped from his chin and fell to the ground unnoticed. "Not a prayer in hell! This time I will not be so easily cuckolded. This time I take no risks. You are coming with me now. We will travel to a small cove southeast of here, where a boat waits to take us to France."

"My lord, I cannot possibly go with you until I gather my wardrobe." Fanny's voice trembled as she realized how dire the circumstances truly were. No one even knew she was here save the maid who had summoned her. She gasped. "That maid who came to my room! You sent her, didn't you?"

Bland smiled smugly. "Yes. I met Lucy at the Anvil on my way here. We got friendly, and it seemed she, too, had a bone to pick with you, my dear. She couldn't imagine why the duke preferred you to her."

As if seeing her for the first time, Bland's eyes drifted toward Fanny's sheer bodice. He smiled ominously. "Well, well. Do you know, for the first time I think I can see what the duke wanted you for. You're not entirely unattractive. What do you say that before we go, we make absolutely certain your devoted duke never wants to claim you again? Tell me, my lady, are you still a virgin?"

Fanny's heart froze in her chest.

"No need to reply. I can see by your expression you are still pure. What's the matter, couldn't your precious duke manage matters? He'll never be the man I am, as you'll soon see."

Fanny felt the blood in her face drain to her feet. "You wouldn't dare!"

Bland frowned. "Dare? My dear lady, it isn't a matter of daring. It is a matter of survival. I have to take you with me, and I have to make certain that after he pays me, the duke wants nothing further to do with you. I do not see that I have any alternative. Now then, the sooner we get started, the sooner we will be finished.

"Oh," he said, as if in afterthought, "please don't run away or try to fight. I will only be forced to hurt you if you struggle unduly. And I can guarantee I would love to have an excuse to cause you part of the pain you have caused me." Reaching down, he began unbuttoning his filthy buff unmentionables.

In all of this, what caught Fanny's eye were Bland's hands. His treasured hands, with their formerly polished nails, were now cut to shreds and black with grime.

A hysterical mix of a sob and a giggle rose in her throat. To lose her virtue like this, after escaping the kidnapper's embrace and then being unable to seduce Malen, seemed almost ludicrous.

Bland's pantaloons now hung open, exposing his dingy silk undergarments. Looking up, he said disinterestedly, "You're going to have to do something to help me. Unless I get properly excited, I will be unable to complete the deed." He stared at her disapprovingly as she stood motionless, gaping at him in disbelief. "Come on, do something!"

His words jolted Fanny out of her trance, and she did do something. She ran. As fast as she could, heading deeper into the woods.

Bland cursed as he stumbled after her. Glancing back, she saw him trip over a log and fall headlong against a large rock. But then he was up again, his unmentionables slipping down his thighs to twine about his skinny legs. Not pausing to pull them up, he ran on, his shouts of rage rending the night.

A crack of thunder nearly deafened Fanny as she fought her way through the thicket. Then the sprinkling clouds split open fully, rain slashing down in blinding sheets. The earth grew slick and treacherous, pulling at her slippers, sucking her down.

As Bland gained ground, his expletives grew more vicious. He caught her just as she neared what she recognized as the cliff just beyond the manor, his hand seizing the stuff of her skirt and pulling her down to the sodden earth. With a cry of triumph, he threw himself on top of her.

19

The wind whistled fiercely, blowing bits of twigs, leaves, and debris from the ground and into Malen's eyes as he followed the wolfhound. Not realizing Dagmar had paused momentarily to sniff the air, he nearly ran over her. Sliding to a halt on the muddy forest floor, he watched her stand very still, nose raised to the wind. A clammy chill touched his stomach as he realized they stood not far from the edge of the cliff.

Before he could call the wolfhound back, she was off again, baying loudly. Just as she faded from view, her keening wail changed pitch. Malen paused and tipped his head to one side. Through the thundering rain, he almost thought he could hear voices. Breaking into a run, he hurried after the dog, catching her collar just before she broke through a stand of trees and into a clearing—the same clearing near the edge of the road where he and Fanny had paused to gaze over the chasm on their way to Inveraray Castle. The voices grew louder.

"You stupid bitch! How dare you run from me? I'll teach you some manners! And I'll enjoy bringing you to your knees! Hold still, damn it! You can't say I didn't warn you!"

"Let go of me!"

Malen cursed. Fitch! He listened, horrified, his eyes frantically seeking the darkness for the source of the voices.

"Oh, stop struggling! You're going to love it!" A masculine scream of pain rent the night. "Aargh! You'll be sorry for that, bitch! Forget about becoming my wife! You're not going to live long enough!"

209

Malen and Dagmar rushed forward as one. They reached the couple wrestling together on the sodden earth at nearly the same moment, just in time to see the man wrap a slender black band around the woman's slim neck. Throwing herself forward, the wolfhound wrapped her jaws around the man's right arm, wrenching her head back and forth until the man released the riband.

"Aargh!" Bland screamed again. "Let go, you nasty beast!"

Consumed with rage, Malen caught the man by his greasy hair and pulled him to his feet. Exposed, Bland's male member swung stiffly in the breeze, shrinking abruptly as the baronet recognized the duke. As if realizing Malen had the situation under control, Dagmar released Bland's arm and bent to lick Fanny's pale face.

Malen plunged his fist into the dandy's teeth, and Bland let out a howl as he flew backward. He crashed to the ground and lay still. Kneeling, Malen nudged Dagmar out of the way and brushed aside the black velvet riband that clung to Fanny's neck. "Duchess? Can you hear me?"

Whimpering, Fanny allowed him to wrap her in his strong arms and hold her close. "Oh, Malen, I was so terrified. He wanted to take me to France and force an annulment. Oh, my love," she confessed brokenly, pressing her face into the shelter of his neck, "I was wrong! I do need you! I never thought I'd need a man, but I do need you! I shouldn't have said all those terrible things today. Please don't let me go!"

"I won't," Malen murmured softly against her wet hair. "I won't, darling. I'll never let you go. And you were right about nearly everything, except that I respect you more than anyone else on earth. I'm so sorry I didn't come for you years ago. I loved you so much, it almost killed me to stay away. It took forever to put you out of my mind, and even though I thought I'd forgotten you, I never did. Never. Mere hours after I saw you again at Carlisle Cottage, I realized I still loved you more than life itself. And I'm sorry I tricked you into marrying me, I'm sorry for everything I ever did to cause you pain."

"I know," Fanny whispered, glorying in the feel of his rough whisker-stubble against her cheek. Happy tears filled her eyes as she tipped her head back to look up at him. His hair hung loose about the masculine planes of his face, gleaming blue-black like the fur of a panther.

Unable to staunch the flow of words, Malen rushed on. "I love you more than anything in the world. Oh, Fanny, if you still want to go back to Dumfries, you can go, even though it would kill me to lose you. If staying with me will make you unhappy, I will let you go. But if you stay with me, I promise to make you the happiest woman in the world." Finally he paused. "And I promise to listen very carefully to what you say, and not to make your choices for you."

Fanny smiled. "Just promise to try, my darling, and I will be happy. A leopard cannot change his spots overnight, after all."

Their lips met in a sweet, fierce kiss and Malen and Fanny clung together as if they couldn't bear to part. When the kiss ended, both were breathing heavily. Then Malen grinned roguishly. "My dear, if we do not return home at once, I fear I will behave almost as badly as Fitch. Another kiss like that and I won't be able to wait to love you until we're married in the morning."

Fanny gazed at him, astonished. "Married? But we're already married!"

"Yes, but I felt it would be best if we were married before a priest as well. You deserve a real wedding ceremony, my love, with all the pomp and circumstance I can give you. Your parents and a large number of your fellow MacDonalds will be arriving in Inveraray tomorrow, as will a group of Campbells, and we're going to be married in state in the castle chapel."

"Oh, Malen, I do love you." Eyes sparkling with happy tears, Fanny reached up to kiss him again. "Even if you *have* made yet another choice for me," she pointed out. He groaned, and she hastened to reassure him. "But this time, my love, you made the right choice."

Smiling in relief, he tried to deepen the embrace, but she laughed and evaded him. "I don't think that's a wise idea, my dear. If you kiss me like you did a moment ago, *I* will be the one who refuses to wait to consummate our marriage!"

"If you mean to frighten me, you're failing miserably." Malen laughed. Getting to his feet, he reached down and took her hands. "But I can show you something that *will* frighten you. Come here." He led her the edge of the cliff and held her waist tightly as she swayed against him, horrified.

"Good Lord! I knew it was close, but I didn't know it was right behind us!" Then something occurred to her. "What happened to Pegeen? I sent her outside with Dagmar, but she never came back in. Your old friend Lucy was recruited by Bland to appear dressed as a housemaid and tell me something had happened to them out near the stables. I came out to investigate, but when I heard barking in this direction, I came this way instead. I guess I was lucky I didn't run off the edge of the cliff!"

"Lucy from the Anvil was in on this?"

"Yes. Apparently she thought she deserved your attentions more than I did."

Malen frowned, then nodded as everything became clear. "Fanny, I must apologize. I rebuked you for flirting with the ruffians there because I thought it was dangerous, and now I find that my own flirtation was every bit as perilous." He sighed. "I guess I really do order you around as though I were the wisest man on earth. I'm sorry. I honestly *will* try to do better."

Fanny smiled again. "It would seem both of us have a great deal to learn about considering the other, but I think we're making great progress."

"I agree. I love you very much, Fanny, and if you're willing, I'll be more than happy to spend the rest of our lives working on mutual understanding." Unable to help himself, Malen kissed her again. After a time, he lifted his head. "As for Pegeen, I left her sleeping in the stable." He explained what he'd found when he discovered Fanny missing from her room.

Fanny shook her head as the tale came to a close. Suddenly a movement in the shadows drew her attention. "Look out!" she screamed as Bland lurched out of the darkness toward them, arms outstretched to shove the duke over the cliff.

Spinning, Malen caught the baronet against the side of the head with his fist, and the dandy's feet slipped in the mud. For what seemed an eternity he teetered, motionless, over the black void. Then, with a wailing cry, he plummeted over the precipice. His scream ended abruptly.

Fanny paled and shivered, and Malen took her elbow and gently led her away from the cliff and back toward the castle.

It was late when Fanny finally awoke the following morning, and Pegeen, none the worse for her misadventure of the night before, hurriedly helped her dress in a morning gown of pale-yellow muslin with matching kid slippers. As Fanny descended the grand staircase, she heard the sound of wheels rumbling over the gravel drive.

Hurrying outside, she was delighted to see that her parents had arrived. Rushing forward as a footman opened the crested carriage door, she threw her arms around her father's neck as he exited the vehicle.

Lord MacDonald put his hands on Fanny's shoulders and held her at arm's length, peering into her face with worried eyes. "Daughter," he said at last with a satisfied sigh. "You look well."

Fanny smiled gently, understanding without needing to be told that the emotion in his eyes was a mixture of guilt and relief. "I am indeed, Father. I have never been happier in my life."

Tears sprang to the earl's dark-brown eyes. "Thank God," he said gruffly. "My heart has ached since you left. Oh, Fanny, can you ever forgive me for tricking you into marrying the duke? Or for treating you as if your opinions were of no consequence? I knew when I posted the banns that you'd be furious, but I was so worried about our clan and so convinced the duke was the man for you that I couldn't help myself."

Fanny laid a hand against her father's cheek. "Of course I can, Father. I love you very much. If I hadn't been so immature and determined to flaunt your wishes, I'd have realized marrying the duke was a wise choice." She smiled. "Not only that, but I've come to realize that having a man around isn't always a bad thing—as long as he's willing to listen to my guidance." Then she became serious. "And you, Father? Can you forgive me for being so willful?"

A single happy tear trailed down Lord MacDonald's cheek. "There is nothing to forgive. I wouldn't have you any other way. After all, if you weren't precisely as you are, the duke wouldn't have been such a perfect mate for you. But I still think it might be a good idea, after your honeymoon, for us to sit down together and have a long talk."

"My sentiments exactly," Fanny replied firmly.

"Where is Argyll, by the way?" Lord MacDonald asked. "Your dog hasn't eaten the duke, has she?"

Fanny looked around, suddenly realizing that neither Malen nor Dagmar were present. "I don't know where either of them are. But I'm sure they'll put in an appearance soon."

"The duke had better. I'll not have my daughter stood up at the altar. By the by, I'm afraid I've some bad news. Your maid, Bessie, finally brought her footman up to scratch and refused to leave Carlisle. Do you think you'll have any difficulty finding another maid?"

Fanny laughed, thinking how relieved Pegeen would be. "None at all."

Lord MacDonald turned to help his wife out of the carriage. After exchanging many hugs and kisses with their beloved daughter, the earl and countess went to their chamber to rest and freshen up.

Several hours later Fanny and Malen took their vows before a priest in the old chapel at Inveraray Castle. The pews were hung with hundreds of flowers and filled with an equal mixture of Campbells and MacDonalds, who cheered the happy couple as the duke pinned the

MacDonald luckenbooth to his bride's bodice for the second time and kissed her soundly.

The Campbells, on the left side of the church, gave their all in an effort to out-cheer the MacDonalds, who made the walls tremble with their hearty highland cries. After the ceremony, the entire horde of clansmen made their way to the grand ballroom, where both food and dancing awaited their pleasure.

The only dark spot on the day was when a fight broke out between the men of the two clans, but Malen assured Fanny that the fight was all in fun, even though many noses were bloodied and a few bones broken. His own nose, he told her, had been bloodied by her father. Naturally, the duke had returned the carl's compliment.

Sitting down at a table to share a light late meal with her new husband, Fanny glanced around, noting, now that the excitement had died down a bit, that the wolf-hound was still not in evidence. Turning to Malen, she asked worriedly, "Have you seen Dagmar? I don't think I've seen her all day."

He smiled. "Yes, I have. I sent her to MacDonald Manor with our luggage. I thought you'd like to honeymoon there."

Fanny laughed and shook her head.

Malen's grin turned rueful. "Oh, heavens. I'm sorry, Fanny. I've done it again. I should have asked if you liked the idea before making plans. I guess a leopard *can't* change his spots that easily."

Fanny returned his smile. "That's all right. Just *try* to remember to solicit my opinion on really important matters. Besides, you seem to be getting very good at knowing exactly what I do want, and I can't complain about that, can I? As it happens, I was wondering how to ask you if we could honeymoon in Dumfries. It seems fitting, since that's where we first met." Then she looked worried. "But do you think Dagmar will be all right until we get there? I wouldn't want her to be lonely."

Laughing, Malen took a sip of wine. "Oh, yes. I make no doubt that she'll be quite content."

The duke and duchess joined their guests for a short

time, then departed for MacDonald Manor. Traveling
with all possible speed, they arrived in Dumfries two
days later, as if by unspoken agreement delaying
consummating their marriage until reaching their desti-
nation.

When they pulled up the long, familiar drive and
stepped out of the carriage, Fanny sighed happily.
Seeming to understand that she needed a few moments
alone, Malen moved into the house.

As if drawn by an invisible magnet, Fanny stepped
onto the path leading toward the apple tree and bench
where she and her grandfather had sat so many years
ago, and where she had first laid eyes on her future
husband. She had some unfinished business to tend to.

Hesitating as she neared the familiar spot, she gazed
at the beautiful garden. She could almost feel her
grandfather's presence. Glancing around, she saw that
nothing had changed since the day she'd left so many
years ago, save that it was a gloriously sunny day
rather than stormy.

Stepping toward the bench, Fanny seated herself.
Raising her tan-gloved fingertips to the luckenbooth
brooch where it rested over her heart, she drew a deep
breath. "Oh, Grandfather," she whispered. "If only I
could explain to you how much I love Malen. If only I
could tell you that he's a wonderful man, just as you
were. You'd have liked him, I know. Even though he is
a Campbell."

Suddenly she gasped. Hazy and dreamlike, the figure
of a man dressed in full Scottish regalia appeared next
to her on the bench. It could be no one but Ian
MacDonald! He smiled at her, and in that moment,
Fanny knew that nothing needed explanation. The spirit
nodded and seemed to whisper as if from across a great
distance, "Argyll is a good man. And noo that the
MacDonald luckenbooth is back in its rightful owner's
hands and peace is ours, all is forgiven. But what are ye
doin' here, lass? Ye should be wi' yer husband, creatin'
the future!"

As abruptly as he had appeared, Lord MacDonald
faded back into the eternities from whence he had

come. For a long time Fanny gazed, speechless, at the spot where her grandfather had appeared. Had she really seen anything, or had it all been in her imagination? She did not move until footsteps on the gravel path heralded a visitor.

"Woolgathering, Duchess?" Malen smiled tenderly at his beautiful young wife.

Fanny looked up blankly.

Seating himself at her side, he put a finger beneath Fanny's chin and tipped her lips toward his. As so often happened, the kiss, meant to last only a moment, deepened until both trembled with desire.

At last Malen cleared his throat. "So what were you thinking about so hard, my love?" he asked softly.

Fanny smiled. "I was thinking of my grandfather and how much he would approve of our marriage."

Malen looked surprised. "I thought he hated all Campbells."

She blushed. "He did. But I—er—have the distinct impression that he would approve of you. And the thought of grandchildren always appealed to him."

Malen's eyes flickered. "And does the idea appeal to you as well, love?"

"Very much," Fanny replied as her body responded to the flame smoldering in his sparkling aquamarine eyes, the sudden surge of desire threatening to melt her very bones. "After all, we have the future to think of."

"Yes," Malen murmured as he pulled Fanny into his arms. "*Our* future." Then he started, as if he remembered something. "Oh, I have a wedding present for you."

Fanny gave a delighted laugh. "What is it?"

Extending his arm, he rose and took her hand in the crook of his arm. Leading her toward the stables, he held a finger to his lips. "Shh. Don't disturb them. I think they're in love."

Fanny's eyes widened with stunned surprise. There, lying atop a large pile of fresh straw and oblivious to everyone else in the world, an enormous male Irish wolfhound gazed adoringly at Dagmar, who kindly allowed her admirer to place a loving lick on her nose.

Dagmar's eyes were brilliant, and in a moment she returned her new mate's caress.

Quietly drawing Fanny back outside, Malen raised his eyebrows questioningly. "What do you think of him? I had him brought in from Ireland, but if you don't like him, I'll have him returned and you can pick out your own dog. After all, it must be your choice which male helps propagate your grandfather's bloodline." He grinned. "You see? I am learning!"

"Oh, no! You mustn't send him away!" Fanny exclaimed ecstatically. "He's perfect!"

Malen beamed. "I hoped you'd think so. I bought him from a friend of mine, one Lord O'Hara from Dublin. Lord O'Hara's dogs are the best in the world. Save yours, of course," he hastily amended. "And I'm sure their pups will surpass even their quality."

Fanny threw her arms arolund her husband's neck. "He's the most wonderful wedding present anyone ever had. And you are the most wonderful husband!"

Tenderness for his young bride rushed through him as Malen lowered his mouth to hers. At last he pulled away. Nuzzling her neck with his lips, he said gruffly, "I'm so happy you like him. But now, Duchess, if you don't come inside with me at once, I won't be held accountable for my actions."

Fanny smiled. "You know, a moment ago you told me it was my decision which male would best help me propogate my grandfather's bloodline."

Malen's eyes sparkled. "Yes?"

"Well, I've made my choice, and I'm eager to get started."

His eyes rapidly darkened with barely restrained passion. "You know we won't be able to get an annulment afterward."

Fanny laughed. "True. You'll never get away from me now."

Laughing, the Duke of Argyll swung his MacDonald bride into his arms and ran for the house, determined to fulfill his vow of making her the happiest woman in the world.